1/5

THUNDER MOON STRIKES

"THUNDER MOON STRIKES,

Max Brand, max

Western

②DODD, MEAD & COMPANY
①NEW YORK
③1982
④263p   LC: 82-5087

Thunder Moon Strikes is comprised of the following stories, which
were originally published in *Western Story Magazine* and written
under the name of George Owen Baxter: *Thunder Moon-Squaman*
and *Thunder Moon Goes White*.

Library of Congress Cataloging in Publication Data

Brand, Max, 1892-1944.
    Thunder moon strikes.

    (Silver star western)
    I. Title
PS3511.A87T46   1982   813'.52   82-5087
ISBN 0-396-08081-2   AACR2

PART ONE

1

Thunder Moon had ridden his great stallion, Sailing Hawk, a thousand miles. Soon he would reach his goal—the home of Colonel Sutton and his wife. Twenty years before, a Cheyenne chief, Big Hard Face, had kidnapped the Sutton's infant son, taking the child to his lodge, where he had brought him up as his own. As the years passed, the boy, Thunder Moon, earned a reputation as the finest young warrior of the Suhtai, one of the tribes of the Cheyenne nation. Never had he taken the war trail in vain.

Then a chief of the Omissis had tricked Big Hard Face into taking his daughter, the beautiful trouble-maker Red Wind, as a gift. Yet when Thunder Moon offered to marry her, she repulsed him. He was white, she said, and he should go back to the white people. Angered by the taunts of the girl, and despite the pleas of Big Hard Face and the old chief's aunt, White Crow, Thunder Moon set out with the brave Standing Antelope to find his father and mother.

Not long after they had left the Suhtai village, Thun-

3

der Moon and Standing Antelope joined a wagon train of white hunters. The time came, however, when they had to leave the caravan and plunge into the lands of the whites as Big Hard Face had done so long ago. Now at last the journey had ended.

It was well past midnight when they reached the Suttons' house. Suddenly a mounted band of youths surrounded them. Led by young Jack Sutton, Thunder Moon was brought before the colonel and accused of stealing Sailing Hawk, his own stallion.

Angered by his parents' bewilderment at Thunder Moon's resemblance to the colonel and by his words that he had come to learn what his name might be, Jack Sutton reacted with fury. It was his sister, Ruth, who ran to her father.

"I know what his name is!" she exclaimed.

"The devil you do! What is it, then?"

"It's William Sutton, and he's your own son. Don't you see? He's come back! He's come back to you!"

Whatever the emotion of the others when the excited Ruth Sutton made this announcement, no one felt more keenly than her brother, Jack, though his sentiment may have differed from the rest. For as the eldest child, the only son, he had naturally expected to come into the majority of his father's great fortune. And though perhaps Jack was no worse than the next man, this announcement thrust him literally to the heart. Whatever his first thought might have been, certainly his first movement was to touch the pocket pistol that he carried with him always, like most of the gay lads of that time. And perhaps he recalled a picture seen a little earlier that morning, when this danger to his hopes then stood with the marsh behind him and fifteen armed men before. One shot would have done a great work, at that lucky time. But now the time was past.

4

There was no opportunity for the others to observe the expression on the face of Jack, for they were all too busily engaged on the subject of this suspected horse thief.

The poor colonel, utterly taken aback, caught his wife and drew her to him, and stared for a moment at Thunder Moon as though he were looking at a leveled gun rather than at a lost son. And Ruth Sutton recoiled. Her keen eyes had seen a resemblance, but the mark of the wilderness was visibly upon him, and she was frightened.

Only Mrs. Sutton went unafraid to the strange visitor. She drew herself out of the arms of the colonel, and, going to Thunder Moon, she took those terrible hands that Pawnee and Comanche and Crow knew and feared.

"You are William!" she cried softly. "Ah, you are my dear boy come back to us! Only tell me! Will you tell me?"

"My heart is sad," said Thunder Moon, and he fought back an impulse to take her in his arms. "My heart is sad. All that I know is what an old man of the Suhtai told me. He sent me here. But of myself I know nothing."

"You see, father," broke in the matter-of-fact voice of Jack, "we'd better go a bit slowly. God knows no one wants him to be the true Sutton more than I do! But we have to have more proof than the resemblance of two faces. We have to have something better than that. You see—he isn't a bit sure himself!"

"How could he be sure? He was an infant when he was stolen!" exclaimed the colonel, who was turning from white to crimson.

"And as for the word of some lying Indian—some old chatterer—"

5

"I tell you, Jack, you mustn't speak that way!" cried Mrs. Sutton. "Isn't there a call of blood to blood? I felt it when I first saw him! Randolf, do something! Let me be sure!"

The colonel hesitated, looked about wildly, and finally said, "Let's try to be calm. Let's make no mistake. It would be too horrible to think that we had him back again and then find it was only a fraud. You understand? Let's try to work out the testimony! Somebody tell someone to give those young fools outdoors some mint juleps—or anything that will keep them quiet! We have to think this out. We have to feel our way to the truth!"

"Here! Here's the truth!" said Mrs. Sutton.

She snapped open a little pendant at her throat and showed a miniature that was painted on the inside, showing her husband as he had been when he was a young man. The colonel looked at it gravely and long; then he raised his eyes as though afraid of what he must see. And the result was a start of amazement and joy.

"By heaven!" cried the colonel. "He's most like! He's certainly most like! Jack, examine this! William, if you are he, forgive us for going slowly now—but once you've been admitted to our hearts, then there'll be no uprooting you!"

"I speak little English; talk slow," said Thunder Moon, knitting his brows with the effort of listening.

"Poor boy!" breathed Mrs. Sutton. "My poor boy! Oh, I believe you!"

"Martha! Will you be still?" cried her husband. "Are you going to make a baby of him before we're sure that the thing is settled?"

"If he's not Indian," said Jack, "I'd like to know where he got that color of skin. He's dark enough to be a red

6

man—or a smoky mulatto, I'd say. Could the sun do that?"

Thunder Moon turned his head and looked calmly, judicially, toward the youth.

"You'll have trouble on your hands in a moment, Jack," said the colonel. "He doesn't like that way you have of putting things, you can see."

"My dear sir," said the boy, "I don't want to stand between a brother and the light. But I'm simply trying to make us all use our common sense. That's only fair and right, I take it. What do you say to that, Ruth?"

She, pale, tense, eager, raised a hand as though to brush the question away from her; all her being was busied in devouring this stranger-brother with her glance.

But Thunder Moon said in his deep voice—a soft voice, but one that filled the room: "I understand. My face is dark. You want to know why. You ask the sun. He will tell you."

Then, letting his robe fall from his shoulders, he stripped off his shirt of antelope skin with a single gesture. Brightly and beautifully beaded was that shirt so that it glistened like a particolored piece of chain mail in his hand; but there were no eyes just now for the fine shirt for which his foster father, Big Hard Face, had paid five good horses, five horses ready for the war trail, a strong knife, and a painted horn. Instead, there was a gasp, as every glance fastened upon the body of Thunder Moon, naked to the waist.

If he had broken any conventions, he was totally unconscious of it. He raised an arm along which the interlacing muscles slipped and stirred, and he pointed to his body.

"See," said he, "that my skin is not all dark. This is paler. Yet I see that it is not as pale as yours."

7

With that he waved his hand toward them as though inviting their closer inspection.

The colonel, indeed, had taken a quick stride toward him, with an exclamation of admiration; but Jack moved back a little and became rigid, as though he were responding to a challenge with proud defiance.

"It isn't all a question of color," said Jack firmly. "Of course, if he's an impostor, he wouldn't be such a fool as to come to us unless his skin were actually white. But the thing to decide on is the testimony. I don't know. It's rather queer, though. Taking a fellow on the strength of his face. Such things have been tried before. Clever devils! Use a striking family resemblance to worm their way into a million or so. Cheap at twice the price, you know."

"Would an impostor be ignorant of the English language, Jack?" asked the colonel sharply.

"Ah, sir," and Jack smiled, "of course he'll *say* that he is a Cheyenne. Why—that's not hard to say. Just be reasonable, please. You know that I could learn a bit of Indian ways, pick up a few of their words, and then say that I had passed most of my life on the prairies. Why not? Then I wouldn't have to answer a lot of embarrassing questions as to where I'd spent my days. Isn't that clear?"

It was, after all, a telling point. Some of the enthusiasm faded from the gentle eyes of Mrs. Sutton, and she looked anxiously to her husband.

He saw the appeal in her glance.

"I know, Martha!" he said. "I'm doing my best. But I'm not a prophet, and I can't look through the secrets of twenty years as if they were glass, you know. Look here, my young friend, tell us how we can be sure that you have spent all of this time with the Cheyennes?"

8

"I cannot understand," said Thunder Moon simply.

"I thought he wouldn't," sneered Jack.

"I say," repeated the colonel more loudly, making a vital effort to be clear, "will you tell us how we can know that you really spent those years with the Cheyennes?"

"And by the way," said Jack, "if you can talk just as well, you might put on your clothes, you know."

Thunder Moon with one gesture, as he had removed the shirt, donned it again. He swept the robe around his shoulders.

"Young man," he said sternly to Jack, "what coups have you counted and what scalps have you taken that you raise your voice and that you talk when chiefs are here?"

Even Jack blinked a little at this, but recovering himself instantly, he said coldly, "That's well done. Clever, by gad! Worthy of the stage, and a big stage. But we want some good, and sound, actual proof that you've been with the Cheyennes all this time."

The color had been growing slowly in the face of Thunder Moon and now it became a dangerously dark crimson; and his eyes glittered as he stared at Jack.

"Do not ask me; do not ask my friends," he said at last. "Ask the enemies of my people. Ask Sioux, ask Comanches, ask Pawnees, ask Crows. They know my face. They have seen it in the battle. No man has asked, Where is Thunder Moon in the battle? No, for they have seen me. So ask them and bring them here. They will tell you if I am a Suhtai!"

There was a stunned silence after this remark so filled with conviction and disdain.

But Jack, who in a way was playing desperately high for stakes that were worth winning, now broke in, "After all, my friend, you can't come over us as easily as

9

that! Of course, we're a thousand miles or so from the hunting grounds of the Sioux and the rest of 'em, whatever you called 'em. Facts, however, are facts. And it seems to me that you should be able to give us some proofs—some plain proofs—that you've been with the Cheyennes all this time under the name of Thunder Moon, or whatever you may be called, or say you are called!"

"Steady, Jack," said the colonel. "By gad, he looks a bit dangerous, just now!"

2

Now the excitement of Thunder Moon had been growing with great rapidity, for he felt the constant check of the questioning and sardonic Jack. It came in such a manner, too, that he was half maddened by it. Since he was a youngster and first distinguished himself in feats of arms among the Suhtai, his name had been known far and wide, not in his own tribe only but all through the Cheyenne nation and among the neighboring tribes. But now his very identity was questioned—not so much as the son of this stern-faced Colonel Sutton but as Thunder Moon himself.

He could endure it no longer. The passion that was rising in him must find some outlet, and since he could not act he must speak. And since he must speak, it had to be of himself. It was a theme on which he was not much practiced, for when the other braves at the end of the warpath danced the scalp dance and told of their

10

exploits, or when the coup stick was passed around, Thunder Moon was nearly always silent. Something in his nature had prevented him from joining in these self-acclaiming outbursts. But now he began to speak. He drew back a little until he stood close to the wall. He did not dance, as a pure-blooded Cheyenne would have done, but as passion and fury and exultation mastered him, his voice became a sort of chanting rhythm, and his whole body swayed in unison. Much of what he said came in Cheyenne; sometimes he used what English words he had absorbed into his vocabulary; but in some manner, as a very intense speaker usually can do, he made his audience realize what he was saying.

"I do not talk of common warriors. I only speak of chiefs who have counted five coups, and taken scalps. Make medicine and call down their spirits! Let them tell you what I am.

"I am Thunder Moon, of the Suhtai!

"The eagle feathers flowed behind the head of Little Wolf, and the bravest Pawnees were around him. The hearts of the Suhtai were sick, seeing those heroes charge. But a young warrior went out to meet that charge. He called to the Sky People and they gave him strength; they turned the bullets and the spear points. Like a snake through grass he wove through the men of the Pawnees. He came to Little Wolf. 'Pawnee, your spear is headed with burned wood; its point crumbles on my shield. My lance is in your heart!'

"And all the Suhtai shouted, 'Thunder Moon!'

"Three hundred warriors followed Waiting Horse. Among the Comanches he was the strongest man; scalps dried continually in the smoke of his tepee, and with scalps all his clothes were fringed. He did not go upon the warpath alone; but I, alone, met him. The eagle stood still in the wind and the buzzards circled

11

above us, watching. 'Waiting Horse, your medicine is weak. The Sky People fly with my bullet and send it into your brains. You lie on the plain with a broken forehead and your spirit slips out and flies on the wind.' 'It is Thunder Moon!' cry the Comanches.

"Now in his lodge a great Pawnee was very sad. His brother and his two uncles were dead, and when he asked his heart who had killed them his heart answered, 'Thunder Moon!' He made great medicine. He asked the greatest medicine men of the Pawnees to help him, and they gave him strength to go out and harry the Suhtai.

" 'Ah-hai! What is wrong with the horses of the Suhtai? Why do they throw up their heads and gallop away? The cunning Pawnee wolves are among them!' Fast they ride, but faster rides Thunder Moon. 'Turn back, Three Spotted Elks! Turn back and avenge your three dead kinsmen. Their spirits are crying to you in that strong wind. They are giving you power.'

"He is a brave man. He has heard their voices and turned back from among the flying horses. Now, Sky People, how shall I kill this man? I offer him to you as a sacrifice!

" 'Kill him only with your knife, Thunder Moon.'

"So let it be! His arrows stick in my shield. His arrows hiss at my ear. He has thrown away his bow and seized his strong war club, stained with blood. Your war club is strong, Three Spotted Elks, but my hand is stronger. My knife is in your throat! Sky People, accept his blood; this is my sacrifice!

"Behold, now, the Comanches' camp sleeps. All the lodges are white under the moon. All the new lodges are shining and bright. There is a shadow among them. Beware, Comanches, for it is Thunder Moon! He steals

12

from lodge to lodge. He comes to the medicine tepee and there sits the Yellow Man grinning, the great spirit, the metal wizard. I take him up and carry him away. With his medicine he calls his people to follow me. Your medicine is weak, Yellow Man. I throw you into the deep water. I carry only your arm away with me so that the Sky People may laugh when they see you with only one arm. I ride away, and with me I carry the fortunes of the Comanches.

"But who are these men whose hair flows to their waist or waves in the wind behind them as they ride? They are Crows, tall and noble of aspect. But none is so tall and none is so noble as Gray Thunder.

"Noble warriors, brave Crows from the mountains, my heart swells to see you. Come swiftly. I am waiting. I shall not run away. In my hands are guns having six voices apiece. Now they speak to you. What, do you fall down when you hear them? Three men fall, and the rest are daunted, but not Gray Thunder.

"Sky People, save him for my hands! With my hands I shall kill him. My bare hands must destroy him. Ha, Gray Thunder, your bullet has missed me. Your rifle as a club is lighter than a piece of rotten wood. I pluck it from you. Now, my hand against your hand! Ask mercy, and you shall live to die by the hands of the Suhtai women. He will not ask mercy. He bites like a wolf at my wrists. But now it is over. He is dead. Come back, you Crows, and bury your dead chief. Why do you run away so fast? He is dead, and his scalp will be taken, and his soul will vanish in the wind!

"Such things I have done. Hear me, you people! My name is not something that has to be asked after on the plains. All the tribes know it. Sky People, give these white men a sign that I do not lie! Sky People, if my medicine is strong, hear me! If ever I have sacrificed to you guns and strong lances and painted robes and beaded suits, send them a sign!"

To this strange narration, half story and half mad chant, the Suttons had listened with great eyes, silent, crushed with wonder and with fear. But now, as the speaker raised his voice in a shout, there was a tremendous answer from without: a horse neighed like many trumpets blowing together; hoofs clattered on the wooden steps; the porch quivered; and through the window was thrust the head of Sailing Hawk, searching for the master whose voice he had heard.

Thunder Moon laughed with joyous triumph.

"Sky People, I thank you!" he cried. "This is the sign. Now will you believe me?"

Believe him? They were almost too frightened to disbelieve.

Mrs. Sutton and Ruth drew closer to each other, but the colonel listened with shining eyes.

Before he could speak, however, it seemed as though the Sky People, to whom Thunder Moon appealed, had sent a more visible sign and one more easily understood. For up the driveway came young Standing Antelope, his hands tied behind him, his feet bound in his stirrups, and a smear of blood on one side of his head. With him were the half dozen men who had captured him—not spruce young gentlemen like those who had hunted Thunder Moon, but rough, brown-faced men in rude clothes.

"Here's number two," said Jack, willing to break the trance that had fallen on all in the room. "Here's the second of 'em. There are the three horses. Now we may get at something. It's Tom Colfax who's brought them in!"

14

They could hear Tom speaking to the scattered group of men in front of the house.

"Here's a rank Cheyenne, gentlemen. Doggone me if he ain't! I was starting out with the rest of the boys here and our guns for a hunt when we seen this fellow jump a fence, but his pony wouldn't clear it. He came down with a slam. And we picked him up. I been enough years on the plains to talk some Cheyenne. And I gathered from his lingo that he might have a friend over here. Anybody know what he means?"

They led Tom Colfax in. He stood at the door, hat in hand.

"Colonel Sutton, sir, the Cheyennes always was the wildest and far-ridingest red devils on the plains, but I never thought that they'd come raiding as far as this!"

The colonel went to him in haste.

"You know the Cheyennes, Tom?"

"I've traded with 'em. I know a parcel of them, of course. This boy opened up when he heard me talk his own lingo, and he says that he's the son of Three Bears. I know Three Bears. An upstanding Indian as I ever seen."

"Look!" said the colonel, and he took Tom by the arm and turned him a little. "Do you know this man?"

He pointed to Thunder Moon, who still stood near the wall. The effect upon Tom Colfax was amazing. He started back with an oath and at the same instant drew a great, old-fashioned horse pistol.

"Know him?" he gasped. "Know him?"

"I mean what I say, man," said the colonel. "This is more important than it may seem. Do you know the name of this man?"

"Know him?" echoed Tom. "I never seen him except once, and in the distance, but every man on the prairies

15

knows him or knows about him! Why, Colonel, this is him that's strung his war trails from the Rio Grande to Canada. If I ain't a half-wit and lost my eyes, this is the right bower and the best bet and the long arm of the Suhtai and the whole doggone Cheyenne nation!"

"His name!" said the colonel. "What's his name, man?"

"Ain't I told you enough to place his name? His name is Thunder Moon. What else would it be? And if I was you, Colonel, I'd have the militia out and bury this Suhtai under ten feet of solid rock. Otherwise you'll be waking up one of these nights—you and about twenty more—to find that you're all spirits singin' on your way to heaven. This is a bad boy, sir, and he makes all his marks in blood!"

3

But Mrs. Sutton had heard and seen more than her nerves could stand, and she broke into hysterical weeping at this point. The colonel bade his daughter take her mother from the room. He left Jack with Thunder Moon, and he took Tom Colfax into his private study.

"Tom," said he, "this is a serious moment."

"Sir," said Tom. "I got eyes and ears enough to understand that. But I feel kind of in a dream—after seeing that red devil in your house!"

"But is he red?"

"Is he red?" asked Tom, more bewildered than ever.

"Why—well, he's a half-breed, maybe. He *does* look a little pale."

"If you know him, do you know his father?"

"The longest hand you ever seen in a trade. Of course I know Big Hard Face."

"Big Hard Face?"

"Their way of saying December."

"Do you know the mother of this boy, then?"

"Her? No, I don't."

"Did you ever hear of her?"

"Matter of fact, Big Hard Face don't live with a squaw."

"Then how does he come to have a son?"

"The ways of an Indian ain't our ways with women and children, Colonel Sutton. Maybe he just picked up the boy someplace. Maybe he adopted him."

The colonel caught his breath.

"That's all you know?"

"No, it ain't half. I can tell you about Thunder Moon all day. Why, they've had articles about him in the papers! He's the only Cheyenne that don't count silly coups and that don't take scalps, and—"

"What of his honesty?"

"The Suhtai are an honest lot. And Thunder Moon's word is better than gold."

"He wouldn't lie?"

"I don't say he wouldn't. But I can tell you how he's raised hell from Mexico to—"

The colonel raised a rather unsteady hand.

"I think that I've heard enough about that already. As a matter of fact, Tom, it begins to appear that this man, this wild Cheyenne, is really the child who was stolen from my house more than twenty years ago."

Tom Colfax opened his mouth and his eyes.

"Does he say that?" he asked.

17

"He does!"

"If it's a lie," said Tom slowly, "it's the queerest lie that I ever heard tell of! For what would bring a Suhtai a thousand miles, pretty near, to claim you for a father? Why should he pick you out?"

"You'd believe him? You know Indian nature, Tom."

"Leastways," observed Tom dryly, "it wasn't *money* that I got out of my stay on the plains."

"Go with me and let him tell the story simply to us. Do you think that you could spot a lying Indian?"

"I dunno. But I could make a fine try."

They went back to Thunder Moon, and found him with folded arms standing against the wall just where they had left him, while Jack, a very nervous lad, fidgeted in a chair.

"Thunder Moon," said the colonel. "I want you to tell us, clearly, just what the old man of the Suhtai told you."

Thunder Moon answered, "He had no squaw. He had no child. He was no longer a boy. So he went off to do some great thing before he died. He rode a great distance. No great thing came to him to be done. He came to the land of the white men. He rode among their lands. Then he came to a great house, and near the house he saw better horses than he ever had seen before. He saw that the great thing he was led to do was to take some of those horses. So he took the best. And he waited until dark in the woods near the house. There he saw a black woman come out and leave a child under a tree. He thought he would go and take the scalp. The scalp of a white man is good to have."

"Good heavens!" breathed the colonel.

"But when he went to the child, it held up its hands to him and laughed. His heart became soft. He carried the boy away and raised him in his lodge. That is the story as it was told to me."

18

"Colfax," called the colonel sharply.

"Sir," said Tom Colfax, "if this here man is lying, I'm a fool that knows nothing!"

The colonel drew a great breath.

"I have gone slowly," he said to Thunder Moon. "Even now, perhaps, we have no testimony that would stand in a court. But you ride a horse that may well have descended from my stock. You have a distinct resemblance to me. Your skin is white. And you have been raised as an Indian. And, more than that, there is something in my heart that speaks to you, William! Come with me, and we'll find your mother!"

"It's settled?" asked Jack, springing up.

"Certainly it's settled, my boy. Do you object to my decisions?"

"I don't know," said Jack Sutton slowly. "It may not be sound reasoning. But—if you've made up your mind, that settles everything. William, I've held back and made things rather hard for you. Will you shake hands to show that you forgive me?"

Thunder Moon paused, and said in his grave way, "In the lodge of Big Hard Face he was called my father, and White Crow, his aunt, was a mother to me; but I never have had a brother. Our blood is the same. Let our hearts be the same, too!"

And he took the hand of Jack with a strong pressure.

They went up to the room of Mrs. Sutton. The colonel rapped, and the door instantly was thrown open by Ruth.

She shrank at the sight of the tall warrior.

"Ruth, my dear," said the colonel, "unless God has blinded me terribly, this is no Cheyenne Indian. He is a Sutton, the heir of Sutton Hall, and your own brother!"

"Mother!" cried Ruth. "It's true! I was right! I was right!"

19

She took Thunder Moon's hand.

"Come quickly! I've put mother to bed and she mustn't get up. Come quickly! Oh, father, what a day for us! William, my dear big Indian!"

She drew him, laughing up at him, to the door of a big room. Inside, Thunder Moon saw a large bed, and a small feminine form half rising from it, and the sunlight streaming through the window, glittering on her white hair.

"Do you mean it, Ruth?" And then, seeing Thunder Moon, the mother cried, "My dear boy!" and her arms went out to him.

The colonel would have entered behind his son; but his daughter, with a finer tact, held up her hand and warned him back.

As she closed the door, softly, they heard Mrs. Sutton crying, "My darling! My poor baby!"

Ruth began to laugh, a little wildly.

"Did you hear?" said she. " 'Baby'—to that terrible man-slayer!"

Father and daughter went to the window together, their arms around one another, and looking down to the back terrace, behind the house, they saw Jack walking slowly up and down, his hands clasped behind him and his head bowed low.

"Poor Jack!" said the colonel. "He's taking it very hard, indeed!"

But Ruth said nothing. She merely watched with an anxious eye, and shook her head a little.

4

Why should sorrow be beautiful or beauty sad?

Thunder Moon in the room of his mother went through such an agony of joy and of love and of yearning that the muscles of his throat swelled and ached.

He sat by her bed and held her hand, and she looked up at him with love. From the steady mask of his face, it seemed that nothing had touched him in the slightest degree in this interview; but she saw that he could not meet her eyes steadily, and by that she guessed that his stern nature was troubled to the bottom.

"William," she said.

There was no response.

"Thunder Moon!"

He looked quickly at her.

"Why are you sad, my dear?"

"Because I have found my people, and lost my people."

"They never really were yours."

"My tongue is their tongue; and part of my heart is their heart."

"I understand. But when you have our speech, then it will be different. But there will be many new things for you to learn. You will have a great deal of patience, dear?"

"Yes."

"Now I have kept you long enough. Go to your father. He is a stern man, William. But you will find that there

21

is a great deal of love and tenderness under his sternness. Also—your brother is young; and he is still younger than he seems. Will you remember that?"

"Yes."

"You may have to forgive him very often."

"I understand," said the warrior. "He has been the only son of a great chief. The lodge and the medicine pipes and all the horses have been his to look forward to."

A faint, sad smile crossed the face of Mrs. Sutton.

"A little time will make everything right," she said. "I trust in time and—in the goodness of men! Now go to your father."

But when Thunder Moon left his mother's room he found that the wild news had gone forth in every direction, and the Sutton ball was being continued through the day as a sort of impromptu reception.

Already half the young blades of the neighborhood had taken part in the chase, and the news of what they had captured had been broadcast. Newcomers began to arrive: farmers on plodding horses; dashing boys of any age; sedate landholders and plantation workers; and just as Thunder Moon came out into the upper hall, there was a screech of wheels turning sharply on the graveled road in front of the house, and Ruth Sutton went to her new brother and drew him to the window so that he could look down.

"You see how many people are happy because you've come home at last?" she asked, and she pointed down to the growing crowd.

Three four-in-hands had just torn up the driveway, one after the other, and the filmy clouds of dust they had raised were just blowing away in snatches under the cuffing hand of the wind. Those vehicles were loaded with people, and Thunder Moon stared at them with wonder. They looked a different kind of beings from those he had been accustomed to. They seemed more delicately made, more slender, and even their voices had a fragile sound in his ear.

Suddenly he stretched forth his long arm.

"What do you see, my boy?" asked the colonel.

"I see," said Thunder Moon, "the woman who should be my squaw!"

Ah, fickle-hearted Thunder Moon! What of Red Wind, the Omissis girl with the braided hair like red metal? What of her? Has her memory been dismissed so quickly?

"Hello!" said the colonel. "That *is* rapid work."

He was not altogether pleased, and he cast a worried glance at Ruth, as though a woman should know best how such an affair as this should be managed, and how serious this symptom might be.

But Ruth, laughing silently behind her brother's back, shook her head, as a token that his was not such a dangerous affair, after all.

"Which one, William, dear?" she asked.

"That one—that one!" said he. "That one with the face like a flower."

"Oh! It's pretty little Jacqueline Manners. Of course it would be she! She *is* a darling, father, isn't she?"

"Is it she?" asked the colonel, beginning to smile in turn. "That one with the flowers in her hat?"

Thunder Moon looked at him with eyes of wonder.

"No, it is that one—she gets down from the wagon now."

"Heavens!" said Ruth Sutton. "It's Charlotte!"

Thunder Moon stepped back from the window with a black brow.

"She is the squaw of another man, then?" he asked.

"You haven't wasted your time with the Cheyennes,"

23

said Ruth. "That's Charlotte Keene. And every young man in the state has asked her to consider him."

At this news Thunder Moon shrugged his shoulders, as much as to say that a battle not already lost still might be fought out.

Then he was taken to his room to dress in a suit of the colonel's.

While the garments were being laid out by the servants, Standing Antelope entered, and his eyes flashed with joy when he saw his friend before him.

"I thought that they were talking and jabbering and getting ready to turn me over to the squaws for torture," said Standing Antelope, "and I thought that they were bringing me just now to the place where I was to die."

"And what of me, Standing Antelope?"

"I listened to hear your death song, but I thought that the wind might have blown the sound of it away from my ears. But behold, brother, our hands are free! Through the hole in that wall we may escape and climb down to the ground. There are fast horses everywhere. Never have I seen so many so fine! And with two knife thrusts we can make these two black men silent!"

"Do not touch them, Standing Antelope. Touch no one in this house; everyone is under my protection."

"Ha?" cried the boy.

"This place is my lodge," said Thunder Moon. "It is given to me to live in!"

"It is very well," replied the boy. "I understand. The great chief understands that you are a part of his family."

"Yes, and so does his squaw, who was my mother."

"That is good," said the boy without any enthusiasm, "and how great a sacrifice will this chief and his squaws and his warriors make to Tarawa because he has led you back to them?"

"I cannot tell," said Thunder Moon, troubled. "All these people laugh and talk much like children in the street of the Suhtai town, but I have not heard them speak a great deal of the spirits. There is not much religion in them, and I have seen no making of medicine, and I have heard no promises of sacrifice. However, you and I must take care of that, for otherwise the Sky People will be very angry!"

"You and I?" said the boy. "Ah, Thunder Moon, you have come home to your tepee, and you have your people around you. They seem to me very strange. And though I hope that you may be happy with them, I must go back to our nation."

"Peace!" said the older warrior. "You are young and you cannot think for yourself. But I have seen many fine squaws and you shall pick out one for yourself, and I shall buy her with many horses. Then, if you must go back one day to our people, you may travel with a woman and with the horses I shall give to you, and many guns, and when you come back to the Suhtai you will be a great and a rich man, and you will tell Big Hard Face and White Crow how to follow the trail in order to come to me."

This conciliatory speech the boy listened to, only half convinced, but the overwhelming authority of Thunder Moon kept him from answering immediately. He said, pointing suddenly, "Thunder Moon!"

"Aye, brother?"

"The medicines of these people is very terrible and wonderful! Look! There is a pool of water standing on one edge!"

For, at this moment, one of the servants had uncurtained a tall mirror that stood at one end of the room. Both the wanderers stared at this apparition with horror.

And Thunder Moon looked suddenly to the ceiling.

"Sky People," he said, "if you are angry with me, do not send this miracle as a sign! If you are angry because I am changing my tongue and my dress, I shall give them up! I shall return to the Suhtai! No, Standing Antelope. I think it is not a bad sign!

So saying, he began to advance, though slowly, and at last stretched out his hand and touched the cold surface of the glass.

"Now I know!" he cried, straightening himself. "It is like the little mirrors that the traders sell; it is like those, made large."

At this there was a convulsive burst of laughter from the two servants. It died in a shriek of fear, for Standing Antelope, recovering from his terror the instant that he learned the true nature of the miracle, seized one of the valets by his head and at the same time presented a knife at his throat!

5

"Black dog!" said the young warrior. "Do you laugh at two warriors of the Suhtai?"

"Don't touch him! Take away your knife," said Thunder Moon, not displeased at this touch of discipline, however. "Does he not belong to my father? The anger of a chief is very great if one of his warriors is touched by the knife of a stranger!"

"Warrior?" snarled the young Suhtai, in great contempt, as he released his captive. "Warrior? A creature like this?"

He thrust home his knife in its sheath with a snapping sound as the hilt rapped the leather.

"What warriors are these, brother?"

Thunder Moon considered.

"We are in a strange country, friend," said he. "Their ways are not our ways, and their speech is not our speech. They are hard to understand. They are even as hard to understand as the tight clothes they wear. However, when in a Comanche lodge, eat like a Comanche."

A bath had been prepared by the servants and Thunder Moon sat in the tub and for the first time in his life scrubbed himself with soap. Burnished and glowing from a rub with a rough towel, he came out to Standing Antelope.

"I am a lighter man," said he. "My heart is better. There is no harm in this medicine, Standing Antelope."

"For my part," said the boy, "I cannot see why men should sit still in a bowl when they might swim in a river. Besides, this is hot water and steam baths are good, as the medicine men say, but hot water always is bad."

"With the Comanches, be a Comanche," repeated Thunder Moon. "Have no fear, Standing Antelope. But what has become of the black men? Have you frightened them away?"

"I only looked at them once or twice," grinned the boy, "and they backed away through that door."

"You are a young wolf among the village dogs," chuckled Thunder Moon. "How am I to arrange these medicine clothes?"

He got them on, in some fashion. They were not a bad fit, for Colonel Sutton was a big man, famous for his strength; yet his coat was very tight upon his newfound son. Up to the neck Thunder Moon was a civilized white man; but he knew nothing of the manipulation of a

27

cravat. His great brown throat rose like a column, and over his shoulders flowed a tide of wild black hair. His toilet was not completed by these labors, however, for, feeling that something still was lacking, made a little paint with the materials which he carried in his belt and decorated his face in a becoming manner.

Then he reviewed himself in the mirror with much gravity.

"How do I appear, Standing Antelope?" he asked.

"Above the shoulders, like a great warrior of the Suhtai," said the boy instantly. "But the rest—"

He made a gesture to indicate his displeasure and disdain.

"You are neither a white man nor an Indian," said he. "You will see! They will laugh at you."

Thunder Moon looked again, anxiously, but he could not see in what manner he was ridiculous. Therefore, he picked up his robe and flung it over his shoulders, and from a packet which was a part of his equipment, he selected a few of his best eagle feathers and arranged them in his hair—an effect which materially increased his height.

When he had finished thus arraying himself, he turned his attention to his young companion, but Standing Antelope, finding that the day was warm, was neatly and efficiently clad in a breechclout, with his robe flung over one shoulder.

Thunder Moon regarded him with attention.

"I never have seen a white man dressed as you are dressed now, Standing Antelope, except the squaw man High Creek, who married the daughter of Lame Eagle. What will they say when they see you?"

"What will the braves of the Suhtai say when they know how Thunder Moon has changed himself!" cried

28

the boy indignantly. "Besides, what is wrong with me? Except that I need a little paint!"

So saying, he borrowed some from Thunder Moon, daubed himself over each eye and turned his face instantly into a hideous mask.

"That is much better," said Thunder Moon approvingly. "Now I think we can go out and let them see us."

"Oh, my father," cried the boy, "you who have harried the Comanches in their far southland, and made the Crows tremble, and the Pawnees to run like dogs, do you wonder how these white strangers may look on you, and what they will say?"

Thunder Moon finished combing his long, black locks and tying again the band that circled his forehead to keep the hair from falling across his face.

He had no adequate answer for the boy, so he merely replied, "There are many things you are too young to understand, my son. Give me my war belt, and then go down before me."

Standing Antelope handed to his companion the belt that supported the two heavy Colts and the hunting knife of Thunder Moon. This the warrior fastened about his hips and gave the finishing touch to his costume.

With Standing Antelope leading the way, they left the room and crossed the hall.

A moment later they were in the midst of a sensation.

All the lower rooms of the house were now filled with eager-eyed, whispering friends and neighbors, all come to congratulate the colonel upon this miraculous recovery of a lost son; and even Mrs. Sutton, recovering rapidly from her weakness, had come down to be among her kind friends.

Into that audience walked Standing Antelope, garbed

chiefly in the clothes God had given him at birth, and with a beautifully made buffalo robe, flung lightly over one shoulder, because the day was warm. Standing Antelope was very young and he did not respect these strangers; otherwise he would have stalked in as Thunder Moon did behind him with his robe gathered carefully around him.

People were stunned, and they managed to keep their faces only by looking down at the floor.

Mrs. Sutton, amazed, though she had tried to prepare her guests for something strange, was unable to stir, but the colonel rose valiantly to the situation. He took his newfound son in tow and escorted him around the rooms. And the introductions were not altogether without result.

"Mr. Kilpatrick is a very old friend of mine, William."

"And of yours, too, my dear boy," said old Mr. Kilpatrick. "Remember me, William?"

"If you are my friend," said Thunder Moon in a grave, loud voice, which reached to every corner of the room, "tell me if all these women have some big medicine? Why do they sit, while the braves stand?"

At this blow, the colonel flinched a little; and the murmur of conversation ceased for an instant, but was immediately resumed.

"Here are Mr. and Mrs. Stanley Graham, our neighbors, William."

"How," said Thunder Moon; and then adopted the white man's etiquette by seizing the hand of Mr. Stanley Graham and nearly crushing its bones in his terrible grip.

"Is this your squaw?" asked Thunder Moon, as the face of young Graham went white with pain.

"Yes," said Stanley Graham politely.

"Tell her to bring me water, friend," said Thunder

30

Moon. "I am thirsty, for the clothes of a white man are hot to wear!"

"One moment," said the colonel, biting his lip. "A servant—"

"I'm very happy to get a glass of water," said Mrs. Stanley Graham, and went off with the pleasantest of smiles, and returned with the water.

Thunder Moon took it at a draught.

"Thank you," said he to Stanley Graham.

"I think," observed old Mr. Kilpatrick, "that the weaker sex is about to be put in its right place!"

6

A moment later Standing Antelope, who was following his leader through these mazes, spoke abruptly to his companion, and Thunder Moon translated to his father, "What is wrong with the legs of Standing Antelope? Why do the braves and the squaws stare at them?"

There was a stifled burst of laughter and Thunder Moon turned a dangerous eye to locate the noise. The laughter ceased.

"There is nothing wrong," declared the colonel in much haste. "All is well, my son."

And he carried Thunder Moon farther into the crowd. Faces began to blur in the eyes of Thunder Moon. He was a stranger in a strange land, and yet all these people spoke to him with the utmost cordiality. Sometimes, at his replies, there were little compressions of the lips, and sometimes there were slight changes of color, but on the whole he noticed nothing very wrong.

It did not occur to Thunder Moon as strange that the party began to break up suddenly and that people began to hurry away. So Indians came and went at a feast.

There was only one ominous form to him. And that was his brother, Jack, who was always somewhere in the background, with a white face that wore a continual faint sneer, or a smile that was like a sneer.

Then there was his sister, Ruth, who seemed half amused and half pained. It was easy for him to speak to her. And as the last of the guests moved away, he crooked his finger.

Obediently, she came to him.

"Are the strangers all gone?" he asked.

"Yes."

He sat down cross-legged on the edge of the carpet. He produced his pipe and filled it.

"Bring me a coal," he commanded.

Readily, she brought what he wanted. He blew a puff of smoke toward the floor, and another toward the ceiling.

"Peace to this lodge," said Thunder Moon, "and peace to all the people in it! May their robes never rot with mold and may the buffalo never fail them in hunting season! Now, sister, tell me what came of the woman with the flower face."

"Of Charlotte Keene?"

"You called her that. The name is hard to say."

"She was here with the others. Didn't you meet her?"

"Sometimes many clouds hide the mountains," observed Thunder Moon gloomily. "Where is the colonel chief?"

"Do you mean—our father?"

"Yes."

"I'll call him for you."

Thunder Moon leaped to his feet and touched her shoulder with his iron hand.

"Girl," said he, "is it proper for a great chief to be called to his son; or for a mother to be called to her daughter? Go, and I follow you!"

So Ruth led the way, and did not smile; and soft-footed Standing Antelope followed to where the colonel and his wife sat in the library, in close and anxious consultation.

Thunder Moon, in the doorway, paused.

"Oh, my father, is this tepee filled or is it free for me to come in to you?"

"Come in, William. Come in!"

Thunder Moon strode in.

"Send away the women!" said he.

"You had better go for a moment," said the colonel. "And you, Ruth. These ways will have to be endured for a time. Then we'll begin to make a few alterations!"

Mrs. Sutton and her daughter left; but Thunder Moon, turning a little, followed the form of his mother with a smile. And she, looking back at the doorway, saw the smile.

All was well between them!

The door closed. Thunder Moon had sent Standing Antelope away; he was alone with his father.

"Shall we smoke together?" asked Thunder Moon.

"Yes, if you will. Sit on this chair, my boy, not on the floor!"

"I am not an old man," said Thunder Moon, "and my legs are still strong enough to support me. However," he added with instant and instinctive courtesy, "do sit on the chair, my father. You have fought in many battles. How many coups the colonel chief has counted and how many scalps he has taken! But he has been wounded, and he has had the spearhead of the enemy in his flesh.

33

Therefore, sit on the chair, my father. It will be easier for you."

"Have I been wounded? Who has told you that?" asked the colonel, turning curious.

"My eye is not the eye of Standing Antelope," said Thunder Moon, "and it is true that the Suhtai have called me a blind man. Yet I can see what is put in my hand—or a cloud in the sky—or the rising sun. And, therefore, my father, I could see that your left leg was more tired than the right."

The colonel started. Many and many a year ago a bullet had torn through that unlucky left leg, but he had thought that all traces of a limp had disappeared from his gait long since.

"And when the knife," went on Thunder Moon, "cut in the soft flesh of the throat it is a danger."

"Could you see that scar? My boy, you're a hawk!"

"And the right side of my father is weak. Perhaps he was struck there, also?"

"By heavens," said the colonel, "your mother has been telling you about these things!"

"My mother?" said Thunder Moon, surprised. "We did not talk."

"No?"

"Except with our eyes and with our hearts," said Thunder Moon gently. "What are words? They cannot speak of love!"

The colonel looked intently at his older son. In another this would be a speech something more than flowery, but the grave honesty of Thunder Moon could not be doubted. He simply was translating as well as he knew how from his old dialect into his new one.

"She did not tell you that I was wounded in the right side? How do you guess it then? Do you look through cloth, my boy?"

34

"The old pine is still strong," said Thunder Moon. "It will not fall during the lifetime of a man. And yet it has begun to lean. It is not standing on a mountainside, and yet it is leaning to the right. Why does it lean, my father?"

"You mean that I incline a little to the right?" said the colonel, straightening his shoulders. "I don't think so, William."

"When you stand," said Thunder Moon, smiling.

"You are a mind reader!" said the colonel. "Well, sit on the floor if you insist. Will you have some of this tobacco?"

"No, father, but shall we smoke your pipe or mine? This tobacco of mine is a good medicine. It is a dream tobacco. Old Flying Crow had a dream, and the head of a buffalo rose above water and told him where to get the bark to mix with this tobacco. He gave me some, because I had helped his son in a battle."

"Let us smoke your tobacco then," said the colonel, interested. "But why should we have only one pipe, my lad? I'm fond of this old black pipe of mine!"

"How does wisdom come except with time?" asked Thunder Moon. "Lo, I am young! The years have not carried me very far down the stream, and it may be that your pipe is better. But a long stem makes a cool smoke," he went on, fitting the stem into the pipe bowl. "Also, this is a gift of the Sky People. Low Cloud made this pipe in the old days. The Crows took it from him when they killed and scalped him. Then Sleeping Wolf, the Pawnee, got the pipe and took the scalp of the Crow who had it, and with that scalp he took the pipe of Low Cloud. And then the Sky People gave Sleeping Wolf into my hands. As he died, he told me the story of the scalps and the pipe. I found the body of Low Cloud, two days dead. I fitted the scalp back on his head. I raised

35

him on a platform. I put weapons beside him and killed a horse beneath him. So his spirit rode off to hunt the buffalo over the blue fields of the sky. And his pipe has been good medicine to me ever since."

The colonel was silent for a moment. He had loved war and battle all his days, and yet this calm reference to a triple killing as a mere part of a story about a pipe made his blood run cold.

"All this is well," said he, "so we'll smoke your pipe, my boy. This old one of mine? Why, I've never done a thing for it except to cut out the cake once in a while, and polish it up a bit. And it hasn't a bit of meaning except that I've smoked it these many years!"

"It is not really medicine, then?" asked Thunder Moon, opening his eyes.

"Not a whit!"

Thunder Moon blushed for his father, and he said hastily, "However, many a strong and rich man will use a cheap thing. But let us smoke this pipe of mine!"

He lighted it with a flint and steel, showering sparks on a bit of dry tinder. Then he blew the customary puffs to the earth spirits and the Sky People, and passed the pipe reverently to his father.

"Now I shall tell you why I have come to speak to you this morning. Are you ready to hear me?"

"Yes."

"In your keeping there are many horses, my father. You have harried your enemies and wisely stolen their horses. Many a brave walks to the hunt because the colonel chief has stolen his horses and his mules. I have seen them on your lands!"

"Bought and raised," broke in the colonel, growing a little hot of face. "I hope that not one of them has been stolen."

At this Thunder Moon opened his eyes a little. Again

he blushed for his father and said hastily, "Well, let it be so. I have heard before of men who love a bought horse as well as one that is nobly stolen from an enemy!"

"*Nobly* stolen?" gasped the colonel.

"What is nobler?" asked Thunder Moon. "What is better than to ride, and make an enemy walk? Well, but the truth is that you have many horses and many mules?"

"That is very true. I am mighty glad to say that I have many of them."

"In my own land and among my own people," said Thunder Moon, "I, also, have many ponies. They are of the best Comanche breed, small and strong and tireless. Now give me ten of your horses, and I shall give you in return as many of my ponies as you wish to have in payment when I can send for them."

"You want ten horses?" asked the colonel. "You shall have as big a riding string as you want, dear lad, as a matter of course. But I'm curious. Why do you want ten horses?"

Thunder Moon stirred a little, and impassive as he kept his face, he could not prevent a slight shadow from crossing it.

"I understand," said he. "My father is about to ride on the warpath. He has need of all of his horses to mount his young men when he goes to take scalps. I am sorry that I asked. Forget that I have begged ten horses from you!"

"Good God!" exclaimed the colonel. "Am I refusing you the first request you've ever made to me? No, no, William! A hundred horses, if you want them! Take a hundred! I only asked—why, lad, there's no harm in a question, is there?"

"A hundred?" said Thunder Moon, smiling. "This is very well. I do not think that I shall need so many. But

37

you are kind. Only tell me where I can find the lodge of the chief who is the father of the young girl, Charlotte Keene."

The colonel glanced sharply at his son, and then he smiled a little.

"I think that you'll want to call there before long," said he. "Well, when the time comes, we'll take you over, or have the Keenes in for dinner. They live five miles down the road. It's the white house with the long front and the columns in front—very like mine. You couldn't miss it."

The colonel went back into the house and Thunder Moon said to Standing Antelope, "Go with me, Standing Antelope, and show me if you have forgotten how to catch a horse."

"My feet still carry me," and the youngster smiled, "and I am not blind. Let us go, Thunder Moon."

At the fence of the broad pastures, they looked over the horse herd, and Thunder Moon, sitting on the topmost rail, checked over the ones he wished to select.

"There is no reason," said he, "why a man should spend the finest horses in a herd to make a purchase. A horse is a horse. Take the young mare, yonder, to begin with. Ah, Standing Antelope, what horses these are! No wonder that the heart of Big Hard Face swelled in his breast when he looked on these chestnuts! And how many dozens of generations have men lived and worked to breed such animals?"

"They are the gift of Tarawa," said Standing Antelope, coming back and leading the mare that had been selected first. "They are the gift of the Sky People, because it is plain that no men could breed such horses as these. The great chief, your father, must have very strong medicine!"

38

"He has," said Thunder Moon, proud of his family for almost the first time since his return to the home of his race. "It is not hard to catch these ponies, Standing Antelope."

"Look!" said the boy. "They come to the hands like dogs. They have fine eyes. And see how the muscles work in their shoulders! Ha-Hai, Thunder Moon, if they did not belong to the father of a friend of mine, I should slip down to this field some black night and in the morning—well, they would be eating grass in another place!"

Thunder Moon smiled in broadest sympathy.

"Young wolf," said he, "follow another herd. This is not the place to fatten your hollow ribs! Now get that tall gelding that looks a little weak in the flanks, and the colt that is low in the croup, also . . ."

So the ten were selected and gathered in a group, and Thunder Moon mounted his war horse, the great Sailing Hawk, and rode off, with Standing Antelope on his own pony.

They went straight down the highway until they came before the long, low façade of the Keene mansion.

They turned into the driveway, and Thunder Moon tethered the horses to the hitching rack that stood at one side. That done, he and Standing Antelope swung into the saddle and galloped back—not directly back to Sutton House, but through the country by a winding way that carried them carelessly and freely here and there. For they needed to talk to one another. They had not been long in the house of the white man, but already they were feeling the galling bondage of civilization.

7

In the meantime, a string of beautiful chestnuts, sleek and bright in the sunshine, was being conducted back to Sutton House by the Keene servants, and Judge Keene himself, mightily perturbed, hurried on ahead, riding his fastest mount.

When he came to Sutton House, he asked to see his neighbor at once, and was brought into the presence of the colonel, on whose face there was a mingling of brightness and of shadow.

"I'm glad to have one moment alone with you, my dear Randolf," said the judge. "I've wanted to have a chance to congratulate you again, quietly, personally, on the great joy that has come to you today. God knows, Randolf, that no man ever less deserved that such a tragedy should come to him as came to you twenty years ago! No man deserves more to have the effects of it undone. And here your boy is back among us!"

"Thank you, thank you!" muttered the colonel. "But I hardly know how long he'll stay!"

"What?"

"I mean it. He's like a wild tiger. He starts away at everything or shows his claws. I only pray that he doesn't murder someone—he or the little devil of a Cheyenne that's with him!"

The judge rubbed his chin.

"I understand you," said he.

"And I suppose," said the colonel, coloring a little,

40

"that the entire countryside is still laughing over this morning's affair?"

"Laughing?" cried the judge hotly. "Laughing at such a thing as the return of my dear Sutton's first-born son? By heavens, Randolf. I'd horsewhip the rascal who dared to laugh at such a thing in my presence!"

"Would you? I think that you would. But everyone in this neighborhood is not a Keene."

"No, sir," answered the hot-headed judge, "nor would we want to include every Tom, Dick, and Harry in our family, I hope!"

"You always must eat a bit of fire," exclaimed the colonel. "Well, God bless you, Dick! You do me good. At the same time, it was a shocking thing, rather, to see him come down the stairs—civilized up to the neck—and wild Indian above!"

"Shocking? Not at all! Of course, every man is a little oversensitive about the appearance of his family. But every man and woman in your house this morning must have known that there was a Sutton heart in the wild man who came down those stairs!"

"What, with horrible paint on his face?"

"What the devil is paint, Randolf? What has that to do with the mind of a man? He needs to learn other ways, that's all. All you need to do is to work on the surface. He's already a man and a leader of men!"

"I might try to send him off to school," suggested the colonel. "He's a bit old for school, but—there's the place that that cousin of yours runs—"

"As a matter of fact," put in the judge hastily, "that school has some very sacred traditions it clings to. And—and—"

"Don't say another word! I understand perfectly. And every other school worth sending him to would have the same!"

41

"Besides, Randolf, there would be something absurd in sending a great chief, a famous warrior, to sit with schoolboys. You'd better try a tutor!"

"I'll try a tutor," decided the colonel, "and I'll be the tutor myself, by heaven! What better have I to do in the world than to see that my son has the proper chance in life?"

Here the judge was compelled to turn his head and to clear his throat with violence.

He put in, "But, by the way, colonel, there's another matter that brought me over here. It's only some practical joke among the grooms, I suppose, but you don't want your grooms to take liberties with your thoroughbreds, I imagine?"

"Certainly not! What have the rascals been doing?"

"Which ones were up to the mischief, I don't know. But a while ago we walked out and found a string of ten of your chestnuts tethered to the rack in front of the house!"

The colonel sat down suddenly, and with violence.

"Ten, did you say?"

"Ten!"

The colonel passed his hand across his brow. "Heavens!" said he.

"What's wrong? It's not so serious as all that, I hope?" exclaimed the judge.

"I—Dick—before anything more happens along this line, I think that I'd better tell you my suspicion."

"Go on, my dear fellow."

"The fact is, that this morning when the people were arriving, William looked out the window and saw only one face, really."

"Well."

"You can imagine what face would stand out in any crowd. It was your girl, Charlotte."

42

"Charlotte!"

"Yes. Charlotte. 'A face like a flower,' he said, and he was quite right. And, later on, he asked me for a gift of ten horses—would give no reason for his request; simply wanted them—I suppose that you begin to see the connection?"

"The connection between Charlotte and ten horses? No, sir, I confess that I don't understand what you may mean!"

"Simply this. I hate to say it. But the fact is—as I've heard it—that when the Indians on the plains decide on a girl they want for a wife, they simply lead out a string of their horses—one horse for an ordinary squaw who may have been married before; two horses for a fine young girl; five horses for a beauty—and—you understand now, I hope?"

The judge's face was purple.

"Extraordinary!" said he.

"Extraordinary, of course," agreed the colonel. "But in a case like this, with a man just from the plains—twenty years as an Indian makes an Indian, in a way. That ought to be clear enough, my dear Dick!"

The judge made a turn up and down the room. He cleared his throat. He had turned from purple to a fiery red.

"There is something to be said—" he began, and stuck.

"For what?" said the colonel, very good-humored.

"For a natural sense of delicacy and decency where women are concerned," said the judge.

"Dick, you're rather running on a bit, it seems to me!"

"Am I? Am I? Colonel, I want you to remember that we've mentioned my only child—my dear Charlotte!"

"It seems that we have," said the colonel, becoming a trifle dry.

43

"And in connection with—er—"

"In connection," the colonel took up the sentence and went on, more dryly than before, "with my oldest son and heir."

"Hmm!" said the judge. He added stiffly, "I don't quite follow you in this, Dick. Do you suggest that you are making a formal proposal of marriage on behalf of your son?"

"I?" said the colonel, raising his bushy brows. "By no means! By no means!"

"Ah!"

"Marriage among all the plains Indians is rather an informal matter," said the colonel.

"Really?"

"Yes. As I understand it, a man gets a wife almost as casually as he gets a horse. And, of course, I don't imagine that William's ideas about marriage differ much from those of the people he's been raised among."

"A very unusual idea," said the judge. "I can hardly imagine that any son of mine—that is to say—"

The colonel rose.

"Perhaps you'd better not hunt for the word, Judge," said he.

"No?"

"Perhaps I understand you well enough as it is!"

The judge was silent. But when the thunder clouds are piled high in the sky, though there may not be either rain or lightning, at least the thunder must rumble, here and there.

"By Jupiter!" exclaimed the judge. "A price of ten horses for my daughter's hand! My Charlotte!"

"I attempted," said the colonel, growing stiffer still, "to explain away an embarrassing moment for both of us. It seems that you don't follow me. I can only assure you that I never shall be a party to any attempt to

44

inveigle your daughter into exchanging your house for mine."

"Colonel Sutton, you use decided language."

"Judge Keene, you suggested the terms to me."

The judge was silent. For a moment the friends stared at one another.

"I think," the judge said softly, at length, "that the ten horses have, by this time, been returned to your paddock."

"Sir, you have shown the most neighborly—thoughtfulness. I thank you."

"Don't mention such a small matter, sir. Good morning!"

"Good morning, Judge Keene!"

The judge bowed, turned upon his heel, and left the house. Precisely, rapidly, he went down the front steps. He approached his horse. He mounted and thanked the groom who held the stirrup for him.

The colonel, from behind a curtained window, watched all of this proceeding, and he marked how his old friend raised his eyes and glanced quickly and searchingly over the face of Sutton House, very much in the manner of one who wishes to take away a clear mental picture of a thing he never may see again. Then the judge rode off.

And the colonel went slowly back to his library and there sat down and pondered. Already he was beginning to pay a price for the return of his son. He had been made ridiculous in the eyes of the neighborhood. He could endure that. But now it had cost him the friendship of a very old and dear friend.

The heart of the colonel began to sink.

8

As for the judge, his irritation increased all the way home. No very honest anger sustained him, and for that reason his temper became worse and worse, for he could not help telling himself that the colonel must have meant no insult to him. And, after all, the alliance that had been proposed had been with the eldest son of the most honorable family in the neighborhood. If that eldest son appeared to be more Indian than white man, the appearance was doubtless rather seeming than actual. So the judge got to his house in a white-hot temper, much more out of patience with himself than with his oldest friend.

Straightway, he did what a sulky person usually does. He began to burn his bridges behind him and thereby made the possibility of reconciliation with the colonel more impossible than ever. He sent for his daughter, and Charlotte came to him. He heard her singing through the big echoing halls of Keene House. She came in wearing a riding habit with the long, trailing skirt of that prim day.

The judge looked upon her with a dull eye, for he was seeing not only his daughter but all his dreams of what a woman should be, and in nothing did he find her lacking.

"Charlotte," said he, "I have broken with Colonel Sutton."

He waited to let this terrible tidings take effect.

Charlotte merely said, "You silly dear!"

46

"You don't understand," explained her father. "I have severed our old relations with Colonel Sutton!"

"How long have we known the Suttons?" she asked.

"Since you were born, my dear."

"But before that there were Suttons and Keenes, I take it?"

"Naturally!"

"And they've always been friends. They were neighbors in Virginia. They were neighbors in England in the musty old days, weren't they?"

"Naturally," said the judge, and he blinked a little as he saw the direction his girl was taking.

"So I don't see how you and the colonel can break off such a friendship in one moment, father."

"I'll show you the reason," said the judge.

He gathered his evidence in his mind. It was not quite as black as he wanted it to be, and therefore he fell back upon artificial stimulus and brought his brows together darkly.

"Now, Charlotte," said he, wishing for the sake of his anger that she were farther away from him, "do you know what the colonel has had the audacity to suggest to me?"

"Well, dear?"

"That I give you in marriage to a wild Indian—a Cheyenne—a bloodthirsty—"

"To William!" said the girl.

Her father paused and stared at her. The name came pat enough from her lips.

"You may call him William. His real name is an infernal Indian jumble that means Thunder Moon!"

"That's delicious, don't you think?" said she.

"Good grief, Charlotte, how can you take it so lightly? A man who has worn war paint and has stolen up on enemies. Stabbed men in the back while they slept—"

47

"Not a bit!" said the girl. "The Cheyennes thought he was a fool because he insisted on giving his enemies fair warning!"

"How do you know so much about him?" asked her father.

"Simply that I've talked with Tom Colfax. Tom knows all about him. He can talk for hours about Thunder Moon. I've heard—"

"The fact is," said her father stiffly, "that at this time I'm not particularly interested in what you've heard about that young man. We've both seen him, and I'll trust the evidence of my eyes rather than the gossip of an ignorant—"

"I never saw a finer man," interrupted the girl.

"Charlotte, you insist on being contrary! Admit that when you saw him come downstairs you were shocked and frightened!"

"Of course, I was frightened! That's why he's so wonderful! But how silly of the colonel to want to marry him off at once. Besides, he's not the sort of a man who would marry at his father's bidding. Or is that Indian manners?"

"I show you a nightmare, and you smile at it!" exclaimed the judge. "I show you a wild red Indian—"

"Whose name is William Sutton, who has white skin, and who is heir of Sutton House! Go on, father."

"Bah!" snapped her father.

He glared at her. Then he played his trump card.

"You talk about his savagery without realizing what it is!" said he. "I'm going to show you. Do you remember the ten horses that were brought here today?"

"Of course! How beautiful they looked, standing together there! I wish we could get some of the Sutton strain, father."

"Damn the Sutton strain!" said her irascible father.

48

"Those ten horses were brought here by Thunder Moon—to buy him a wife!"

"Oh!" cried the girl, and caught her riding crop in both strong hands.

"Yes, sir! Brought over to buy you with, Charlotte!"

"Then he wants me of his own will!"

"The young brute looked out of the window of Sutton House and saw you—and said something about a flower-face—and swore that you must be his wife. Straightway, he takes ten horses and ties them at our door!"

She hesitated.

"Well," she said at last, "Bob Sherman sent me flowers one day and perfume the next, and the third day he asked me to marry him!"

"Do you think the cases are parallel?" shouted her father, losing his temper.

"Fundamentally about the same," said she.

"Gracious, Charlotte!" cried the judge. "I believe that you want to marry this barbarian from the prairies!"

She puckered her forehead.

"The idea is rather attractive," said she.

"Charlotte!"

"Well?"

"What do you know about him? This stranger—this wild—"

"I know that he's a hero, a brave and strong man, a glorious rider, a wonderful fighter, and—and—"

"What else, if you know these things?"

"That he's kind to his horse."

"Charlotte, I think you are mad!"

"Not a bit!" said she. "Let him tie ten horses at the door of any other girl around here and see if her head doesn't swim."

"I hope not!" said the judge. "I have a higher respect,"

49

he went on bitterly, "for our young women, raised with such care and nurtured so delicately! I could not attribute such thoughts to them!"

She was not insulted. She merely smiled at her father.

"We look very fine," said she. "We're not cut on such broad, strong lines as men. But never think that we're so delicate, dear. Because we're not, and besides—ah!"

She broke off and pointed through the window. The judge looked and saw two riders sweeping like the wind up the driveway of his house, and one of them was Thunder Moon!

9

Never had such a person appeared at the door of Keene House!

Gone were the clothes in which Thunder Moon had startled the neighbors that morning. Now he was clad in one style only, and that was the style in which he had been raised for twenty years.

Over his head towered lofty eagle feathers, which hung in a double row down his back and to his heels, well-nigh. Around his forehead was a narrow band of doeskin, set with a complicated pattern of colored beads worked by the masterly hands of White Crow herself. But the rest of his outfit was not the product of Cheyenne craft. He had drawn upon half the tribes of the plains to gain his wardrobe, and he had paid for it by heroic daring, and not in gold. His beaded shirt, heavy as mail, was taken from the body of a Sioux chief who had fallen in battle under the bullets of Thunder Moon. His trousers, of softest leather, intricately fringed, were decorated with beadwork of another kind, laboriously sewn on by Crow women; and lost when one of their warriors lost his life in war. Upon his left arm he carried that dream shield, which, as he thought, had so often brought him safely through the dangers of battle. Some few deep scars were upon its face, showing where bullet had glanced or lance head failed from the front of the thickened buffalo hide. The shield wore its mysterious paint; but the face of Thunder Moon was without that adornment.

The servant who opened the front door to this apparition grinned at first, feeling that there must be a game behind such a festival appearance. Then he almost fainted as he realized that this was not a sham or a mask.

The next moment, the judge himself confronted the tall young man.

The right hand of Thunder Moon was ceremoniously raised. From the wrist dangled the long canine tooth of a grizzly bear, slain valorously in single combat, a prize not less in the eyes of an Indian than the scalp of a chief.

"How!" said Thunder Moon.

"How!" said the judge, answering dignity with dignity, in spite of his irritation. "Will you come in— William?"

Thunder Moon pointed to the sky.

"I have to speak a great word," said he. "In your lodge that word might be lost, for the eye of the judge chief will look on many things that are big medicine and that are his already, and so he will not regard the medicine I offer him. But there is a place where we may stand and talk!"

He pointed to the lawn in front of the house.

51

"Very well! Very well!" said the judge, and he walked uneasily down the steps behind the tall visitor.

He felt that he made a very poor second to such a lofty fellow. And he was all the more annoyed by this consideration because he knew that from some window nearby his daughter must be spying upon them with a curious eye. He would have liked to tell himself that she was above such childish eavesdropping, but in his heart of hearts he knew that she was not. The judge knew not whether to sigh or to swear.

Upon the plot of grass, Thunder Moon took his stand. Nearby Standing Antelope sat upon his pony, the butt of his war lance resting on the ground, his hand grasping it near the head, both man and horse apparently turned to stone. Only, from time to time, a touch of wind fluttered the single feather that adorned his hair.

The great stallion, Sailing Hawk, followed his master upon the lawn, and the judge was about to make a pettish remark as he saw the hoofs digging into his favorite bit of grass, but he felt in this situation an element of almost tragic dignity and importance that kept him from speaking of smaller things.

Thunder Moon struck instantly into the main current of his message.

"You are my father's friend," said he, "therefore you are my friend. My father is your friend, and therefore I am your friend. This must be true. The blood of man is not as cheap as the blood of buffaloes in the spring hunting, and such friendships do not come and go lightly."

The judge could have said something very much to the point about this matter, but he restrained the desire to speak, and listened, merely nodding a little in polite assent.

"This day," said Thunder Moon, "I looked out from the lodge of my father and I saw the woman who lives in your tepee. I was troubled. In my home I have no woman. I never have looked after them. But we are in the hands of Tarawa. He guides us where he will, and what he wishes, he puts into our minds to do and to speak. I felt him touch me when I saw the maiden. He touched my heart and put words on my tongue. I said to my father, 'There is the squaw of Thunder Moon.' After that, I took ten horses and I brought them to the lodge of my father's friend. For I said to myself that sometimes between friends a woman is given out of mere friendship, but never such a woman as this maiden. I left the horses at the lodge of my father's friend. I hoped that he would accept them, and that he would come again leading the maiden and leave her at the entrance to my father's tepee.

"But I was a fool, and a great fool, for I did not understand that what is greatly desired by the heart must be paid for from the heart. He who desires glory must risk his life for it. He who desires love must pay for it with sorrow.

"For a long time, I did not know what to do. That which we love is like a part of the flesh. We cannot think of doing without it. So I did not know what to do, but at last I had a great thought. It made me very sad, but also I saw that it must be accomplished before I could have the maiden. My friend, behold!"

Thunder Moon stepped back a little and threw out his hand with a gesture of much dignity, pointing to the stallion.

And Sailing Hawk, unmindful of the solemn occasion in which he had been included, playfully pricked his ears, and nibbled fearlessly at the hand of his master.

Now the judge looked more earnestly at the stallion.

Hitherto, he had been wishing only one thing, which was that the strong voice of this young warrior might be lowered so that it would not reach the girl who, somewhere, surely was listening and drinking it all in. What devil had prompted this reclaimed Suhtai to act his play upon such an open stage?

But a sense of courtesy chained the judge. Much, he felt, was due to his own dignity, but still more was due to the conventions in which he had been raised.

He regarded the stallion now, more intently.

The animal was, in truth, the most glorious bit of horseflesh that the judge—an expert in such matters—ever had looked upon. He himself had bought beautiful horses, and he had raised them. But never before had he seen such an animal as this.

So the judge looked and looked again, and for a moment he forgot the foolish situation in which he stood; he forgot his anger at the colonel; he forgot the watching girl who was drinking in all these happenings.

"What a king of horses!" cried the judge. "What a grand fellow he is!"

"In all his life, he never has failed me," said Thunder Moon solemnly. "When his mother foaled him I, Thunder Moon, riding the plains and watching, saw the colt and knew that he was great. It was known by the white star in his forehead and by the bigness of his bone and the goodness of his legs. And from his back to his belly there was also room for a good heart and strong lungs.

"Now this foal grew into a colt, and when the herd galloped, he ran in the lead, until the old mares threw their heels at him. And from a colt he grew into a horse. He was so filled with fire that when he was only two years old he met the greatest stallion in the herd and beat him, and he became the king of the herd from that day.

"I watched him. When he was three, Big Hard Face said, 'Let him be ridden!' But I watched and waited. I said that no man should ride him save me. I watched him, and when his fourth year was almost ended, one day I saw the herd running at full speed, and all the fastest stallions and the swiftest mares were working with their heads stretched straight before them and their tails whipped straight behind by the wind of their going. But in front of them ran this great horse. His tail was arched, and his head was high, and he looked carelessly from side to side as he galloped, and yet for all their straining they could not gain upon him. It seemed that the wind blew him forward.

"Have you seen a hawk with broad, still wings sail swiftly, even against the wind? So it was with him, and at that moment I shouted with all my might. He ran on as though he did not hear me, but I knew him, and I would not call again. Yet I began to grow a little angry, and to fear that he had become too proud from running unmastered so many years. However, all was well. He presently threw up his head, and came heading back for me. Then he ran indeed. The herd could not stay with him! He leaped away from them! They disappeared in his dust! So he rushed up to me. He stopped and put down his head and began to pretend to crop the grass carelessly, but all the time he was watching me from the corner of his eye to make sure that I had noticed his greatness.

"Truly, I was not blind. I stretched up my hands to Tarawa, and I gave him thanks for the horse and the friend he had sent to me!"

When Thunder Moon had said this, he made a pause and gathered himself in great composure for a moment, for his eye had begun to shine wildly. And even though he commanded himself with some difficulty, he could not wholly master his enthusiasm as he went on, "Since that day, I have hovered over all the prairies like a sailing hawk dropping from the sky on a victim, and then sweeping away again out of sight when pursuit was attempted. The warriors have praised me many times when the glory should have been to Sailing Hawk. For with a sound of the voice or a pressure of the knee he can be made to swerve, to turn, to halt, to leap onward again. With him beneath you, you think your way through danger. Where you would be, there you already are in an instant.

"I have said many things, O my friend, though I know that he who praises his horse is praising himself. But look on him for yourself, and you will see that all I have said is true!"

The judge stared enviously and hungrily upon the stallion. He was a round man, built to fill a most comfortable chair, and his weight staggered the beam of the scales to an amazing figure. When the rest of his neighbors, and even the ponderous Colonel Sutton, floated across the fences on their thoroughbreds, the poor judge was forced to labor in the rear upon some stiff-shouldered nag whose hot blood had grown cold. As a rule, therefore, he broke down more fences than he cleared, and he could not help knowing that he was more or less of a joke in the hunt.

Now, when he looked on the tall horse from the prairies, he had a dazzling mental image of his stalwart form blown forward against the wind and leading the hunt at a terrific pace, with a good double wrap taken upon the pulling jaw of the stallion.

To the judge it seemed, at the moment, that there was nothing in the world comparable with the beauty of this thought.

He turned to Thunder Moon with a sigh.

56

And the young man went on, "You have heard and you have seen, and I see that you believe what I have said. Now, O my friend, I give you this great horse. I separate myself from him. I thrust his spirit away from me—"

He was slightly interrupted in the midst of a dignified gesture, for the stallion caught at his beaded sleeve and held it mischievously in his teeth.

"I give him to you," said Thunder Moon, increasing the volume of his voice as it became suddenly a little husky. "I give him to you," he went on, his arm under the head of the big horse, "and in exchange, I ask you to remember that if your daughter comes to my lodge, she does not come to be the common squaw of a common warrior. The fleshing knife need not strain her hands, and the back of my woman shall not bend under heavy loads. I go, my friend. Take my horse and this thought into your heart and consider well!"

He laid the reins in the hand of the petrified judge, looked once full into the eyes of the horse and then turned and hurried away.

Behind him, as he walked down the drive, Standing Antelope turned his pony and followed his chief respectfully.

"Wait!" called the judge.

But his voice did not carry far.

"Wait!" cried the judge again, but this time Thunder Moon had turned the curve of the driveway, and a rising breeze drowned the call.

Mr. Keene looked helplessly around him, and now he saw in a lower window of the house the grave face of his daughter, who said, "It seems to be settled, father."

"Settled? What is settled?" asked the judge, growing crimson.

"The exchange seems to be made," said the girl.

57

"Hang it!" exclaimed the judge. "What exchange do you mean?"

"I don't think you've done badly," said Charlotte. "After all, I was bound to marry before very long. And, ordinarily, you wouldn't have such a horse as that to fill my place in the house—in the stable—or at the hunt, you know."

"Charlotte," declared her father, "the fool of an Indian—"

"Indian?"

"He is. An infernal, wild, red Indian. My dear, what am I to do? Tom! George!"

Two grooms instantly appeared.

"Take this horse," said the judge, "and get him back to the Sutton place as fast as you can. George, jump on his back and take him over. You can walk back across the fields. Hurry!"

Into the saddle went George.

The stallion did not seem to move violently; but though George was an expert rider, out of the saddle he sailed far more gracefully than he had swung into place. Out of the saddle he went and reached the lawn in a sitting posture with an audible thud.

"You ride like a fool," said the judge. "You, there, Tom, get into the saddle and ride that horse home!"

Tom, setting his teeth, cautiously got into place. The same swift, soft move of the stallion followed, and Tom rose into the air with a screech like a skyrocket and landed with a louder yell.

The judge looked on in amazement. These two grooms rode as well as any men in the district.

"How did it happen?" he gasped.

"Big medicine," suggested his daughter.

"I would have been murdered!" breathed the judge. "That last fall—it would have broken my back! Tom, if you can walk, you and George take the head of that ugly brute and lead him back."

He turned his back resolutely on the stallion and stamped into the house, where he found his daughter.

"You were in here listening?" he asked savagely.

"Of course," said smiling Charlotte.

"A lady—" began the judge hotly.

"Is always human," said Charlotte. "And when one is being sold—"

"Charlotte! The ignorant, bland-faced ruffian!"

"I thought he was a glorious figure!" said she.

"Glorious, child? Glorious? A man who is fool enough to think that I would exchange my daughter for a horse and—"

"Not a horse," interrupted Charlotte, shaking her head. "Not just a horse. He was offering you a part of his greatness. He was offering you half his glory. And, besides, I've an idea that he loves that horse about as well as most men love their wives. And—why shouldn't there be some exchange?"

"Do you think I want a horse to help me take scalps?"

"Look at it from Thunder Moon's viewpoint, not the viewpoint of a Keene or a Sutton."

"Charlotte," cried the judge, "I think that you want me to marry you to that man!"

"I don't know," said she. "But certainly it's true that I've never seen a man before that I could think of marrying so easily!"

The judge recoiled in horror.

"Little fool!" he shouted. "Go to your room! Go to your room at once!"

Charlotte went. But even before she was upstairs, she was singing most cheerfully, and the judge, agape, listened to that cheerful voice as to a voice of doom.

10

As the weeks passed, the rift between the families of Sutton and Keene continued, simply because the heads of the families refused to take a step toward a reconciliation. Charlotte Keene was less worried by the alienation; handsome Harrison Traynor filled her days and most of her evenings with his attentions, and, for his part, he was perfectly well contented with the progress of affairs. And in the household of the Suttons there was happiness for everyone save young Jack. Traynor saw him at a coursing match one day, and touched his shoulder.

"You're out of sorts lately," he suggested.

The youngster looked keenly up at him.

"Can you guess why?" he quickly asked.

"I can more than guess."

They were old acquaintances, and besides, the bitterness of Jack's heart required a confidant.

"It's not the idea of the split inheritance," said he. "It's the blindness of everyone, not seeing that it's all a sham. My father's tutoring has turned a wild Indian into a copy of a white man. Because he looks and acts like one of us now, people believe that he has changed."

"It's always easy to believe what one wants to believe," agreed Traynor. "But I'll tell you, Jack: a wolf looks like a dog until it shows its teeth!"

"What do you mean by that?"

But Traynor already was moving off; and Jack stared earnestly after him. It was not difficult to put that suggestion into a plainer form: the way to make the so-

60

called William Sutton reveal his true nature was to stir him up with a violent stimulus. Advice easy to give, perhaps, but who would want to scratch such a tartar? However, the idea ate deeply into the memory of the younger man, and he lodged it in his heart for the future.

In the meantime, a most unexpected stimulus was injected into the lives of all concerned by the arrival of Adler and Kahn's Greatest Circus on Earth. They sent vast red bills ahead and splashed the countryside with streaks of crimson advertising their hordes of dangerous jungle beasts and their dazzling air acts. They were only to be in town for a single day, and for that day the entire countryside turned out to be thrilled.

There was not much thrill to be found in the performance, however. There was one splendid young tiger, with huge, supple shoulders, which looked mighty enough to rip out the bars of its gilded cage, but the rest of the beasts were a mangy lot. There was a moth-eaten lion minus its teeth; a sleepy bear, which ambled through some stupid tricks; a few acrobats in dingy white; and the very popcorn and the pink lemonade were stale. Even the children pronounced it a poor show and dozed in their seats; and the evening performance was attended by the merest handful.

Before midnight, however, the show of Adler and Kahn had given the countryside a thrill and a start. The big tiger did exactly what had seemed so impossible. He ripped out two bars of his cage, battered aside two others with blows that would have done credit to a grizzly, and then squeezed his way out and paid a visit to the bear's cage. Half a dozen frightened, shouting attendants fired blank cartridges into the face of the jungle monster, but they could not keep it from sweeping open the cage and going in after the snarling bear.

61

It emerged quickly, leaving a dead carcass behind, and now it left the circus and loped softly away into the nearby woods.

An alarm was sent out. The community armed itself. Excited searchers went out in bands.

But the tiger had melted away in the shadows among the trees, and for a whole day there was no slightest report of it.

Then a fine three-year-old thoroughbred was found with a broken neck in a corner of the Harmon pastures, and the body had been partly devoured.

The trackers followed the prints of huge feet away from the spot, but they led to a creek, and in the waters of the creek the trail was lost. In vain the hunters watched around the carcass. The tiger did not visit it again; and the following day but one, Judge Keene lost a beautiful young mare, slaughtered by the savage destroyer.

Panic seized the horsebreeders. They had in their midst an enemy with a special taste for horseflesh, and they shuddered with fear. A price was laid on the tiger's head. Five days later the price was doubled, so that it stood at two thousand dollars, for three more animals had gone down before this crafty jungle-devil. One was a common mule. But two were high-priced hunters.

People ventured out in the evening only in large parties, and there was a general panic at every stir of shadows even during the broadest daylight. Every midnight creak in every plantation house was felt to be caused by the stalking foot of the tiger.

Then Standing Antelope came to Thunder Moon and, squatting on his heels, he made a great print upon the ground.

"That is the foot of the striped one," said he. "I shall find him, O brother, and we will kill him, and take the

62

price. It is the value of forty ponies. And I am not a rich man!"

Thunder Moon smiled and shook his head. He felt that he was pledged to more serious work; but in the middle of the night he wakened, and the bright moon was shining in his face. He got up and entered the adjoining chamber where the boy slept.

Standing Antelope was already up, bringing a hunting knife to a fine edge, and with a rifle laid out before him. He glanced keenly at his leader.

"I have been waiting a long time," said he, "but now let us go."

And Thunder Moon, rather sheepishly, went with him out of the house and into the woods.

Just at the verge of the moon and the shadow, they lighted a pipe and smoked, with puffs to the Sky People and puffs to the earth spirits, alternately. Then Standing Antelope took up a handful of dust and pebbles and blew the dust away.

He closed his hand and face to the north, the east, the south, and the west. Then he opened his hand and counted five little stones.

"It is luck and medicine, brother," said he. "Four days I have followed the sign of this great one. This is the fifth day. Four times I rode behind you in the other times, and the fifth time you noticed me and took me with you and made me a man. Hai, Thunder Moon! We shall kill before the morning!"

And he turned and began to run across the country.

Mile after mile they put behind them until they came to a group of wrecked buildings, the site of a deserted farmhouse. There Standing Antelope paused, and said, "Look at the great trees, brother, that go up against the sky and the moon. All underneath them is thick, thick brush."

63

"Good!" gasped Thunder Moon. "Is he in there?"

The boy smiled at him.

"You are fat, O my friend," said he. "You are fat and your wind is not good, if a little walk such as we have taken steals it away from you!"

The long arm of Thunder Moon reached for him, but with catlike speed Standing Antelope avoided it.

"Did you follow the tiger here?" asked Thunder Moon.

"I have followed it for four days, and each of the four tracks disappeared. And each time the tracks pointed in this direction from different quarters of the horizon. He could come by that stone ledge and lose his tracks. Or he could jump from one fallen log to another, there. You will see! Something will happen before long!"

They followed the line of the logs the boy had pointed out, and at the end of the last one, where the ground was soft, Standing Antelope lifted a little patch of fallen leaves. He made a quick signal, and Thunder Moon peered over his shoulder. There, plainly visible in the moonlight, was a great round print of a foot.

They spoke no more, except with signs.

"This was not here this morning," said the boy. "And surely he is inside!"

Like snakes they advanced, writhing softly through the brush, until at last Thunder Moon was gripped in the small of the back by a deadly chill. He jerked his head over his shoulder and saw behind him two phosphorescent disks of light, huge as lanterns in the dusk beneath the shadow of the trees.

And he knew that the hunted had turned hunter. He touched the leg of the boy who was crawling in front of him with the flying tips of his fingers, and made the sign, "Danger is behind us!"

Then he gripped his rifle.

64

But the brush confined him on either side, and he felt that before he could swing the gun through the crackling leaves, the monster would spring. So, he drew from either hip holster a long-barreled Colt, and cast up through the boughs above him a single glance to the moon-flooded brightness of the sky.

Then he turned and planted a bullet straight between the eyes of the beast.

The answer was a roar that made his nerves leap. And the giant shadow lurched forward at him. He fell, firing as he dropped, and as he twisted on his side a striped belly drove above him.

Into it he sent a .44 caliber slug, and got to his knees again.

The thought of Standing Antelope was in his mind, but now he saw that the boy was safe at one side of the path. The great tiger had leaped blindly and cleared the bodies of both its enemies. Now it stood in the midst of a patch of stout brush such as that through which Standing Antelope and Thunder Moon had been forcing their way. It seemed like a vast cat, gone mad with rage because a mouse had escaped it, and at the slashing strokes of its forepaws the brush was uprooted, beaten aside, knocked flat.

Something more than rage had blinded it, Thunder Moon could guess. Standing Antelope's rifle spat fire. The tiger stood like a soldier at attention. And then, with a quick shot from the gun he had just picked up, Thunder Moon drove a bullet behind the shoulder of the monster and through its heart. So that battle ended.

11

The moonlight was failing as they began to skin the tiger. The dawn was gray in the east when the pelt finally was stripped from the body. Still much had to be done to clean the hide, and by the time the preparation was complete, all the sky was rosy with the day. They had carried the pelt outside the brush for better light, and here they were observed at a distance by one of Paul Leicester's farmhands, who went to report to his master. Leicester, riding over the meadow, came on the final stage of the work, and saw William Sutton, stripped to the waist, laboring with a will. It was Leicester who looked on the scene of the combat, and saw where the fight had taken place, where the hunters had been hunted, where the tiger had battered down the brush, and where it had fallen. It was he, also, who had a pair of horses brought for the victors so that they could ride home with their pelt.

There had been what seemed to them an equitable division of the spoil. The reward for the killing was to go to Standing Antelope, as also the twenty knifelike claws of the great cat, which, their points blunted, already were strung as a necklace to ornament the boy's neck. Like a young savage he went, rejoicing in the bloodstains that covered his body, his hands, and his clothes. But William Sutton, stepping out of the role of Thunder Moon, was properly clad when he mounted the borrowed horse and tied behind his saddle the share of the loot that went to him—the head and pelt of the tiger.

Already he knew what he wanted to do with it, and he went straight as an arrow across the countryside to the house of Judge Keene. It was still early morning, but the judge and his daughter were at breakfast under a pergola in the garden when Thunder Moon rode up.

He raised his hat, dismounted, and bowed to them again. Judge Keene came hastily toward him. He was only waiting for some such chance as this to show that he regretted the words he had spoken in heat on the subject of this young man and his novel courtship. He took the hand of William Sutton with much warmth.

"You're up early, William," said he. "I'm delighted to see you! And isn't that the Austrian horse of Mr. Leicester. Isn't that Fregoli? Hello, though! What have you been hunting?"

He saw the roll of fur bulked behind the saddle, and a moment later Charlotte screamed with excitement, for Thunder Moon had taken down the pelt, and the huge, grinning head of the tiger appeared.

At the feet of the girl Thunder Moon laid down the spoil. He unrolled it, and the pelt glimmered like black-striped velvet. Though the hide was empty, the great fangs seemed locked with power and malice upon the stout stick Thunder Moon had placed between the jaws.

"This is for you," said he. "If you will take it, I shall leave it here."

She stared into the terrible mask of the jungle beast.

"How can I take it?" she asked.

"Why not?" broke in her father. "It's a most magnificent present! Sit down here, my lad. And ask your wild young friend to come here, too. I want to hear all about it. By heaven, there's still blood on that youngster! Did you fight hand to hand? Sit down, William!"

67

Thunder Moon glanced toward the sun and marked its height.

"In a few moments," said he, "my mother will ask for me, and she will be frightened if I am not there. I must go back at once."

He stepped to his horse and gathered the reins. Then he turned toward Charlotte for a last word.

"I'm glad that you'll keep the skin," said he. Leaping into the saddle, he bowed to them over the horn with bared head, and presently his horse was scattering the gravel down the driveway, and Standing Antelope was galloping in the van.

The judge could hardly finish his breakfast. He jumped up from the table again and again to look at the trophy. Suddenly he said, "Charlie, the scoundrel really loves you."

Charlotte did not answer. She leaned over and felt the hide.

"It still seems warm with life!" said she.

So a double sensation was given. There was the filling of the tiger to talk about, and more than that, there was the presentation of the pelt to young Charlotte Keene.

"If he hadn't done it quite so soon—in a few days—but to take it there straightaway—why, my dear, it was almost as though he had been hunting the tiger for the sake of Charlotte Keene!"

So said the colonel to his wife, and she answered, "Well, and perhaps he was!"

"But we don't publish our affairs of the heart for the attention of the entire world!"

"Let him go his own way," said Mrs. Sutton. "It will turn out right in the end!"

"Let me have another month with him," said the colonel fervently, "and I think it will. Let me have another month to train him, and then I think he'll understand what law means, and real self-control!"

Now while the colonel was making this prayer aloud, young Harrison Traynor rode through the woodland with Charlotte Keene. He was saying to her, "This fellow William Sutton—or Thunder Moon—or whatever his right name may be—"

"We'll call him William Sutton," suggested Charlotte coldly.

"I thought he was quite sidetracked," said Traynor. "But he seems to be one of the sort who never fires single guns. Silence or a broadside, from him!"

"You're speaking very frankly."

"Of course I am. What could be franker? I'm afraid of how he may get on with you with these odd presents, given at odd moments."

"There's something devilish about your frankness," said the girl. "It always makes it harder to guess what you're really thinking."

"Like Iago, you mean? But tell me, my dear, when a fellow gallops out of the heart of the morning, so to speak, and lays a handsome tiger skin at your feet, doesn't it open your soul to him a bit?"

"You may be as frank as you please," said she; "I'd rather talk about the weather."

"Yes," said Traynor, "he's gaining ground with you, I see. One can feel his cleverness. He won't stay in the field for steady maneuvers, but he lays ambushes, makes night attacks, and carries forward in five minutes farther than others go in years of effort."

"Do you think he's simply crafty?"

"Of course he is. Plenty of brains, he has! He's not so sure of his rhetoric, you see. Won't trust himself entirely to words. So he sets up a tiger skin to speak for him with

69

all its stripes! And, By Jove, it seems to have worked most successfully!"

"I think," she said, "that he's simply filled with impulse!"

Mr. Traynor laughed gaily.

"You wouldn't be so charming, my dear," he declared, "if there was not so much of the child in you. It's delightful to see the way you trust people! Mere impulse? In a fellow clever enough to play such a role as he's carrying off and—"

Charlotte Keene checked her horse.

"I shouldn't have said that. I really apologize to him and to you. My tongue simply stammered it out, confound it!" said he.

"It wasn't fair!" said she.

"Of course it wasn't! It was like hitting from behind, and I never do that! I'm eternally sorry, Charlie!

"You're angry, Charlotte," Traynor said softly, breaking the silence between them.

"I am," she confessed. "I think I'd better ride on alone and get rid of my temper."

"Do just as you think best," he answered.

"Then I'll turn back. Good morning, Harry."

"Good morning, Charlie."

He raised his hat to her and kept it off, watching her around the turn of the road.

12

"I am no more to him than a schoolmaster to a pupil," said Colonel Sutton gloomily. "If there is any emotion in him, I have failed to see it! And what does he do when he sits with you here in the evenings? Does he speak at all?"

The family was on the small side veranda of the house, facing the rose garden.

Mrs. Sutton touched her husband's arm.

"I'm not worried," said she. "He cannot show himself to you as he does to me. Sometimes he says nothing at all. Sometimes he says such things as no one else can say."

It was after dinner, and William Sutton had not yet come down to the porch. But when he appeared, a little later, the father and the others excused themselves. Mrs. Sutton settled to her needlepoint close to the hooded lamp. Thunder Moon, when the rest were gone, stretched himself on the porch floor, with his hands behind his head, so that he could stare up into the star-strewn vault of the sky.

For many minutes nothing was said.

There was some sound that was inaudible to the listeners inside the window in the dark.

"What was that?" asked Mrs. Sutton.

"A night hawk."

Another silence.

"Who taught you the calls of the birds, William?"

"Big Hard Face taught me. Mostly when we went away to hunt eagles."

"To hunt eagles?"

"Yes. For their feathers. They are a good medicine, you know."

He still used some words out of his old Indian vocabulary, even when he was calmest. When he was excited, they came forth in troops.

"But how can they be hunted?"

"It is best to go with a very wise and patient man. One learns to be patient. Big Hard Face used to say that was the better part of wisdom."

"Was he a patient man?"

"He is a patient man," replied Thunder Moon, quietly correcting the tense. "For many years he wanted to make me a great warrior and thought that I was a coward. I could not stand pain."

"But I have seen—why, William, of course you can stand pain!"

"No, I cannot. Even to think of it makes me sick. When Snake-that-talks was young, someone dared him to pick a coal out of a fire and hold it to light his father's pipe. There is a way of handling a live coal so that it will not burn. He did not know how. It stuck to his skin. The smoke went up from his flesh while he held the coal to light his father's pipe, but he would not make a sign. Afterward, when the burn healed, his fingers were stiff for more than a year. And there were many other young men among the Suhtai who despised fear, but I never was like that."

"I am glad you were not!" said Mrs. Sutton. "Such absolute folly! Such ridiculous pride in self-torture! I am glad that you were not so foolish, dear boy!"

72

Thunder Moon was silent for a moment, watching the waving branch of a climbing vine, like a dark arm against the stars.

"Ha!" he said softly, at last. "That is the way with mothers. I have listened to the women among the Suhtai, and even when many spoke at once, I always could tell when a mother spoke to a child. Now I have another thing to say to you. My brother and my sister do not love me. How shall I win their love?"

"Now you are very busy with your studies. When you have more time, then you will be able to talk with them."

"I shall find what they wish and learn how to give it to them," he replied. Then he sat up.

"That owl is very near," said Mrs. Sutton, listening also.

"Yes, it is near."

"Are you going to bed, dear?"

"Yes."

He kissed her good night, and disappeared into the house.

He tapped at the door of Standing Antelope. There was no answer. He opened the door and saw that the room was empty. And, as though that made him hasten, he slipped out the window, peering keenly among the shadows of the garden beneath.

Halfway down the side of the house, Thunder Moon clutched a drainpipe and hung by one hand, listening, for the long, soft hoot of an owl again drifted through the air. The next instant he was on the ground, and, heading back through the shrubbery, he worked swiftly around toward the point from which the call had seemed to drift.

A shadow stepped from behind a tree trunk. Thunder Moon swerved as if from a pointed gun, but the quiet voice of Standing Antelope said, "I shall watch for you and wait here, brother. Let me be your eyes!"

Striding forward, Thunder Moon stepped into a little open space among the trees and saw before him a shadowy outline, and the starlight glinted faintly upon two copper-red braids of hair.

"Red Wind!" said he, gasping out the words in Cheyenne. "How have you come here? Who brought you here?"

"Someone who rode this trail before."

"Someone who rode this trail before? But no other person ever came here from the Cheyennes except—ah, do you mean Big Hard Face? Is he here with you? Did the old man bring you?"

"The tepee of Big Hard Face is empty and sad," said the girl. "I could not fill it. So he came away to find you."

"Bring me to him, then. Where is he? What could have made him come into such danger, Red Wind?"

"He has many things to say," she answered, "and it is not fitting that a woman should speak the mind of a war chief! This way, Thunder Moon!"

Full of excitement, he hurried with great strides, and the girl began to run to keep up and show him the proper direction, only murmuring to him, "Thunder Moon, your feet fall on the ground like a stick on the face of a drum. Everyone will hear in the great lodge. They will all come out and look for you! Hush! Hush! Go softly!"

Suddenly he saw a tall form hooded in a great robe.

"My father!" cried Thunder Moon.

"How!" said the old chief, and raised his hand.

But Thunder Moon rushed in under the saluting hand and clasped the old warrior in his arms. It was no trembling, time-worn skeleton that he took in his grasp, for the years had fallen thickly upon the head of the chief but they had neither bowed his shoulders nor made his step infirm. And the arms with which he embraced his foster son were like the arms of a bear.

"Come in with me," said Thunder Moon, as they separated a little. "I want to have light so that I can see you, my father."

"Would you take me into the lodge of the strangers?" asked the chief.

"It is my lodge also," said Thunder Moon, "and if—"

A gruff exclamation of anger stopped him.

"Your lodge stands among the Suhtai," said the chief with emotion. "How can a man have lodges among two people? Your place is back on the plains where the Suhtai wait for you! How many warriors ride behind your white father into battle?"

Thunder Moon replied, "He does not ride to battle, and there are no warriors behind him. Only friends. Things are not with the white man as they are with the Indians, father."

"Ha!" cried the chief. "This is good! What has kept you so long, then, among people where there is no glory to be gained? What has kept you here, Thunder Moon? Honor and fame call you back to the plains. The Suhtai await you! Listen to me while I tell you a true thing. They let you live among them and gave you only a little praise. But now that you have gone, the Pawnees and the Comanches know of your going. The leaders of the Suhtai look at one another and no man wishes to take the war path. We have no strong medicine left. The Comanches are coming up from the south, and they sweep away our horses by hundreds. Before long, the Suhtai will have to walk on the plains. Dogs will pull their travois. All the Indians of the plains will laugh at them. They will be beggars. They will have to creep up to the buffalo by stealth. They no longer will be able to ride among them like warriors and hunters!"

"Be silent for a moment!" broke in William Sutton. "You fill my heart with trouble and misery, father. Let me think and draw my breath again."

Red Wind, as though she read his mind, stepped close and drew about his shoulders her own robe, made of the lightest skins, delicately prepared and dressed.

He pulled it like a hood over his head, and covered his face in the age-old sign of grief and suffering.

Big Hard Face seemed touched by this, and he went on in a gentler voice, "Now that our enemies scorn us, the Suhtai are beginning to talk to one another and they say, 'It was not like this in the days when Thunder Moon was among us. When he led out our young men, they came back with scalps and they counted many coups. He was himself like a strong war party, able to dash into the camps of our enemies and fill them with terror. He was like a fire upon the fields. All the nations fled from before him!' "

The imagery of the chief had taken wings.

But Thunder Moon said suddenly, "Still there is the medicine man, Spotted Bull, who hates me and turns the hearts of the people from me."

"Spotted Bull is like a young man who never has counted a coup," said the chief. "A few old women still listen to him, but the men have turned away from him, for they know that it was he who drove you from us!"

"He did not drive me!" said Thunder Moon. "And ten like him could not have driven me! Tell me! Is it true that the chiefs and the young warriors speak of me and wish me back among them?"

"Ha?" cried Big Hard Face. "Is it strange that their

76

prayers for your return have not walked even this far through the air to you! Come back, for you will be made the chief of all the Suhtai. Come back, and by lifting them from misery to greatness you will make yourself great also! At the last council of the Cheyennes, the other tribes shrugged their shoulders at the Suhtai, and the Omissis chief, Walking Horse, even the father of this wretched girl, offered to take us among his people and add our tepees to his!"

"Ha?" cried Thunder Moon. And his strong fingers, in the darkness, found the haft of the hunting knife that was always somewhere in his clothes.

"It is true, and the young men of the Suhtai listened and are disturbed and they said that perhaps it would be wise for them to join the Omissis, and so they could escape from the Pawnees and from the terrible Comanche riders!"

"You spoke, however!" said Thunder Moon.

"I spoke," admitted the old chief, "and I restored their hearts to them for a little. But they will change again."

"Ah, my brave and wise father!" said the youth. "How much I honor you! I shall go out with you and find my people again, and when I come, let the Comanches and the Pawnees make their prayers to Tarawa, and let them offer up their sacrifices, for I shall take them with a vengeance that our grandchildren shall speak of! I shall carry off their horses and leave their dead without scalps! I shall make the Pawnees howl like wolves! Do you hear me, my father?"

"I hear you!" said the old man, his voice trembling with joy. "Tell me that it is a promise and a true thing that shall happen, Thunder Moon!"

"I tell you," began Thunder Moon, when the soft voice of the girl broke in upon him. "Do not promise!

Our people are red men, and your face is white. Live here among the men of your own blood. You must not leave them. What right have we to ask for your life!"

The riding whip of old Big Hard Face hung by a noose from his wrist. He raised it with a groan of fury and lashed the girl heavily with it.

She did not stir. It was as though she had not felt the stroke.

"Stay here," said she, "and send the old man away. He has a name; but he is no more kin to you than the dog that howls there in the darkness!"

For, somewhere in the night, a dog was calling mournfully for a moon that had not yet risen.

Thunder Moon was too amazed by this speech to speak a word; and his foster father stood with arm and whip suspended, ready to give the second stroke but held back by some inexplicable force. At length he dropped his hand and said bitterly, "I know, now, why this woman followed me, and trailed after me for two days before she came up to me on the plains. I know now why she cared for me as a daughter cares for a father. It was because, out of her malice, she wished to be with me when I spoke to my son, and then she would destroy whatever I said. For that is the curse that she brought to the Suhtai—she has lived only to send Thunder Moon away from us, and now she will prevent him from ever returning!"

Thunder Moon stepped close to the girl and stood above her in the darkness.

"Why is it that you have hated me so?" he asked her. "What is the harm that I have done to you? When have I struck you or reviled you? I brought you back when you would have gone away with a Pawnee wolf from our tepee. Otherwise, I have not injured you. But now you

78

hate me terribly. You would lay down your life, I think, to keep me from going back to the Suhtai!"

"You will not go back," said the girl. "They are not your people. Even when you lived among them, you were not one of them. And now, if you went back, you would see that they eat raw entrails of freshly killed game. They would be horrible to you! No, you will not go back!"

"Why do I not strike her dead?" asked Big Hard Face, panting with emotion. "Why do I stand and listen to her, as if my hand were numb? There is nothing but evil in her. You were about to give me a promise that you would return with me to your people—to our people, Thunder Moon. Let me hear you speak it now!"

"I have heard you," said Thunder Moon. "Someday, of course, I shall return to the Suhtai, but it is true that my skin is white, and now the great lodge is my lodge, and I have a place in it. Let me at least stay until I know a little more of them."

"No good journey can be made when the face is turned in the wrong direction," replied the old chief. "It is the voice of the girl that has changed you! Leave me, Thunder Moon! There is no joy in my heart. Go and leave me alone with my sorrow!"

And he turned his back resolutely on his foster son and strode away, but so blindly that he would have crashed against a tree, had not Red Wind, with instant care, drawn him to one side. She sprang back to Thunder Moon.

"Go back!" she said. "I shall come to you again. Now, go back, for there is nothing more that you can do tonight!"

He turned gloomily, and went toward the house. A dozen times he paused, and a dozen times he was about to return to the spot where he had left the old man. But each time he remembered the words of the girl, and the strange surety with which she had spoken.

Whatever was the strength of Big Hard Face, or whatever was his own might, Thunder Moon could not help feeling that in this girl there was an uncanny influence stronger than either. He acknowledged it, and he wondered greatly.

13

The estate of Colonel Sutton was so far-flung and his interests were so many that he himself had only a vague idea of all that was going on over his domain. He felt that while it was due to the property to show it a respectful attention and interest, it was due to himself not to be troubled by details.

And what details there were! There was lumbering and lath-making at one mill and shingle-making at another. There was wheat-raising and the growing of barley and oats and corn. The chief crop was tobacco, and to the tobacco the colonel gave some attention, as to a matter about which he had intimate knowledge. The other crops interested him very little, and when Thunder Moon said, as they rode through the estates, "This tobacco is very much. It will fill many pipes. All the Comanches and the Sioux and the Cheyennes could fill their pipes from that one field. But still, those trees are very many, and the creeks turn the wheels of the mills, and the wheat grows thick and tall. There must be a great profit from those things, my father." The colonel merely answered, "The rest are nothing. Look at the book of profit and loss! Curly thinks I ought to sell out everything except the tobacco land, and I'd do it, except that the fellow who wants to buy is a Yankee. I can't have a Yankee for a neighbor. However, it's a temptation to sell to this one. He offers a great price! For the timber alone he would pay—well, enough to make your head swim."

"Why should he offer so much?" asked William.

"Because the Yankees know how to make money."

"What profit do you make from the lumber each year?" asked Thunder Moon.

"What cash return? I don't know. I leave those things to Samson. Samson handles the books. He could tell you, I suppose."

"Next to you," said William, "Samson is the chief of all these lands and the people who live on them?"

"Chief? Well, he has many responsibilities. Takes a vast load off my shoulders. Don't you like Samson? Pleasant fellow!"

"Among the Suhtai," answered William, "they do not choose a war chief because he is kind, but because he can get scalps for the young men who follow him. I do not think that Samson would be made a chief among the Suhtai."

The colonel made a wry face at this comment.

"Don't mix your standards of judgment," said he. "Remember that what's true for the Suhtai on the war path is not true for white men living in peace!"

To all of this William listened intently, but he reserved judgment. It seemed to him that some lessons learned among the Cheyennes would be useful among the white men.

In the meantime, he wanted very much to speak to his

father about the two visitors who had come to him from the plains; but the last speech had, in a sense, made it impossible for him to talk of what was nearest to his heart. A man who held that the white man and the Indian were different humans could not be expected to sympathize with Big Hard Face and Red Wind.

This conversation had taken place during a recess of the morning's work, and after it the work began again. Labor, labor, labor! Thunder Moon's head was bowed, his brain staggered as it approached new problems of infinite smallness. Of what real use was *any* of this book learning? Did it teach one to strike harder, stand straighter, hit the mark more squarely?

Revolting for the thousandth time, he started up from his table in the little summer house and strode impatiently to the window. Through the vistas of the mighty trees he could see the distant fields and the laborers moving through them.

He shuddered with sympathy as he watched them.

"It is true," said a voice. "It is a smaller horizon than that of the plains!"

It did not startle him; it was no more, hardly, than an echo of his thoughts. But then he remembered that he had not spoken and he stared wildly around him.

He saw nothing, at first, but then, not three steps away, hardly screened by the showering tendrils or by the copper-bright blossoms of the big, climbing vine, stood Red Wind!

His face darkened as he looked at her.

"Where is the old man?" he asked.

"He did not sleep all the night. But now he is sleeping."

"Why are you here where everyone can see you?"

"No one will see me. The people here are blind; even Thunder Moon does not see very clearly."

Only in her eyes a faint smile appeared.

He rested a hand against the side of the trellis and looked calmly, thoroughly at her.

"No," said he, "a thousand men could look at you and never see the truth about you."

"What truth, Thunder Moon?"

"I, in my life," said he, feeling the familiar Cheyenne speech like a charm upon his tongue, "I in my life have not sat all my days in a lodge and looked at old women painting images of the world. I have ridden out and beheld many things. Is it not true?"

"Men say among the Suhtai," said the girl, "that Thunder Moon has ridden from the great south river to the northern snow. However, a blind man could ride forever and see very little!"

"Peace!" said he, stamping with anger. "I say that I have seen many things, splendid rivers, and noble mountains, and glorious horses, and young and old people of the white men and the red, but never have I seen so much beauty as there is gathered together and made into Red Wind. She is like a thing molded of fire; and the image of her is burned into the mind. By day and by night the thought of your beauty has blown through me. What I see of you is good. But the mind sees you more clearly than the eyes! Now, that vine falls over you with grace and with beautiful blossoms, but there is more grace and there is more beauty in you; and yet with my mind I know you. Among the Omissis you were a shadow of trouble and to the Suhtai you have brought disgrace and ruin, and you have sent me away into a distant country. And what man in the world can speak good of you? Do not call me blind, Red Wind. For I see you and know you!"

"However," said the girl calmly, "the bad horse suffers from the whip, and I have suffered also."

She drew aside her robe at the throat, and he saw the livid streak left by the whip stroke Big Hard Face had given her the night before.

"Big Hard Face," said she, "is a kind man. When he strikes, he uses only a whip, and after a while the mark of the whip is healed and goes away; but other men strike heavily with words, and the marks that they make never are healed and they never go away. Do not blame your father too much. I have almost forgotten that he struck me!"

Thunder Moon gritted his teeth.

"You say that I am cruel and wicked," said he. "Then come into this small lodge and sit down with me. I shall talk to you. Tell me about my wickedness. I shall listen!"

14

There was no chance for Thunder Moon to receive an answer to this, for hoofs spattered sharply up the driveway, and two riders came to a stop not far away, where Mrs. Sutton was busy with her trowel in the garden.

"Dear Mrs. Sutton," called the voice of Charlotte Keene, "how lazy you make me feel! And what a beautiful garden you have made here!"

"I only potter around, child," said Mrs. Sutton. "We have such an industrious member of the family now, you know, that he shames the rest of us into some sort of labor!"

"That's William, I suppose. Have you heard about the present he gave me?"

"Oh, the skin of the tiger, you mean? And he gave all the reward to the Indian boy."

"He has no business sense, dear Mrs. Sutton. But he couldn't give away the glory of such a killing, could he? Where is he now?"

"In the summer house, there. In this fine, warm weather he prefers it to indoors."

"May I speak with him?"

"Please do."

The hoofbeats crashed closer; through the lattice-work Thunder Moon saw Charlotte swing to the ground, and now she was standing before him at the little arched entrance over which the climbing vines streamed.

She came to him smiling and took his hand.

"Are you too busy to see me for one moment? Thank you! May I come in then? What a lovely place for work!"

Somehow he hoped that she would not look through the other window and see Red Wind standing among the shadows; in the distance he heard the quiet voice of that young aristocrat, Harrison Traynor, speaking to Mrs. Sutton in the garden.

"You have it decorated, too, I see!" said the girl. "*What* a lance! Like a knight in the old days, isn't it?"

"What is a knight?" asked Thunder Moon.

"Ah, your father will tell you! But—a real bow and real arrows! Don't tell me that you've actually used them—not with your own hands!"

"I have!"

"But can you hit anything with them? Will they really go straight and pierce through?"

For answer, he slipped the bow from the wall, saying, "I never could handle a bow as the rest of the tribe managed it. But, still, you can see how rapidly they work—at short range they're very good! You see?"

85

And with a swift and easy motion he drew the bow, an arrow on the string. Strong were the Cheyennes, and strongest of all were the Suhtai, but no hand, save that of Thunder Moon, could wield this mighty war bow. The twang of the cord was like the stroke of a finger upon the harp. And there the arrow quivered in the heart of a sapling twenty yards away.

She ran to look; the keen steel point had pricked through on the farther side. And though the tree was young and slender and the wood was soft with youth, yet Charlotte could not help a shudder when she thought of how that arrow would have driven through human flesh. She touched the shaft; it still was quivering in its lodgment.

Then she came back to Thunder Moon.

"Well," she said, "of course you make everything possible! But if every Indian can shoot as well as this, why aren't the white men wiped out of the plains country?"

"I'll tell you," he answered. "Every Indian shouts as he fights. The white man shouts afterward. The Indian fights so that he may tell about it afterward; but the white man is willing to die in the battle. That is the great difference, and that is why the white man grow stronger and stronger!"

"You say it sadly, William."

"It is a vast country," said he for answer. "And there should be room for everyone in it. But the white man is a king, and so is the Cheyenne. They cannot live beside one another."

He fell into gloomy thought, in the spell of these reflections. And Charlotte had an opportunity to turn her clear, bright eyes from one thing to another in the room, and finally to the fatal book of geography over which he had been poring. She smiled at him, then, partly in amusement, and partly in pity.

"I'm giving a dance tonight. Not a real ball. Can you come, William?"

"The Suhtai do not dance like the white men, who go around and around with a woman in their arms," he answered.

"You may dance as you please," said she. "But there are a great many young people in our neighborhood who want to know you better. Say that you'll come!"

He thought of Big Hard Face in the woods nearby, of Red Wind, of all the trouble that lay before him, and of the many decisions he would have to make.

"I cannot come," said he.

"Is it your father?" she asked, tilting her head a little. "Is he still very angry with my father?"

"My father?" he answered, with a start. "Which father?"

Charlotte stared.

"Which father?" she asked in bewilderment. "Oh—but if your foster father is here also—"

"I don't—" he paused.

Among the Cheyennes social lies were not in favor, so he checked himself in the midst of a denial. He glowered at her, and she drew back a little toward the door, almost as though she were afraid.

"Everyone said that you wouldn't come," she declared. "Of course, you wouldn't have to dance, unless you wished to. You could sit and talk. My father would talk with you. And I'll talk, too, if you'll let me, and if I'm able. I wish you'd think it over!"

He began to smile a little.

"You're relenting, I think," said she, and her smile was much broader than his.

"Why do you talk like a child?" he asked her suddenly.

"I?" cried the girl.

"Yes. You make your eyes open wide, but your heart is not so open. You speak very simply, too, like a child; and yet I am sure that you are much wiser than I am, and that you know a great many things I do not know. Why do you talk to me like a child, when you are *not* a child?"

She bit her lip. It was the first time since early girlhood that anyone had spoken to her after so blunt and frank a fashion. Her color grew high. She was about to make a quick and keen retort, but she checked herself and said, "I suppose I *do* play a part and that I'm not always entirely honest. But, really, that's what we're expected to do, you know. However, I see that you want me to go—"

He stepped a little closer and did a thing no other young man would have dreamed of doing. He laid a hand upon her shoulder in order to detain her. And the other hand he put on top of her head, and bent her head gently back, so that she was forced to meet his eyes.

Why she did not exclaim angrily at this familiarity, she herself could not have told. Yet there was something about his manner and his air that was not in the least rude.

"Do you think it would be well for me to come?" he asked her.

"Only if you wish to."

"If I come, it would not be to see the others, but only to see you. Because of all the people I have met here, there is no other who puzzles me so much as you do. And of all the people in the world, only one has seemed stranger to me."

He released her.

"I shall come," said he.

"I am glad of that," answered Charlotte, much sobered. "Who was the other strange person, William?"

"An Omissis girl who came like a curse to the Suhtai," said he. "She lived in my lodge and brought the curse into my life also."

Miss Keene grew very white.

"She was your squaw, your wife, William?"

"She? No, I would not take her with that curse on her. Besides, she would not have taken me. She hated me."

"But you were a great and rich chief!"

"No chief was great or rich enough for her. The rivers that run from the mountains to the sea are filled with wisdom, but they are not so wise, as she. They are beautiful, but not so beautiful as she. Nothing in the world, I think, is so beautiful as she."

"Ah?" said the girl coldly.

"Nor so evil," he finished.

"It makes an attractive portrait," she replied. "What was her name?"

He stopped at the door and picked up a bit of dust.

"May her name be forgotten and may she disappear like this dust!" said he, and he blew it into the air, where it hung in a thin mist, and then dissolved.

"That seems like magic," said she, and laughed a little shakily. "You will come, then? Please do. Good day, William."

She got to her horse and rode from the place.

"You were hardly civil to Mrs. Sutton when you said good-bye," remarked her companion, Harrison Traynor, "and you look like a thundercloud just now. Nothing went wrong with your talk with William, I trust?"

"I'm not going to bother with him," she exclaimed. "He's simply too different to understand. He—he makes my head spin! Do you know, I think that his foster father—the Indian one—has come out of the plains! Think of that! But—he talked to me as if I were a little fool, Harry. And he actually made me feel like one!"

Harrison Traynor said not a word. The least syllable might break the train of thought, and he wanted her to utter her thoughts aloud.

"He put his hand on my head and looked into my eyes and said that I shouldn't try to talk like a child! Am I such an affected fool? Heavens, it makes me furious when I remember! What unutterable impertinence!"

Again he was wisely silent; and very grave was Harrison Traynor then.

"I've half a mind to go back and tell him that I can do without him at the dance tonight!"

Traynor checked his horse. "Shall we turn back?" said he.

"Of course not!" she said. "I can't be so rude as that! But, oh, Harry, what a man among men he is! There's no other like him, is there? Did you see him drive that arrow through the tree? The point came through on the farther side! It would have gone clear through a man, I think!"

"No doubt!"

"He told me about a fascinating and beautiful Indian girl, too. Do you think that Indian girls ever are truly beautiful?"

To have resolved that question, she should have looked not to her companion but back to the summer house, where, at that moment, Thunder Moon turned from the door and saw Red Wind standing at the opposite latticed window.

"You have stayed to listen to me, then?" he asked.

She smiled at him and glided away. "Come back, Red Wind! I have something more to say and to hear!"

But when he strode to the window, she was gone, and instinct told him that he could not overtake her.

Afterward, he puzzled for a long time above his book, but he found that the letters were dancing before his eyes.

15

Harrison Traynor was a polite man, but also he could be astonishingly direct. He was when he saw young Jack Sutton later on that same day.

"No one seems to see through him," exclaimed Jack peevishly. "It's as plain as day that the fellow is a sham and a farce, but no one seems to be able to make it out. Not even," he added with a touch of keener malice, "not even Charlie Keene. She's come over to ask him to her dance tonight, you know."

"You're right." Traynor nodded. "You have me there. Or rather, Thunder Moon has me. It seems to me, old fellow, that something should be done about him before long. And I have, in fact, the idea of how we can work it."

"Good!" said Jack Sutton, a glint in his eyes. "What shall we do, then?"

"Nothing. But make him do something."

"I can't guess my way through that puzzle. Be a little more explicit."

"Well, Jack, we both know that the fellow is a ruffian at heart, eh?"

"Naturally."

"And the great idea is to make him act like a ruffian, too."

"But how to do that?"

"I had the key to the situation today, I think. From a hint that was dropped, I believe that the father of Thunder Moon—the Cheyenne father—is hanging around in this vicinity. Well, the last time he was here, some horses were stolen. And lately Patterson missed that good bay mare of his. One might put two and two together."

"It was three weeks ago that Patterson lost his mare."

"That makes no difference. It isn't the matter of a horse that's important to us. It's the chance to get Thunder Moon into trouble."

"Get his father into trouble, you mean?"

"My dear fellow, you follow me at a great distance. Consider this. They've put the fighting talents of young Larry Marston into service by making him constable, and he's doing the work for the fun of it. But we all know that he hates William Sutton, so-called, and would do anything to take a knock at him. Now, then, go to Marston and let him know that a vagabond Indian is hanging around the Sutton place—and isn't it likely that he'll find the man and lock him up?"

"So far, so good. William will be annoyed."

"Is that all? My boy, he'll be so annoyed that he's apt to rip that jail apart in order to get the red man out."

"Hello! I hadn't thought of that. And if he does, why there's an excuse for Marston to raise a posse to help him capture the escaped criminal! And then Thunder Moon intervenes to protect his father—and then there's grand trouble—and perhaps father is tired of the disgrace of the thing and cuts Thunder Moon off—or comes to his senses and sees that the man is a mere pretender!"

92

"Jack, you argue like a sleuth. The next thing is to carry the message to Larry. Will you do it?"

"As fast as a horse can take me to him."

"Not too fast, though. It's just a casual thing thrown out—an old vagabond Indian has been seen near your house, you've heard. Let Larry think out the rest for himself. At any rate, he's as keen as mustard to make every arrest that looks dangerous, and I suppose that arresting a Cheyenne chief ought to appeal to him."

Those were the instructions under which Jack rode to find Larry Marston, and found him, luckily, in the very act of galloping from his home.

Young Mr. Marston had become a new man since he had taken over the office of constable. However wild his antecedents had been, he now proved that excitement and not mere trouble was what he wanted. Ruffians dared not group in their familiar gangs, and the solitary criminals who drifted across the country looking for houses to rob rapidly began to desert this hot region. Larry Marston had been considered a black sheep, not many weeks before. Now, he was an honored and most valued member of the community.

He frowned a little as young Jack Sutton came up to him. For the marks of William Sutton's fist still were on the face of Marston. He had not forgotten the day he had tried to shoulder William Sutton out of his way. William had jumped on him like a tiger, but fortunately the colonel had intervened. So Marston scowled now as one of the hostile family came up to him.

"Well met, Larry," said Jack Sutton cheerfully. "Are you hot on a trail?"

I'm riding over to Everett. Old fool there has got a jug of moonshine and locked himself into his house; threatens to blow off the head of anyone who comes near him!"

"That's an ugly job for you," said the boy. "Why don't you wait for him to sleep the jag off?"

"He has a wife, you know, and it's really not right that he should be allowed to keep her out in the cold, is it? Besides, he's defied the law, and we can't stand for that for a minute."

The businesslike tone of Marston made Jack Sutton smile a little.

"Best luck, old fellow," said he. And he began to turn his horse. "Hold on!" he cried as an afterthought. "If you happen to come by our way, you might have a look through the woods for an old vagabond Indian who's hanging about there."

"What? An Indian?"

Marston brightened with keen interest.

"You don't mean it, Jack! A red man—in this part of the country?"

"It's not the first time that they've come this far from the plains—according to history," said Jack. "Horse stealing, I suppose. You know Patterson lost his fine mare not so long ago."

"Of course, I remember all about it. Let Everett sleep off his jag. No use making blood flow for the sake of a fool like that! I'm coming back with you, Jack!"

Back he turned, bubbling over with questions—and looking to his rifle as he went!

He wanted to know when the Indian had been seen, and where, and how he looked, and how old he was, and how he was mounted—or was he on foot?

To all of this, Jack returned vague answers. If Marston found an oldish Indian, it would be sure to be the right man; and once the fellow was safe in jail, then it would be time to ask many questions. And Marston agreed.

Straightway he cached his horse in the woods, and he

94

started out on foot through the late afternoon to comb the place for the suspect.

There was no keener hunter in all the district. From the days of his boyhood, by himself or with his dog, he had worked every inch of the country. With Indian woodcraft, he knew how to stalk with speed and with silence, and it mattered not that the evening came and thickened the woods with shadows.

Once, coming close to Sutton House, he saw the big carriage rolling off beneath the stars with Jack and Ruth and William Sutton in it.

He heard the gay laughter of the girl, and could make out distinctly the wide, strong shoulders of William. The sight of them made him touch his bruised, scarred face, and he gritted his teeth in revengeful anger.

Someday, fate willing, he would make the fellow pay for that. And yet how it would be managed he could not tell. Strength of hand and skill with weapons were his chief attributes, but he knew that in neither quality could he stand for an instant before this newly reclaimed hero of the plains.

So he stood among the shadows and stared, and saw the carriage wheel away, and then he was left alone with his gloomy imaginings of the future.

No, not quite alone.

Presently there was a stir not far from him—hardly to be heard but rather to be guessed at. Out of the woods stepped a tall man wrapped in a blanket up to the neck. His head was distinguished by long, flowing hair such as Thunder Moon had worn; and in silhouette, the watcher could perceive several long feathers at the crown of the man's head.

This, undoubtedly, was either a masquerader or an Indian; and what masquerader would show himself like this, at the verge of the silent woods?

The young constable was about to steal up from behind, gun in hand, to make his challenge, when he saw a second form come out of the darkness, and then a woman's voice addressed the first comer in language Marston never had heard before.

His heart jumped. If a woman were here—why, it was as though an entire Indian tribe had slipped through the settlements and come to this rich and cultivated section of the country! Fear thrilled the constable; and then keen eagerness for the work he saw before him.

He heard the man answer in gruff, unintelligible words; and the girl went swiftly away among the trees. So skillfully did she step that after one or two slight sounds, there was no further trace of her. The mere whisper of the wind had been enough to efface all trace of the noise she had made.

He listened again; then he stepped out behind the statuesque giant. Not William Sutton himself was wider of shoulder than this man; and again the heart of the constable failed him a little. But he went on, fearing shame more than danger.

When he was very close, "Who are you, friend?" said he in a firm voice.

The answer would have surprised most men, but Marston was nerved for almost anything. He swerved to avoid the knife thrust that was aimed at his throat, and with a sidelong blow of his rifle barrel, he felled the giant.

Kneeling above him, he bound the hands of the unconscious man. Then he felt for the place where his blow had fallen, and found that no blood was flowing.

After that, he waited for consciousness to return. He knew that a shout would bring help from the Sutton place, but he scorned making any appeal; and, in the meantime, he watched the woods behind him with a scrupulous eye. A dozen times he felt that he saw forms drifting to the edge of the trees, stealthily preparing to spring out at him, and a dozen times he told himself that he was mistaken, and steadied his nerves by gripping the rifle harder.

But no danger leaped at him from the wood. The fallen man stirred, at last, and groaned faintly; but as consciousness returned it was easy to make him stand erect, and then to walk forward, impelled by the muzzle of a rifle pressed against the small of his back.

They came to Marston's horse, which he mounted, and so he rode on into the town, and the big man still walked with a long, soft tread before him. The first lamplight from a window on the outskirts of the village glinted on him, and Larry Marston felt his heart bound. This victim was older than he had expected; but also there was an air of surpassing greatness about him; and Marston felt very much like some Titan who dared to grasp the thunderbolt of Jove and found it obedient to his hand.

Just before them was the jail.

16

It was Thunder Moon's formal entrance into society, and the rumor that he was to be at Charlotte Keene's dance made every other invited guest certain to be present. He was unused to many of the ways of the white man, but he was familiar enough with the peculiar hum of voices that arose when he entered the Keene house. That same hum, less subdued, he had heard many times before, as when he entered the lodge where the wise men of the Suhtai held council, or when he stood in the center of the circle at the scalp dance. There was a little pressing toward him, but Judge Keene captured him the moment he appeared and carried him off to his library.

"You're not interested in dancing, William," he said, confidentially. "And I had to chat with you a moment. I want to bury the hatchet. Naturally, I'm referring to the first visit you paid me. On that day, frankly, I played the fool. It takes a wise man to look through surfaces to the inner man. I was not wise. Now, William, I want to tell you that I've changed my mind. Because you killed a tiger? Not at all! But because you've shown conclusively that you're going to become a respected member of our society. You've changed yourself profoundly, most profoundly, and in a few short weeks!"

He scanned William Sutton from head to foot; certainly nothing was wrong with the costume of that youth. The soberness of his clothes merely added emphasis to the dignity of his demeanor.

The judge continued: "You came to me, on that first day, to tell me that you wanted to ask for, er, in fact, that you looked rather kindly upon my girl, but, since that time, of course you've seen a great many of the beauties of this county and no doubt you've changed your mind."

It would have required a duller wit than that of William to fail to understand the drift of the judge, and he said quietly, "I have seen many other faces; they are like pictures that stay in the eye for a moment and then are rubbed out by a little time. I haven't seen another woman like your daughter."

"Well said!" exclaimed the judge heartily. "And I hope, my lad, that no matter how long you live among us, you won't lose the outland flavor you have in your speech. Now, William, I shall come straight to the point, for I'm a man who hates circumlocution. You saw Charlotte on the first day and wanted her. What she feels about the matter I really don't know, and even if I did, I wouldn't be free to speak about it. The girl has a mind of her own and she's only too apt to use it. But from my viewpoint, I don't know of another young man in the community who would suit me better as a son."

He held out his hand, and William grasped it firmly, and, leaning forward a little, looked deeply into the eyes of the judge. "No matter what she says when I speak to her," he declared, "tonight we have become friends. And my father will be happy!"

"Of course he will," said the judge. "Randolf and I have been as close as brothers all our lives, and we'll be close again. I was an ass, that was all. I've half a mind to ride over to see him now, but first I want to know what Charlotte says to you. Find a chance to slip out into some quiet corner with her and tell her what's in your heart. And the best of good luck to you, William!"

William Sutton stepped from the library and into a swirl of light, of music, of color. Kind eyes smiled at him and welcomed him. And he heard the murmur of compliment and light laughter, as though pleasure overflowed in these people at the sight of him.

"The tiger was a half-wit to tackle such a man!"

And the heart of William Sutton swelled in him, and he felt for the first time since coming to the new world that he was a part and portion of these people. They were his, and he was theirs. The universe in which they lived, so petty once in comparison with the war and the hunt on the distant plains, now seemed a universe indeed, not bounded by physical horizons but stretching dimly on the endless plane of thought. As for the

99

dry labor to which he was confined, it no longer seemed dull or pointless, but rather it was the alphabet through which he would eventually become conversant with the vital spirit of this strange life. And as the immensity of all these new dimensions crowded in upon his brain, so he felt a mental strength waken in him and expand to meet the new necessity.

Yet, something was lacking, something was out of joint. He stood in a corner, watching gravely the whirl and the gaiety of the dance, and the sound of the violins pierced his mind like arrows pointed with sweet pain.

The circles of the dance dissolved into confusion as the music ceased, and the floors were filled with couples moving toward the chairs or toward the lighted coolness of the garden beyond. Charlotte came by him with a red-faced youth.

"Run along, Jimmy," she said to him. "There's Mary waiting for you, and I have to talk to William Sutton."

Jimmy grinned affably at William and nodded as he vanished.

"Do you like it?" said Charlotte.

"It is a pleasant thing to see, but not to take part in," said William. "I am used to people who are happy and celebrate because they have done something real. But here the people are going through motions and imitating happiness in order to be happy. But I think these are jumbled words that make little meaning."

"Not the sort of things that usually are said at dances," she said, looking up to him and frowning a little. "You seem to be an extraordinarily serious person."

"Is that a fault?"

"No. But, come out in the garden and let the night wind blow the taste of the dance out of your mind."

They went into the garden. The great bare face of the night pressed close down above them and subdued the

100

voices of the girls and boys; even the fountain in the farthest corner dared do no more than whisper, and the wind lifted its falling spray and shook it out like silver hair. They paused beside it. As they watched, the music began again inside; the crowd swept back into the house; from indoors they heard only a throb and rhythm of music, and the night noises began to grow audible, the rattle of leaves, and the booming chorus of the bullfrogs around the pool in the next meadow.

"Now you are thinking of what," Charlotte asked.

"This wind comes from the west. It has blown over the lodges of the Crows; over the tepees of the Suhtai; over the Father of Waters; and it comes to us here. I breathe of it and try to smell the wood smoke from our fires; but a man is less than a coyote and cannot read the wind with his nose."

She began to laugh a little, though her eyes were still grave.

"You still want to be there," she suggested.

"A frog goes by land and water both," answered William. "He lives in the water, and yet he is not a fish. I have been taken out of the water; I never could be happy in the old life again; but still I want to get back in the pool. I am used to it. Sometimes I crave for unseasoned meat and air in a tepee, choked with wood smoke, and the harsh songs of the young men at night. I shall always turn back to those things, even when I am an old man among the whites. That is a weakness."

"No, that is a strength, I should say. You have two ways of being happy. Other people only have one."

"But a man cannot divide his body or his spirit into halves and live in two lives at once."

Charlotte was silent.

"No," she said at last. "One has to make a choice. And if I were you, I'd hardly know what to choose. I've never

101

known anything else, but still I'm frightfully bored with life here more than half the time. Perhaps that's because we're never satisfied with what we are; we want to step around the corner. But around the corner there are other people just as restless."

"Horses, guns, men, women are real," said he. "We fill our hearts with such things on the plains. Well, there are horses, guns, men, and women here. But they are not real. The horses do not give you speed to escape from an enemy, or to catch him. They simply help you to follow a fox. The guns do not save your life or kill your foe. They simply make a noise and drop a bird or a squirrel. They do not even give you food. The men live in chairs. The women do not make the tepees or take care of their children. Even the shadows of the dead Cheyennes chasing the shadows of the buffalo through the sky live more really. But still, there is something else in this land and among you white people. I first guessed at it when I leaned out of a window at Sutton House and looked down into your face."

He turned as he spoke and looked down in her face again. And her eyes grew larger to receive his glance. The talk had taken this personal turn so quickly that she caught her breath.

"Ah," murmured he. "Whenever I look at you, I see the thing again. It makes me want to take you and possess you. It makes me want to come close to you. I wanted you for my squaw when I first saw you, but even then I knew that if I had you even in my tepee something of you would not be mine. Still I would be trying to capture you. I might be a hundred marches away from you, and yet closer than when I stand beside you near this water! Do you understand?"

She did not answer, still receiving his glance.

"Hai!" cried William Sutton softly, like a hunter on the plains. "Stand farther away from me. My arms open to receive you. I have a song in the hollow of my throat. I want to tell you—well, that I shall kill many buffalo for you if you let me take you to my tepee. You see, I forget that you do not live on buffalo meat. Let us go back to the house. There is nothing that I can say to you!"

He turned away in obedience to his own suggestion, but the girl did not stir, and, stepping back to her, he saw that she was smiling.

"Are you laughing at me?" he asked.

"Not altogether."

"You had better come back into the house with me."

"I can't," said she, "I wouldn't dare to show my face to them all."

"You wouldn't?"

"No. I'm frightfully red."

He touched her face.

"Yes," he said, "your face is hot. You tremble. Are you afraid?"

"Heavens!" cried Charlotte. "You will drive me mad!"

"Are you angry?"

"I am so excited, William, that I'm almost fainting. My heart is beating like ten hammers. I can't possibly go inside."

He paused.

"I almost think," said he, "that you want me to talk to you some more."

"I thank heaven," said the girl, "that you see that much!"

She made a little gesture as she said it, and he caught the hand deftly and none too gently in midair.

"Charlotte!" said he hoarsely.

She began to laugh brokenly, and William was draw-

103

ing her closer and closer when the steady soft hoot of an owl sounded from the nearest woods; and he dropped her hand as though at a spoken order.

17

"There is danger?" asked the girl, with a gasp, not of fear but from the strain of recovering suddenly from her emotion.

"Go inside," said William Sutton. "There is always danger," he added bitterly. "No, not danger to my life, perhaps!"

And he waved her toward the house.

She started in instinctive obedience. Halfway to the door, she turned and glanced back, but he was waiting, tall, stern, passive. And realizing somehow that a crisis was upon him that was a crisis for her also, she hurried on to the house and closed the door behind her hastily, almost like one who has escaped from pursuit.

William, as he saw the door close, turned from the garden, leaped the hedge with a single bound, and upon the farther side, touched by a faint glimmer of the light from the house, he saw Red Wind.

"I did not mean to drive you away from your squaw," said the Omissis girl quietly. "Only, I came with something to tell you."

"It is something evil," he answered sternly. "You never have come to me with good of any kind."

"It is neither good nor evil to you," replied Red Wind. "When Thunder Moon was a Suhtai, the lives and the happiness of the Suhtai were life and happiness to him, also. But now he is changed. What happens to them is nothing. They are like a dream. And he is awake!"

"It is Standing Antelope!" exclaimed Thunder Moon. "He has stepped into some trouble. Tell me, Red Wind! He has struck a knife into someone. That is it—and nothing can tame him!"

"It is not Standing Antelope," she answered, and he saw that she smiled faintly. "It is Big Hard Face."

"He is sick?"

"He is worse than sick."

"He is dead! Sorrow and trouble have broken his heart!"

"No, he is worse than dead!"

William was silent. He waited for the great blow to fall.

"To be shamed and captured is worse than to die," said Red Wind. "He has been taken. I followed as fast as I could. It was hard to follow without being seen, but I saw him closed into a house and I saw armed men come to watch at the entrance. They have taken him, and he never will come back to us! I went to Standing Antelope; he said that you were here. So I left Standing Antelope putting on his war paint, and I came on alone to tell you. I am sorry that I troubled you. Go back to your squaw and forget the Suhtai. Alas, they never can forget you!"

But Thunder Moon laughed softly.

"That is a small thing," said he. "My father has great power. I shall say a word to him, and he will set Big Hard Face free."

The girl shook her head.

"You will see," said he. "Go back toward the Sutton House. I come at once."

105

In the Keene stables he borrowed a horse easily enough, and sweeping down the driveway, with no pause to make excuses to his host, he drove the poor animal at frantic speed up the highway until the lofty trees that clustered around his father's house were visible.

He was out of the saddle and on the front steps with a single movement, and then into the high, hushed hallway, where a maid in white uniform shrank with frightened eyes from before him.

"Where is the master?"

She seemed too disturbed to answer. But she ran before him and stopped at the library door.

William tapped softly at the door and waited until the deep, familiar voice bade him enter. So he went inside the room, and saw two pools of lamplight, where his mother sat with her needlepoint, and where his father sat, poring over the white pages of a book.

"Now what's up, William?" asked the colonel. "What's happened to bring you back so soon?"

"My foster father has come back from the Suhtai," said William, "to find me. And he has been taken and closed into the jail in the town. Will you set him free?"

The colonel and his wife started up, she with a faint cry.

"Be at ease, Martha," said her husband. "There'll be no trouble about this. You go along to bed—William and I shall handle this little matter, eh?"

He drew his wife from William and ushered her up the stairs.

He was back at once. Not a word was said while he swung into an overcoat and ordered a rig. But as he drove his high-stepper toward the town, he said to his son, "Did you know that Big Hard Face was back?"

"Yes."

106

"When?"

"Yesterday."

That was all. But the silence of the colonel was eloquent to William. He could feel the criticism it implied—the lack of perfect confidence in his parents that had led him to keep back the fact of the Suhtai's arrival. And, for some reason, the sense of opposition in his father caused in him a swift revolt. He set his teeth and looked down at the hands of the colonel as they held the reins tight upon the trotting horse. The trees shot back behind them on either side, and the road spun inward, as though upon a reel.

The lights of the town loomed up before them, and presently they were within the fencing rows of houses, within the mingled sounds of many voices, lost upon the colonel but audible to those wilderness-trained ears of William Sutton. No outlying guards rode post around that swarm of people. All their wealth of horses, cattle, sheep, of garnered grain, and all the treasure within the houses was open to the hand of violence to strike and take where and what it pleased. But the mysterious spirit of the law had extended its arm around the place and kept it secure; yes, and now that same spirit of the law had taken within its grasp the wandering chief of the Suhtai—what then?

The jail loomed on the left, squat, dark, with little windows like many eyes in ranges, regular and level. Within it lived the very spirit of the law itself.

They drew rein, they dismounted, and went up the steps of the building, William last, after tethering the horses, the colonel in the lead.

William, looking at the squared shoulders of his father, felt that surely there was no force, even in the law itself, to withstand the dignity and the power of this man.

The colonel rapped at the door. A heavy sound came back, and he could guess at the strength of the solid slabs of wood that made the door. With the silence of oiled hinges, with the slowness that testified to its weight, the door swung open. Out to William came the thick, strange air of confinement, like the air of a cave, but without the fresh earth scent.

Before them stood the jailer.

"Good evening, Colonel Sutton," said he, touching his hat.

In his other hand he held a sawed-off shotgun, ready for instant use. William knew that weapon. At close range, three rifles and half a dozen revolvers could not make up the sum of its deadliness. And then he looked into the face of the jailer, calm, square, lined, with the dull eyes of a fighting man. Such were the ideal warriors upon warpath; such were the enemies most to be dreaded.

"You have a man here," said the colonel, "an Indian. I want to know what charge he's held on."

"Mr. Marston just brought him in," said the jailer. "Horse stealing is the charge, I think. That's the usual Indian thing, ain't it? Will you step in, sir?"

The colonel passed in, and William entered, guardedly, behind him.

He did not like the place. Neither its odor nor the solemn sense of strength it exuded like a human being. He became all eyes, and though looking only before him, he saw every detail of the interior as he walked.

They were shown into a little office where Marston was sitting. He rose to meet them with no air of surprise, so that William guessed he had expected this visit.

The colonel repeated his question.

"You know that we've been missing horses in the neighborhood, sir."

"I didn't know that."

"No? There was the Patterson mare."

"That was weeks ago!"

"Of course, these fellows steal and then send their spoil west by their confederates. As a matter of fact, you've suffered at their hands yourself, Colonel Sutton, I believe."

"A good many years ago, Marston. May we see the man?"

"Certainly. You have some reason to be interested in his case, I suppose?"

The colonel looked at William, and the latter said slowly, "He was my foster father among the Suhtai."

He half expected to see the face of Marston harden and his eyes glitter, and he was not disappointed. Quite by accident, the young constable had been able to strike a blow at the man he most feared and hated, and it was plain from his expression that he relished the accident.

"Certainly you may see him then," said Marston, politely. "Just come this way. Of course, I'm very sorry. Very!"

He led the way with a lantern. There was no other light in the place, and as he swung it the shadows of the bars of the cells striped the ceiling and the walls in crazy patterns.

There was no other person in the jail except one old vagabond, lying face downward on his cot. He reared on one arm and blinked at them. They came to the cell where Big Hard Face sat Indian fashion on the floor. He rose to greet them and raised one hand above his head.

"How!" said he.

A little silence came over the group; there was such a world of uncivilized dignity about the chief that they could find no words to answer at the moment.

Then William said in Cheyenne, "We have come to help you out of this place, father. This man declares that you have stolen a horse."

"He says a thing that is not true," said the Indian.

"Big Hard Face," translated William, "says that he stole no horse. He has been in this neighborhood only two days. How could he have taken the mare?"

"I'm glad to hear it," said the constable. "But of course I can't set him free—not on his bare assertion! We'll have to have some proofs!"

"My dear Marston," replied the colonel, "the burden is put on the state in maintaining that the man it suspects is guilty. Isn't that the law?"

"We have to have special ways of handling the Indians," said Marston. "You surely realize that. If he didn't come to steal horses, why did he come?"

"To persuade me to come back to the Cheyennes," said William.

"Ah, yes," murmured Marston. "We'll pan the whole thing out at the trial. I wish the man all the luck in the world, of course!"

But his eyes were grim, and it was plain that he would not relax his grip on this prisoner if he could help it.

18

The colonel, in the meantime, took stock of the situation in silence, looking once or twice straight at the captive, but giving more of his attention to his son; for William seemed profoundly troubled, and, gripping one of the bars, he frowned in at the Cheyenne as though about to tear a way open through the steel and take the chief away with him.

He could see that Marston had marked the same instinct in his enemy; and he could make out, furthermore, that the young constable was not unpleased. Why, could be understood without too much difficulty. A long revenge was what Marston wanted, and any attempt at violence on the part of William would give him his opening.

"Marston," said the colonel at last, "even if Patterson may prefer and prove a claim against this man, I'll stand good for the price of the lost mare if need be. Turn the Cheyenne loose, like a good fellow, will you?"

The constable flushed a little. Colonel Sutton was a great man in the community, and it would not be the wisest of political moves to win his hostility. However, his heart was set. He took refuge behind a legality.

"It's my job to bring in the suspects," said he. "It isn't my part to turn them loose again. You must know that, sir!"

The colonel made no further effort.

"You see, William," said he, "that nothing can be done. Just tell your friend that we'll do what we can for him, have a lawyer to defend him, of course—and that everything doubtless will turn out all right!"

The deep voice of William, strangely musical now that it was burdened with the language of the far plains, translated obediently. The chief was greatly moved, though he wore his usual mask of indifference. "Tell him," he said to William, "that I had no reason to expect kindness from him. I have raised my hand against him! But behold, Thunder Moon, you are armed! The enemy is only one. You and your father are two. Strike him down! He wears the key that opens this door. Take

111

me away now, because otherwise you never will free me with words and with money!"

"Let me be alone with him for a moment," said William to his father and Marston. "You can let the jailer watch to see that I pass nothing to him through the bars," he added scornfully.

Marston flushed as he withdrew to his office with the colonel, but nevertheless he took the suggested precaution and placed the jailer on guard at a little distance from the occupied cell.

"I cannot shoot him down," explained William, when he could speak freely, without danger that his meaning might be guessed by the gestures of the prisoner, or by his own. "Here in the land of the white men, weapons are not used except to kill cattle or birds. It is the law that holds you, father, and the law cannot be broken!"

"Is it medicine?" said the chief solemnly. "One man came and stole up behind me and struck me down; yet I am not on the warpath. I have done no harm to these people. They lie about me and say that I have stolen horses. But I came not for horses but for you. If they have medicine, you have medicine too. You have a greater medicine than their law. Pray to the Sky People. They will tell you what to do for me!"

"Farewell," said the foster son sadly. "I shall come again in the morning. Perhaps there will be some way. My father is a great chief; through him I shall work."

"Farewell, my son," said the old Suhtai. "But beware of a gift from the hand of an enemy."

William, moving away, from the corner of his eye saw the chief draw a blanket over his head.

He went to the office. The heavy door that closed it against the interior of the jail had been left accidentally a trifle ajar, and as he came closer, he heard a phrase in the voice of his heart stop.

112

"—but what I really want is to see this Cheyenne jailed the rest of his days."

William halted, aghast. The warning of Big Hard Face was yet in his ear, and now he heard this!

"I hardly follow that," said Marston.

"My lad," said the colonel, "there's no doubt that the Suhtai deserves something worse than a cell. If he had justice for his murders, probably he'd hang at once. I don't want that. But so long as he's in jail, I have assurance that my son will not be turning his heart west. He's still restless. This civilization of ours is a heavy load on his shoulders. I know, Marston, that you have no reason to like him. But in this case you and I can work together, and afterward perhaps I can show you that my help in this country is not worthless."

"Colonel Sutton," said Marston, "nothing possibly could please me more than to feel that I had won your confidence. If I can do it in this way, which lies right in line with my legal duties, of course I simply welcome the work. In the meantime, you'll let William think that you're really working for the freedom of Big Hard Face?"

"Naturally. We'll keep the little secret, you and I. You might let the judge know beforehand how I stand on the matter. I'll have a lawyer hired. But you can let the judge know that I'm against the cause I am ostensibly representing!"

"Certainly!" Marston chuckled. "Nothing could be simpler. Judge Whittaker has a sense of humor, as everyone knows!"

A sense of humor?

William Sutton set his teeth and controlled himself sternly, and then he entered the office. There was no purpose in letting the pair know that he had overheard them.

He and the colonel left at once and started back for the house. On the way, his father talked kindly of Big Hard Face, and hoped that the time would come when he could see the chief in his house.

And all the time, as he listened, the heart of William swelled big against this hypocrisy. If love for him occasioned it, and if nothing but care for his welfare was behind this duplicity on the part of his father, nevertheless, he could not forgive the sin.

He made himself answer, but all the time he was telling himself that there was no trust to be put in anything now, except in the strength of his own hand— and perhaps in the cunning of Standing Antelope.

When they reached the house, therefore, and he had gone to his room, he was not surprised to find Standing Antelope waiting for him, hideous with paint, and busily at work cleaning a rifle. He gave Thunder Moon merely a glance.

"I knew that you would fail," said he.

William went to the window and leaned out into the night. He had come to a turning point, he knew, and once having put his foot on this trail, how could he tell how he might withdraw it peaceably? He was about to raise his hand against the whites; and such a raising of the hand never was forgotten and never was forgiven, as he understood. It was not against a mere human; it was against the figure of the law, and in the deathless memory of the law the act would be enshrined and held vividly until penance had been done.

So William thought, staring into the night. Now that he was thinking of leaving it, the house itself appeared to him a thing worthy of love, almost like a human being. And all the broad acres of the estate had a meaning to him—not the meaning of wealth alone, but a sense of the rich pride of a small kingdom.

That estate would, in time, pass into his hands. What was a chieftainship among the Suhtai compared with the overlordship here? The Suhtai could put their swift volleys of warriors in motion across the prairies, but under the first war chief there were other chiefs, each with a personal following. The medicine man, in many matters, was actually the head of the tribe. And the authority of the head chief, in many respects, was limited to the extent of his own lodge.

How different on this place!

Fenced with wilderness here, the river there, and on the other two sides bordered by wide roads, the estate held within its bosom great woods where the ax never had fallen, swift creeks ran chattering across the meadows, and the broad acres were sowed with many crops.

These were things to think of more than once before deserting them. William sighed as he looked out on the dark of the night. The stars were out, but gave only enough light in the central heavens to indicate the great masses of cloud rolling across their faces.

"Bring me," said William, "bring me the dream shield and the lance."

Instantly they were placed in his hands. And he stepped out onto the little balcony outside his chamber.

There he raised shield and spear to the dark face of the heavens. The Christian teaching of his kind mother were blotted from his mind in this tense emergency.

"Sky People, wonder workers, keepers of the medicine of the spirits of the air and the earth," said Thunder Moon, "you have heard my voice on the prairies and given me a sign. If you can hear me and see me now that I stand in the land of the white man, give me a sign here, also. If I may stay here and let Big Hard Face die of a broken heart in the jail, be silent. I shall know that your silence, like death, concerns him. But if I am to raise my hand and strike for him and then flee away from my father and my mother, my sister and my brother, and from all of this life around me, let me hear you, or show me a sign!"

He stretched his hands high above his head laden with the long lance and the dream shield.

For a long space he waited, and he heard behind him the superstitious groan of the boy, Standing Antelope, as the latter read the silence of the Sky People as an eloquent sign.

And then, ripping boldly across the face of the sky, a bolt of lightning split the clouds and dropped jagged to the earth!

There was a faint, choked cry of joy from the boy.

And almost instantly, a vast double roll of thunder shook the very house. The sign had been given in no uncertain form!

19

When William came back into the room, pale, his eyes fixed and staring as one who has been looking into the face of a deity, young Standing Antelope drew back from him, thoroughly frightened.

His opinion of his celebrated companion had passed under some shadow of late months when he saw him taking so swiftly to the ways of the whites, but now he changed his mind violently, for a man to whom the upper spirits shouted in strong thunder and upon whom they looked with flashing lightnings was a dealer in medicine so dreadful and so strong that the boy was overwhelmed.

He had brought out the Indian clothes that Thunder Moon wore when he first came to the house of his father and had laid them upon a chair. Now, since he could not speak, he hardly dared to point toward this costume.

But Thunder Moon, with flashing eyes, went to it and picked it up. In another minute he began to tear off his clothing, saying to Standing Antelope that it was time to get the horses. The youngster was through the window and away in a moment.

The warrior now dressed in the fringed and beaded suit of softest deerskin. Moccasins were upon his feet; about his waist he belted two heavy revolvers; in his hand he took his rifle; and over his shoulders he slung the dream shield.

Even with all this accouterment, he was able to descend deftly and swiftly to the ground. On the verge of the trees he found the boy waiting. There, too, was Sailing Hawk, whinnying softly with delight. And Thunder Moon, rapt in his grim determination, hardly noticed that Standing Antelope had taken for his own use the favorite charger of Colonel Sutton himself! A thing the stern master of Sutton House never could forgive. And the led horse for Old Hard Face was a chosen beauty.

Now they were in the saddle and away. Going softly beneath the trees, they cut out across the meadows, gained the roadway, and then fairly flew toward the town; and the rush of the horses and the keen cutting of the wind against Thunder Moon's face raised his heart to a fierce exultation such as he had not felt before during all these weeks. He wanted to shout, and from the corner of his eye he could see Standing Antelope swaying in his saddle, laughing like a mad creature.

117

They drew rein as the lights of the town glimmered, twinkled, and grew into long, bright rays before them. Quietly they rode into the village. There were no voices now. All was still, but there seemed to be a lurking danger in the silence.

So it was through a strange silence that they went, and Standing Antelope instinctively allowed his mount to draw closer to the side of Sailing Hawk, and his keen glances went eagerly to this side and to that, prying beneath the hedges, seeking in the shadowy doorways.

"The law never sleeps," Thunder Moon had been told by his father, and that they saw no danger before them was no real reason why they should think all was safe, he felt.

Restless as two wolves, the pair came before the jail.

Close under the shadow of the jail wall they halted, the grass muffling the tread of the horses, and there, in a whisper, Thunder Moon told his young companion to hold the bridles and wait for him.

A groan answered him. With all his heart, Standing Antelope yearned to have a part in this expedition; but he dared not protest against the orders of a leader at such a moment as this. He gritted his teeth and remained behind.

Thunder Moon, adjusting a mask over his face, spoke rapidly to his companion.

"Keep their heads turned toward the mouth of that street that leads north," said he. "We must not let a soul suspect that it is William Sutton who takes part in this rescue. But, wrapped in this buffalo robe, I must seem an Indian if I can!"

He went straightway to the front door of the jail and knocked. Had he known it, the instant reply was suspicious.

"Who's there?"

118

"A friend!" said William, his voice going husky.

"Friend? What name?"

Purposely, William made his answer a blur.

"Wait a minute!"

There was a noise of a bolt turning, and then a little iron shutter a foot square was opened near the side of the main door and a ray of light darted out against the masked face of William. His long arm drove through the aperture; his hand fastened on a throat, and as he jerked the victim to the small port, he saw the fear-distorted face of the jailer.

"Give me the keys," said William sternly, pressing a gun against the man's head. "Give me the keys to the door and to the cell. Point them out in your bunch!"

In a choked voice, for the grip that held him was cutting off his breath, the jailer answered as he obediently held up the keys, "Give me air! For God's sake don't murder me! The biggest one for the door—this new one for the cell of the Indian!"

How did he know so instantly which cell was to be opened?

But Thunder Moon did not pause to think of this. His mind was too thoroughly filled with the work that lay before him.

He merely murmured, "If you give an alarm and call for help, I'll shoot you down when I come inside the jail. If you stand fast and make no sound, I'll reward you."

The jailer nodded, he was past speech now; and as William's iron grip relaxed, the poor fellow staggered back, gasping heavily.

The big key fit the jail door, the lock turned smoothly back, and the next instant William stepped inside the building.

There was not a sound. The jailer had sunk into the shadows.

119

William walked lightly down the central aisle until he came to the cell where Big Hard Face sat in the darkness.

"Father, are you there?" he asked in Cheyenne.

There was a moment's pause. His heart stopped with fear lest the old man had been removed. But then the deep, quiet voice of Big Hard Face made answer, "You have come, O my son, and all is well!"

The next instant he fitted the key into the lock and turned it.

It was only a slight, grating sound that the key made, but it seemed to be a signal that was instantly answered, as from three different portions of the big cell room three lanterns were that instant unhooded, and their well-focused shafts of light struck full upon the cell, Big Hard Face, and Thunder Moon.

"Thank God for the mask!" thought Thunder Moon.

But the very first cry was, "William Sutton, in the name of the law I call on you to surrender!"

They knew! And how?

He was acting too swiftly to allow much thought, and he cast the door wide and letting Big Hard Face rush out into the aisle.

"Shoot!" shouted someone—and William thought it was the voice of the jailer. "You've let them get together already!"

Thunder Moon had placed his rifle in the hands of his foster father. A heavy Colt lay in each of his!

And as the warning rang, a gun belched with a terrible roar, not like the metal clang of an exploding rifle, and then they heard the clattering of a charge of buckshot as it scattered among the steel bars of the cells, striking out sparks of fire.

That charge was aimed not at the old chief, but at Thunder Moon, and he heard the keen hum of the shot

120

around him. Something stung his leg, but it was only a scratch. For the rest, the bars of the cells saved him and he was unscathed!

But not relieved from all danger, for as he heard the unlucky marksman cursing, two rifles spat at him with tongues of flame.

"Shoot to kill! Shoot to kill!" shouted the voice of Marston. "The two devils are together, and they're both armed now!"

But though he had laid the trap with consummate skill, he had forgotten one most important item, which was that the light of the lanterns, shining through the bars from different angles, filled the room with a bewildering madness of shadows, and through those shadows two men were running, by no means an easy target, in spite of the close range.

"Straight ahead—the door is open!" cried Thunder Moon, and as his foster father rushed ahead of him, he snapped a shot to the right and a shot to the left at the shadows that crouched near the lanterns.

Either an intervening bar or carelessness made the first shot miss; but the second was answered by a wild burst of cursing and he knew that he had struck his mark.

He knew it, and his heart failed him, and he set his teeth.

All that he had done hitherto might be condoned by skillful lawyers, but nothing in the world, his father so often had said, could make up for the shooting of a fellow man.

The law, now, would follow him like a relentless bloodhound. But, if the man were not dead, he . . .

In that hope, he sped on with his foster father. Again the rifles crashed behind them—two of them. But the door was close before them. Ah! A wheeling shadow

121

swung across the open gap, and the door shut with a heavy slam in their faces.

"Drop! Drop!" commanded Big Hard Face, instantly and coolly. "Drop, and let us kill these devils and take their scalps. Afterward, we shall find a way out of the place! They are only two to two, now!"

Well for them was it that they had dropped to the floor at the suggestion of the old chief; for the straight-focused fire of two well-aimed rifles was now turned toward them. They heard the thud of bullets striking against the iron plates upon the inside of the door; little shreds of lead fell upon them.

The odds still were not two to two, however. Yonder lay one fellow groaning and moaning and cursing, quite out of the battle, but making more noise than a fatally hurt person should be able to do. Marston and some other fellow, with a supply of weapons at hand, were keeping up a steady fire; but now from the side the jailer opened with a revolver. He it was who had mustered his resolution to fling the door shut in their faces.

Knee-high, Thunder Moon aimed his shot; there was a gasp, and the jailer was down.

Big Hard Face, moving sideways across the floor, came to a pause and fired, and the heavy report of the rifle was half drowned and then prolonged by the shout of a hurt man.

"Are you done, Mike?" cried Marston's voice, in an agony of fear.

"I'm a dead man, Larry," said the other. "Make terms with Sutton or he'll murder you too and . . ."

The voice trailed away.

"Will you surrender, Marston?" called Thunder Moon. "Will you surrender?"

"You've got the odds against me," said Marston. "I'll surrender, then, and—no, damn you, I'll fight on to the finish! I have you now, and I'll hang you for tonight's work!"

There was a reason for this change in his speech, for loud and heavily, at this moment, a hand had beaten against the door of the jail, and the sound of many voices could be heard calling from the street.

20

"Shoot low! Shoot low!" whispered Thunder Moon to Big Hard Face. "No, shoot no more. He has stopped firing—"

"Kill him," said Big Hard Face through his teeth. "Now I praise Tarawa! I shall die fighting and leave the dead men heaped around me! There shall be something for you to say when you reach the Suhtai and sing to them how your father died! For now you have killed the whites in their own land, and they cannot forgive you. They will hunt you back to your people, my people, the Cheyennes!"

"It is true," admitted Thunder Moon. "But we shall fight our way out together. How shall we leave this place, O my father? Listen! The people are gathering in the street. Soon there will be hundreds of them with guns. And the coward, Standing Antelope, fired no gun and made no stand against them to keep me protected, or warned at least of the danger."

"That boy is brave and wise," said the old chief. "You will find that good comes of him. Now I see a way, I think. See, they press against the door and beat on it!"

123

For many voices were raised on the outside, calling, "Marston! Marston! Open the door! What's happening?"

And the loud voice of Marston answered with a shout, "Murder has happened! Three men are down in here, dropped by William Sutton and his Indian father! Break in the rear door because that is the weakest!"

"Throw open this door," whispered the chief to his foster son, "and then we shall rush out through them."

"We shall rush through them," agreed Thunder Moon. "The Sky People sent me to you tonight, and they would not send me to my death."

"But first, let us kill the dog who barks at our heels in this room."

"He has hidden among the shadows and waits. Let him live. We have spilled enough white blood, and the white law never forgets!"

"Let your way be my way, then," said the chief. "Here! I have the handle of this door!"

He had been fumbling in the darkness, for under the deadly fire of Thunder Moon and Big Hard Face the jailers had extinguished the lanterns. Now, with a strong pull, the chief flung the heavy door open, and half a dozen men who were beating against it and shouting on the outside, lurched in with cries of alarm.

Beyond, on the narrow platform, clustered on the steps of the jail, and scattered in the street, were fully fifty armed men. In all the adjoining houses lamps were being lighted, casting yellow, glowing streams into the street so that all these figures were faintly illuminated.

"The gun butt," said Thunder Moon, "and save the bullet for the last crisis! Charge them, father!"

And as he spoke, he beat the heavy barrel of his revolver into the face of a big man who lurched toward him, arms outspread.

124

The man went down, and as Thunder Moon fired rapidly into the air the others fell back with shouts of fear and confusion. Guns were raised, but before bullets could be fired, the two had swept on through the crowd and a shot was more apt to strike a fellow townsman than one of the fugitives.

Those behind were hindered by their own numbers. Those ahead had something to do to guard themselves and escape from the rush of danger, for, as Big Hard Face strode forward, the rifle circled with crushing force in his hands, and the revolvers of Thunder Moon spat fire in the faces of the crowd.

How could they mark that the bullets were not aimed at them, but just above their heads?

It was a lost battle, however, and Thunder Moon knew it, and groaned as he set his teeth. These fellows gave back a little, to be sure, but they came again, and their numbers were beginning to mass together.

"Ah hai!" cried Big Hard Face. "We have come to the last battle, O my son! Stand with me, and guard my back as I shall guard yours. Let us pile the dead around us before we die. Stand with me, Thunder Moon. A few great deeds, and then the end!"

It seemed, indeed, that the last moment had come. A knife flicked the shoulder of Thunder Moon; he barely swayed away from the stroke of a clubbed shotgun; and then, piercingly sweet in the ears of the two, the terrible and familiar war yell of a Cheyenne rang up and down the street.

As the startled whites gave back a little, there was heard the volleying beat of many hoofs, and again the screaming, wailing, battle cry of the Suhtai, pitched high, stabbing at the eardrums and curdling the blood.

Four tall horses were rushing into the crowd, and the townsmen gave back with a shout of fear and astonish-

125

ment. It seemed as though a whole tribe were pouring to the attack; and through an opened avenue in the press Thunder Moon made out the familiar front of Sailing Hawk sweeping toward him, and then he recognized the furious voice of Standing Antelope as that young brave fired a revolver blindly to either side and came on, screaming like a demon.

There was a second rider; and as the horse came to them Thunder Moon recognized by the light that glimmered on the copper braids of hair, sleek as metal, Red Wind!

"Brave girl!" cried Big Hard Face, leaping to his saddle.

"Little brother, well done!" called Thunder Moon to Standing Antelope, and all four turned their horses into the mouth of the nearest street, which opened before them a black gulf of refuge from their danger.

Guns were roaring behind them, but roaring vainly, for the street bent sharply to the right, and in another instant the Indians were flying safely through the night. The last lights of the town shot past, and the open country received them.

"Ah hai!" shouted the chief. "Four Suhtai strike through four hundred! This is a night for singing! This is a night the tribe shall remember! But do not ride out your horses, my children. Slowly and softly! The race will be long. The white devils will rise up against us. They will hunt us with horses. Dogs will show them the way that we have gone, and we and our horses shall need much strength!"

They heeded his caution, and drew back to a soft trot. They left the road, and went into a pasture, so that they would not leave behind them a stain of dust in the air to direct their immediate pursuers; and now that the grass muffled the tread of the horses, they could talk.

How the picture of the stern and self-composed Indian would have vanished had that group been seen and heard by many witnesses, and how Big Hard Face laughed and boasted!

"They shut me behind iron," he cried. "There was around me more iron than goes to the making of a thousand guns. But Thunder Moon came and struck the iron, and it turned to rotten wood. He took me by the hand, and I stood up. The white men shot at us; we killed them to the right and to the left. The head man was left. Like a frightened prairie dog in its hold, he dared not speak or move. We threw open the doors. We walked out through hundreds of warriors. We struck at their faces and they were blinded by our might and by our valor. And then a boy and woman rushed at them and made them flee, screaming. But the boy and the woman were Cheyennes! And a Cheyenne woman has more courage than the bravest men of other tribes. Look on her, Thunder Moon!"

"Look on her!" said Standing Antelope. "Yes, you have said that she has made bad medicine. But she came to me and warned me that there was danger gathering in the town and that the people were awake in their houses though they showed no lights. She came to me riding a fine horse, and so when the crowd poured out and the shooting began inside the jail, I would have charged at their faces, shooting to kill, but she was wise and told me that I should go away and wait to help you as you left the jail. I saw that she was wise and I followed her."

He paused.

And the girl, who had ridden with downward head, now turned a little and glanced at Thunder Moon. One glance, and that was all.

"I have been a fool," said Big Hard Face. "I have not

127

seen what was in her. Tarawa sent her to us as a blessing. For her sake, I shall offer up five painted buffalo robes when I return to the Suhtai. She shall have honor among the warriors and even the oldest women and the wives of the chiefs shall stand up and wait on her. On all things she was made to be the squaw of Thunder Moon. Take her hand; ask her if she will belong to you and cook in your tepee and be the mother of your children!"

"Hush! Hush!" said the girl. "You talk and talk!"

And she galloped her horse ahead.

"Go after her, Thunder Moon!" said the chief. "Go after her. She rides just fast enough to be overtaken. Ah hai! Go! Go!"

But Thunder Moon did not go.

He was too filled with wonder at the state of his own mind. For after all these months during which he had felt that the red men were divorced from his thoughts and his life forever at a touch all the old glamor came back to him.

It had not been life. It had been like sleep. Only two faces looked in on his heart—his mother and Charlotte Keene. And though Charlotte was beautiful, she had no beauty such as the wild loveliness of this Omissis girl; and if there were a delicate mystery and the sense of a soul surrounding her, nevertheless there was no such bewildering strangeness as that which surrounded the Cheyenne maiden.

What friend had he won in all his stay among the whites equal to the friendship of Standing Antelope? Ay, and what was the love of his stern, thoughtful, busy father compared with the devotion that had drawn Big Hard Face out of the plains and across the long marches to his side?

He began to breathe deeply. He listened to Standing

Antelope and his foster father laughing together, as though they had struck upon some capital jest, and a lump rose in his throat. Whether it was joy or sorrow he could hardly tell.

But, as he looked at the stars above him, he knew that they were traveling *west, west, west;* and the goal of their travels was the safety and the peril of the open plains. Suddenly he was hungry for it. He wanted again the smell of the lodge fires, and the noise of the dogs and the children in the village, and the chanting of one of the old criers, inviting to a feast. He wanted again the rush and the dust of the buffalo hunt; and the long and terrible marches along the warpath.

Westward, then! And now, at a rousing gallop, they swept down a slope and came upon Red Wind, who was giving her horse water in the brook that glimmered in the heart of the little valley.

She raised her hand, and they halted around her.

"There is no pursuit," murmured Standing Antelope. "Listen! There is no sound of the hoofs of horses behind us. We are safe; the white men are fools, as I have told you a thousand times, Thunder Moon!"

"You are a child," said the girl gravely. "We are all in danger, except Thunder Moon. There is no easy way for us, except through Thunder Moon. He could make our peace and let us go. But then he would have to stay behind us."

"The evil spirit comes into you again, Red Wind," said the old chief in a fury. "You speak with no wit."

"Look!" said the girl. "Up that valley lies the house of your father. Are you willing to leave it behind you?"

"I have killed," said Thunder Moon. "I cannot turn back now!"

"The white men have ways of dodging the white

129

man's law," said the girl with perfect surety. "Do not let fear drive you! Go look at your father's house. We shall wait for you here. For a little while there is no danger to us if we stay!"

21

The pursuers, however, were not men to give up without an effort. But there was not a saddled horse in the street to follow the flight, and by the time mounts were ready, the swift galloping of the four had put them well beyond the reach of immediate detection. They might have followed any one of a whole great network of trails, roads, and bridle paths that was flung down over the face of that country.

Other citizens in similar circumstances might have settled back and cursed the stupidity or the negligence of the officers of the law who had been detailed to guard the jail. But the men of this town were of better stuff.

They paused to inspect the interior of the jail, and there they found Larry Marston busily tying up the wounds of his three companions. One was shot deep through the shoulder; two others had wounds in the legs that would not have kept them from handling guns if they were heroes. But heroes they were not, and they had had enough of Marston's little party.

He himself was grimly set on revenge; his words were few; his face was set; and a glare was in his eyes.

Calmly, in a hard, rapid voice, he told his fellow townsmen what to do. The four had escaped from them. Well, all of them had been seen, and having been seen they might be trailed. There was the Indian chief; there was the Indian boy, Standing Antelope; and there was William Sutton, upon whom the eyes of the entire county had been fixed for so long. In addition, there was the mysterious figure with the dress of a man and the face and braided hair of a woman. She, too, should not be hard to find.

And to find them, let not the townsfolk worry about spotting particular trails, but remember that they could often strike a target by firing rather blindly with scatter shot.

In the meantime, let them go coursing through every road and every path near the town and ride on and on until the morning brightened. Wherever a house stood near, let them rouse the sleeping people and tell them what had happened and describe the fugitives.

So, by the time that morning light came, the entire circle around the town would be aroused, and after that, it could hardly be that the pursuit would miss the trail.

However, should this broadcasting method fail, he, Marston, had another thing to do as a final resource, and let all his fellow citizens trust that he never would give up this work, no matter what days or weeks or years were required. William Sutton had broken open the jail that was in his, Marston's, charge. William Sutton had managed it with incredible skill and audacity in spite of the fact that a special committee had been arranged to lie in wait for just such a raid. And now Marston would have blood for blood in repayment!

The villagers heard these bits of advice and promise which were something more than advice and something less than commands. They hurried to do as they were bidden.

And so it was that the hasty, earnest riders of the town rushed away through the countryside.

Wherever they came to a great house, two or three would strike at the door until the proprietor came down, or flung up a window, usually gun in hand, to find out what the uproar meant.

And then they gave him the word, and sped on toward the next plantation.

It was true that, the farther out they rode from the town, the fewer were the houses. But when the morning came, they themselves would be lying in a great ring, ready to take up the trail should any rumor of its direction come to them. Once a clue was picked up, the whole force of the township instantly could be flung in that direction.

Altogether, it was a skillfully organized effort.

But even a novice could have seen that the work would by no means be easy, for they were pursuing Indians, instinctively wise in all matters of war and concealment, and in addition most nobly mounted! All they needed to do, then, was to fling straight out on their course, and it would be most hard to overtake them.

But Marston was not prepared to trust everything merely to the numbers of his followers or to the eagerness with which they would go about their work.

Several times he had hunted fugitives, on every occasion, with a pack of sturdy bloodhounds. They belonged to one of the oldest settlers in the district, a queer, solitary fellow named Kingston. Men were apt to say that Kingston kept the hounds not for the trail of deer or other four-footed game but for the pleasure it gave him to hunt men.

To him Marston rode now, accompanied by seven of the best fighting men in the town. They were not of the upper class. They were square-jawed warriors, every one, men used to the handling of guns, and too familiar with the shooting of big game to hesitate a great deal in pointing their weapons even at human targets. Now, well mounted, keen for their work, armed to the teeth, they followed their leader down the road to the house of Mr. Kingston.

They did not have to complete their journey, for halfway to the place they encountered the pack, brought forward by Kingston himself and handled by three mounted Negroes. A dozen great beasts, tugging at the leashes that secured them to the horses, they lurched down the road, keen to be at some important trail.

Kingston came rapidly on through the darkness.

"Is that you, Marston?"

"It's I, Mr. Kingston. How did you happen to turn out your pack tonight?"

"I had word from some one passing the place. I hear that young Sutton has finally kicked over the traces. Well, I've been expecting it. I've been expecting it!"

He spoke with a sort of exultation in his tone. He turned back with Marston toward the jail.

"This may be bitter work for the dogs," said Marston, as they cantered on. "We have four people to follow and though one of them is a woman she seems to be an Amazon. I don't think that, if we come up with the quarry, all of your dogs will be alive to tell the tale tomorrow!"

"I've hunted the boar and the deer," said Mr. Kingston savagely. "And I've hunted desperate fugitives and never regretted a dog or two lost along the way. Why should I begrudge a few of my best now that we have something worthwhile on foot? And tell me! If we get at William Sutton, do you think he'll shoot—at men?"

133

The constable laughed harshly.

"It's a point on which I don't think. I don't have to," said he. "Because I know! I've seen something of him as you know. And if he's not a natural killer, then I'll admit that I've learned nothing about human nature from my work as constable. He'll shoot to kill; and, furthermore, he'll kill! We're going to pay, on this trail. We're going to pay, both in dogs and in men. Are you unwilling to keep on the trail, Mr. Kingston?"

Mr. Kingston laughed in turn, a crooning, brooding laughter.

"We have only one life to live," said he. "Sport has been the greatest thing for me, and yet I've never had a chance at real sport before this evening. Is it likely that I'll turn back? Four of 'em—and one a woman! Why, my dear young friend, this is going to be something to remember—or to die for!"

They got back to the jail, and the pack was brought inside the building.

First they were taken to the cell where the Indian had been confined; and after that, they were shown and allowed to smell and mouth the buffalo robe Big Hard Face had been wearing, which had been left behind when he fled from the jail and attacked the waiting mob outside. It was as good a clue as possibly could have been given to them.

Next they were pooled at the spot where many signs of horses showed where the four mounts had been brought up in the street so that Big Hard Face and William Sutton could escape.

The scent of man and beast now was in the nostrils of the pack, and they gave tongue in a mellow thunder the instant they were loosed. Straight down the side street they drove, close together, letting one high-shouldered veteran take the lead.

Behind them rode the constable and his men in company with Kingston. Altogether there were twelve souls, though no doubt the expedition would be reinforced by others who would flock to the music of the dogs as they headed across the country.

"We've started late," said Marston, "but I think this trail will lead to something."

"It will lead to blood," replied Kingston, fiercely prophetic. "I feel it, man, I feel it!"

22

While these things were happening in the town, William Sutton had left his companions and galloped up the way toward the house of his father.

Under the trees nearby, he left Sailing Hawk. Then he climbed up to the top of the front porch and from that point came under the window of the room in which his parents slept. He slipped in through the window and began to cross the floor stealthily.

A dim, white form rose from the farther bed.

"Who is there?" said a ghostly whisper.

He whispered back, "William!"

Instantly he saw his mother rise, saw her throw on her dressing gown and step into her slippers. He delayed no longer in the room, but went softly into the little library adjoining.

There she joined him, her slippers whispering on the deep pile of the carpet. She came straight to him and reached up her hands to his shoulders.

"What has happened, William? What have you done?"

"I've taken my foster father from the jail."

"Ah!" she murmured. And then she added faintly, "I knew that it would happen. I dreamed of it. I told your father; but he wouldn't believe!"

"I couldn't trust the thing to my father," said William sternly. "If I had been able to leave it in his hands, I should have done so, but I overheard him plotting with Marston to keep Big Hard Face in the jail forever! I overheard him betraying my foster father and in that way betraying me as well! But matters have gone too far for his help. *No* one can help me now."

"What do you mean? And what have you done, in the name of mercy?"

"There are dead men lying in the jail, mother."

She clung to him swaying and stunned by the blow.

"The wind is up. The rain will be coming soon," said she. "It's turning into a wild night. I shall die of grief and of fear if you go out into it, my poor boy!"

"Shall I wait here, then? Listen!"

He drew her to the window. As the gale whistled around the corner of the building they could hear something more than the mere spirit of the storm in the sound, for there was a booming voice, and then a chorus of voices, far away, but seeming to run up on them with an amazing speed.

"Do you hear?"

"The bloodhounds!" said she. She added hysterically, "Go quickly. And how shall I let you know when it is possible for you to come back to us?"

"I'll find some safe messenger to send to you if I cannot come myself. But it never will be safe for me to come back openly. Tell Charlotte Keene that I shall never forget her. The lodge where she lives is my heart. But we are drawn into different trails. I must go back to

136

the plains, and she must stay here and work out her own way through the lives of the whites. I feel very sick, mother. I have two hearts. And both of them are broken with sorrow. Good-bye!"

He kissed her forehead and left as he had come, through the window and then down a column to the ground below.

There he did not hesitate, but hurried back to the spot at which he had left the stallion.

He found Sailing Hawk extremely nervous, alternately throwing up his head and sniffing at the ground, very much as he often had acted when on the debatable ground of a warpath in the old days upon the plains. And as Thunder Moon swung into the saddle, he heard the cause of the disturbance of the big horse.

Far on the horizon was a cry of dogs, the unmistakable chorus of a pack; not like the wild calling of a band of wolves in winter running down a blood trail, but filled with the same deathless terror and malice.

It seemed safely distant, but as the wind fell a moment later and atmospheric conditions altered, the full chime of the chorus beat suddenly and fully upon his ear. And he realized that the pack was rapidly closing in upon the trail.

What trail they followed, he did not need to ask. He was familiar with the dogs Kingston was in the habit of donating to the constable and the officers of the law in that vicinity. Therefore he set his teeth, but not in any ecstasy of fear. Rather, he was grimly determined to make those who rode behind him realize that now they were not on the trail of some frightened and desperate fugitive.

He rode rapidly back to the place where the three Indians waited for him, and as he came to them he saw that they, too, had heard the calling of the dogs and had understood it perfectly. Standing Antelope had warned them of its significance. And now the boy called anxiously to Thunder Moon, "How do we ride? Where shall we go do dodge them? They are coming fast, and they never tire!"

They held serious conference upon the matter. Should they ride straight down one of the main roads and trust to the speed and the wind of their horses? Or, should they attempt to take half-known byways and cross water many times in order to delay the hounds behind them as much as possible?

There were other possibilities, also, such as frequently taking a course across some of the farmyards that might lie more or less in their way where the strong odors of many animals might kill their scent.

But this Standing Antelope was against. He had been behind this same pack of hounds when they ran down a fugitive who had tried that very precaution, and they had captured the man and, indeed, nearly torn him to pieces, before the posse of the constable arrived on the scene and rescued the victim.

They continued their grave debate, all speaking in turn except the girl, who looked first at one and then at the other. At length Big Hard Face was addressed by his foster son.

"Father," said he, "on the plains you have been a hundred times upon the trail. These hounds are very swift and their noses are sure, but I think that they are not so sure and not so swift as Pawnees in pursuit. Now tell us what we must do, and we shall attempt it!"

"Each man," said Big Hard Face, "is only wise in his own country and this land is strange to me. Therefore my advice may be very wrong, but I should ride by the broadest and the swiftest way and put a march between us and the enemy swiftly. Let it be, however, as my son wills it!"

"One march," said Thunder Moon, "cannot take us away from our enemies. We have killed white men, therefore the white law follows us. It lies behind us and before us. It will follow us into the prairies. However, what use have we for secret ways in a strange country? Even Standing Antelope is not so familiar with it as are the white men. Father, let us ride straight and fast and trust to the legs of our horses."

He ended, and straightway they headed for the nearest road, and then bore west along it at a brisk gallop.

Presently Big Hard Face called for a slower speed.

"We are not children in the saddle, Thunder Moon and I," said he, "and therefore we must save the strength of our horses, as wise men save water when they cross the desert."

He drew his own mount down to a trot, and the rest imitated the example, reining in their horses.

They made less noise now, and taking the grassy edges of the highway, where the softer ground was better for the hoofs of the horses, they passed along with practically no sound. Like four shadows they drifted across the countryside. Then the moon rose and began to silver the tops of the trees in the woodland before them.

"There may be traps and traps before us," said Standing Antelope. "Phaugh! This country chokes me. If ever I come back to the prairies where the sky is a full half circle above our heads, I never shall leave it again!"

"Look!" cried Standing Antelope. "The woods! The woods! Turn to the side; whips and spurs!"

They heeded his warning and scattered to either side, their horses bounding under the lash. And at the same time a full dozen of rifles rang from the ambush and the bullets sang among them. The treacherous moonlight, and the timely warning of Standing Antelope, however, had made the volley bite empty air only.

23

To understand how that volley happened to be fired into the faces of the fugitives, however, we must go back a little to a time when Charlotte Keene's ball was at its height.

No one could be there and be unhappy. Charlotte herself went around like one in a delighted dream. And Harrison Traynor, pale and grim of face, guessed at the cause of her absentmindedness. He determined to ask the question point-blank, and therefore he drew her to a corner when he could and said, "Perhaps you don't know it, Charlotte, but William Sutton isn't here. He's disappeared quite mysteriously. Hasn't been here during the last two hours, I take it!"

"What makes you say this, Harry?" she asked.

"Someone was inquiring for him. That's all."

"Has there been any trouble?"

"No," said Traynor. "Not that I know of. He's learned his lessons fairly well, it appears, and he knows how to keep his claws masked behind the velvet. He never lets people see the danger in him lately."

"You always have an ugly manner when you speak of him," said the girl coldly. "You shouldn't, Harry. It isn't becoming!"

"Of course it isn't," he admitted, with a disarming smile. "Only—you're the hostess, you know, and you really ought to keep an eye on a tiger after you've invited him to a party!"

"He was called away from the house," she replied. "But I don't think there's any trouble, really."

"You knew he was gone, then?"

"Yes."

"Ah?"

"Why are you so pointed about it, Harry?"

"You've been going about with a mysterious look most of the evening. I don't suppose that his disappearance has had anything to do with it?"

She hesitated.

"I think it has," said Traynor.

"Well?"

"You don't have to tell me anything that's an important secret, Charlie," he continued, "but I have a right to know when it has become actual folly for me to bother you with my attentions. Now, I have an idea that this William Sutton has edged me out. Well, more power to him, if that's the case! But at the same time, it appears to me that I should be informed. Just tell me when the door has definitely been closed in my face!"

"What's made you so serious?" she asked gravely.

"Because," he said, "you look to me tonight exactly like a person who has been made giddy with good news. And I guess that the good news has something to do with what you and Sutton have decided. Perhaps it's connected with his disappearance from the house this evening. I don't ask any details. I only want you to tell me when I must consider myself simply—your best friend!"

"It's true," she said suddenly. "You have a right to

141

know. And you've guessed. It isn't for general circulation, you must understand. But—"

"I'll never repeat until you yourself tell me that I may. Ten thousand hearty congratulations, Charlie."

He shook hands warmly with her. But afterward, he managed to get out into the garden, and there he leaned against a corner of the wall and closed his eyes. He felt rather sick and helpless, for he had fought a long fight for this girl. He was not rich, and she was. He was well placed in their social circle, but not a whit better than the daughter of Judge Keene. From all viewpoints it was a match most to be desired. But beyond this, it was undoubtedly true that he loved Charlie for her own sake. He felt it now as he never had felt it before.

For five minutes he remained there, breathing deeply. But even after that interval, before he trusted himself to return to the house he practiced a smile and rubbed the color into his cheeks. Then he came back with apparent cheerfulness, and had no sooner entered the room than there was a disturbance and general confusion in the front of the house, and immediately thereafter young Luke Masterson came striding into the ballroom.

"Gentlemen!" he said. "I beg your pardon, Miss Keene, but will you ask the ladies to excuse the gentlemen for one minute. I have important news for them!"

"What is the news? You can tell it before all of us," said Charlotte Keene.

Harrison Traynor, tall and erect, came beside her.

"Certainly," he said, "let's have the excitement, Luke. Talk out, old fellow."

"There's excitement enough!" exclaimed Masterson. "The jail's been broken into by William Sutton, three men are lying dead inside the place now, and Sutton has escaped with the Cheyenne Indian who was arrested this evening by the constable. I've come to get you men on your horses. Will you come along with me?"

Dead silence followed this stunning bit of news. All heads turned toward Jack Sutton and his sister, and they themselves stood like statues.

Charlotte Keene held Traynor's arm to steady herself, but her voice was clear and firm enough as she called, "You've made a mistake, Luke Masterson. William Sutton never would shoot to kill."

"By heavens, Miss Keene, I had the word from the constable himself! He said that three men were either dead or dying inside the jail when he started on the trail."

For that was the message with which wily young Marston had sent his emissaries through the countryside.

Afterward, when it turned out that no one had been killed, he could easily say that he thought the wounds all were fatal. But he knew that it made a vast difference. A mere case of jailbreaking was one thing—and, considering the motives William Sutton had for his action, he was apt to meet with a good deal of sympathy—but, on the other hand, if it were felt that he had committed murder, then every man in the community would be willing to ride hard and shoot straight to avenge the deed.

There was little chance that the information he sent out by his messengers would be questioned, for there was no time for the true report to follow on its heels. And so it happened at the house of Judge Keene that the voice of his daughter was the only one raised in doubt.

Among the rest went a gloomy and deadly murmur.

"This comes of trying to domicile a wild man among

143

civilized people. Colonel Sutton should be held to strict account for this!"

And if the men were stern, the women were no less determined.

Murder!

Moreover, Thunder Moon had been too busy with his studies, and his manner was too coldly reserved, to make him many friends. When he ceased being a freak, he almost ceased being interesting.

"What's the murder of three men to a cold-blooded devil who thinks nothing of taking a boy along and trailing a man-eater into a forest at night? Nothing's beyond him!"

Such was the first reaction toward the news that was brought to this house by Masterson.

The constable's call for volunteers brought a notable response, for every man who was able to ride a horse rushed for his mount; and those who had not come in the saddle were furnished with horses from the judge's stables.

He himself, pale and troubled, was met by his daughter, who caught one of his hands in hers.

"Father," she said fiercely, "you sent William to speak to me tonight!"

"And he did?"

"Yes."

"And you?"

"I told him that I loved him."

"Wipe it out of your mind, Charlie. A murderer—a jail brawl—three men dead. Good heavens, how unspeakable! My daughter and such a man?"

"Father," she urged eagerly, "ride with the rest, just to keep them from shooting at the critical moment. Ride with them and try to keep them back! I'm going myself! He's got to be saved. I don't care what he's done."

144

"Charlotte!" cried her father. "I explicitly forbid you to do anything so mad! I—"

She slipped from him. He ran after her, but she slammed the door behind her and turned the lock. By the time he had gone around through the hall, she was lost to sight, and he knew that she would be mounted and off with the hunt before he could prevent.

So, grinding his teeth and groaning, the judge rushed in turn to get a mount at his stables, and there he found a press of hot-blooded youths, cursing William Sutton, and swearing that they would do their part to take vengeance on him for his crime.

Charlotte was nowhere in sight. No one could give him word of her. But that was not strange, for the stables were like madhouses this evening, with men calling for saddles and bridles, and then having to help themselves and find what they could.

Every instant, in little groups of three and four, the riders pushed away into the dark of the night, past the pathetic figure of young Ruth Sutton, who stood beyond the gate imploring each wild-riding band to wait until the next day had given them surer word of what had happened and what guilt belonged to her older brother. But she was unregarded. The judge himself paid no attention to her, and dashed through the gate with a rifle in his hand. Whatever the others had to spur them on, he had before him the high goal of preventing for his daughter a most unfortunate, a mad love affair.

24

First man from the house, on that night, and first to reach the stables, was Harrison Traynor.

He had paused only to take the hand of Charlotte Keene and say to her, with his heart apparently in his voice, "I've said that I was your best friend, and tonight I'm going to try to give you a proof of it!"

"Dear Harry! God bless you!" she cried.

He went away, smiling grimly.

He only paused at the gun room in the back of the house. He was familiar with it and with its contents, and he was able to select, even in the dim light of one small lamp, a fine new rifle, and a quantity of ammunition. He took a Colt revolver of the newest stamp as well. With this equipment, he hurried for the stables, cursing the fortune that had made him leave his riding horse behind him on this night of all nights in his life. However, he was the very first in the stables, and he could take his pick.

He did not have to ask. A big-headed roan had taken his eye long before. It was not a clean-bred one, but it had plenty of hot blood. It was just a trifle over in the knees and went lame for the first ten minutes of a ride. But there never was a gamer horse, a better-winded runner, or a better head for cross-country running, where horse brains truly tell!

He snatched a saddle from the saddle room, and rushed for his prize. He had hardly started work when the pale face of Jack Sutton gleamed under the lantern

146

light, running for a horse in a neighboring box. And fast though the hands of Traynor worked, Jack was a little faster, and they led their horses from the barn together.

Quickly and softly, in spite of the turmoil that was beginning all through the stables, Harrison Traynor developed a little dialogue with his companion on the way to the open.

"Now, Jack," he said, "you have your opportunity. You can help to polish off the existence of this impostor tonight!"

"*I*?" cried Jack. "I'm going to help him if I can."

"Help him? Good heavens, my dear Jack, you don't mean that!"

"What else can I do? What else will people expect me to do?"

"They'll expect you to stand up for law and order, no matter who may have broken the law. A murderer is a murderer, Jack!"

"I'd be outlawed from every decent house!"

"You talk like a fool, Jack. Everyone would understand!"

Eagerly Traynor pressed his point. There was not a cooler head, not a steadier hand, not a deadlier shot in the county than young Jack Sutton, unless it were Traynor himself. And he wanted the services of the marksman, wanted them most terribly. Better one sure rifleman than a hundred bunglers. Better and more to be trusted in this keen hunt, which, fate willing, would end the life of William Sutton, and the love affair of Charlie Keene.

"I couldn't aim a gun at him," said Jack.

"Tell me this, old fellow. Is he really your brother, or is he an impostor?"

"Lord knows, not I!"

"You do know. What's your instinct in the matter?"

"I admit that I can't call him a brother with any feeling."

"Of course you can't, and the intuition always is right. Trust instinct, Jack!"

The boy turned suddenly, fiercely, on Traynor.

"Harry, you're older than I."

"A little, yes."

"You're an honorable fellow, and you know the world. Now, I don't like William—if he really *is* William. Not that he's cut me off from the fortune. I don't think that's what counts with me. But my heart doesn't warm to him. Never has. Harry, tell me on your solemn and holy word of honor, what would you do if you were in my place?"

"I'll tell you," said Traynor. "I'd ride with the boys and I'd tell them that you wanted them to do William no harm. That would gloss over your reputation. But in the meantime, if I got a fair chance, I would say that I wanted a shot at the damned Indians who were running off with your brother and carrying him away to the prairies. I'd pretend to take a shot at them, if the chance came, but, by heaven, I'd see that my bullet found the heart of the impostor and murderer who is masquerading in the name of your house!"

Jack Sutton gasped.

Then, "I'll do it!" he cried. "I want to do it! And you know what's wisest and most right. I'll do it, Harry!"

"Good, Jack! Then ride with me. For if anyone finds him tonight, I've an idea that I'll be the man. Do you hear? I have a premonition that I or Thunder Moon will die tonight!"

They swung into their saddles, and now it could be seen that Traynor had not wasted his life in that part of the world. When he was seen mounting, half a dozen who were in the same act called to him that they would go with him. For whether at the dinner table or in the hunting field, no man had a better reputation than Harrison Traynor for surety and keen wit. These others wanted a leader, and they turned readily to him in the emergency.

He ran them over with his eye.

They were what he wanted. Not so many as to make a clumsy crowd, but enough to push that fighting devil, Thunder Moon, to the wall. And every man of them was armed to the teeth, and every man of them knew how to use his weapons. Whether from the back of a galloping horse or shooting at a mark, there was not one of them but had put in long years of training. Moreover, they looked as thoroughbred as the horses upon which they were mounted, and Traynor knew, as he glanced at their faces, that he could count upon them in the fight that, he hoped, would end up that ride.

For, he told himself, with a swelling heart and with set teeth, that life would not be worthwhile for him if he lost Charlie Keene. And lose her he would, he knew, so long as William Sutton lived. Death alone could end that affair, perhaps, and the touch of the great healer, time.

Traynor had in view a maneuver both simple and practical. Three roads pointed toward the west; west toward the distant prairies he felt sure the fugitives would press; and if he could occupy those roads he would be apt to bag the four. People more familiar with the lay of the land might have been apt to take secret ways and passes among the marshes and through the woods, but the Indians were comparative strangers—even Standing Antelope—and therefore Traynor was fairly sure that the band would take to the highways.

In the meantime, he had only this handful of men. The others from the ball had scattered here and there, each party with some idea of its own. Not far away, there was a low, rolling ridge that crossed the three roads and ran on beyond them. Traynor put one man to watch each of the side roads and he, with young Jack Sutton and seven others, took cover in the trees looking down on the middle way.

They dismounted and Jack Sutton made a speech to the little group.

He told them, with apparent earnestness, that he must beg them not to fire a shot at his brother, William. Let them try to take him alive. As for the Indians who were with him, of course they should be shot down as quickly as possible. It was for that purpose, he said, that he had joined their number.

His speech was received with respect, and Traynor tapped him lightly on the shoulder.

"But suppose, Jack," broke in one of the party, "that your brother opens fire on us. He's not the sort of man who misses a target twice. Are we simply to stand up under his fire?"

"My friends," said Jack with dignity, "I only can ask you to show some restraint and try to give my brother some favor."

"Aye, Jack," said Traynor. "That's spoken like a man, and of course we'll do what we can for him."

A moment later, he found occasion to whisper in the ear of Jack, "Let the rest mark down the other Indians, if we have a chance to fire, but you and I'll train our guns on Thunder Moon. Agreed?"

"Yes," said Jack through his teeth.

After that, silence fell over the party. Out of the west a wind was coming; the boughs above their heads began to sway. Somewhere nearby two branches were rubbing together with a dolorous, mournful sound. Across the stars vague shapes of clouds began to sweep.

The moon had risen now, however, and its light gave more surety and sense of power to the ambushers. But nothing happened until one of the older members of the group declared he thought that he heard the baying of distant hounds like the voices of bloodhounds. The whole group listened intently, but they did not make out the sound again.

In due time, they saw four shadows moving down the road just before them, not with a rush and sweep as they had imagined that the four would come, but merely trotting their horses.

"Cool heads, all of 'em," said Traynor. "They're saving their horseflesh for a brush! Now, boys, there they come. Mark down your men, except for William Sutton. No one aim at him!"

The wind suddenly dropped. Jack Sutton, as he lay beside Traynor, could hear the hard breathing of his companion, and over a fallen log as a rest, he drew his bead with a steady hand upon the body of his brother. He changed from the body to the head, for Thunder Moon looked so utterly formidable as he came down the road upon his horse it seemed impossible that one bullet could take his life.

The four riders drifted closer and closer. They were speaking, and the faint sound of the deep voice of William came across to Jack. It touched him as the sight of the man had failed to stir his heart, and, putting his rifle down, he murmured to Traynor, "I can't do it, Harry! My God, how could I ever have dreamed of trying to shoot such a man—and my own brother! You were a devil to tempt me to it, Harry Traynor!"

"You fool!" said Traynor. "Don't let your heart run away with your head entirely! There is a —"

His voice stopped with a gasp, for suddenly the four riders swept away from one another like dead leaves

151

picked up by a whirlpool of wind. Traynor caught his mark again with a deft shift of his rifle, but as he closed his finger on the trigger a hand struck his arm and made his shot fly wild.

It was young Jack beside him.

"I couldn't let you, Harry!" said he. "I know you mean the best for me. There's nothing for you to gain by his death. You're only thinking of me—but I couldn't let you!"

"Damnation!" snarled Traynor. "You young fool, do you know that you nudged yourself out of Sutton House that moment?"

Springing to his feet, he called on his companions, "We've turned them back. We'll go after them, boys, and ride 'em down, or else turn 'em straight back into the hands of the fellows that must be following from behind. We've lost the first trick; but we'll take the trick that wins the game!"

They mounted instantly, and flying across the open meadow, they drove on into the trees among which the four were now out of sight.

25

Such was the cause of the ambush that would have stopped the flight of the four before it had well begun had it not been for the hawklike eye of Standing Antelope, which detected the shadow of danger that lay before them. Sweeping back toward the trees at one side, they spurred for safety.

Bullets still whistled around them, for the posse was firing as it came hotfoot after them.

Thunder Moon, ranging beside his old foster father, was suddenly aware that the noise of the pursuit had stopped and that the firing had redoubled but drew no closer.

"They are shooting at shadows!" laughed Big Hard Face. "Come, my son. The white men are fools. We shall slip through the hands of a hundred of them."

"Where is Red Wind?" asked Standing Antelope, pressing closer to them.

"Red Wind!" exclaimed Thunder Moon. "She has gone back to make a sacrifice of herself and let us escape. Listen! She is firing on them and drawing their fire! Ah hai! Who would have thought there was such courage in any woman! It is she! It must be she!"

With that, he whirled his horse about.

"Let her be," said Big Hard Face. "Is the life of a woman worth the life of a man? Let her be, I say. She is making a sacrifice that will be accepted; her spirit will find happiness forever, and in our safe lodge among the Suhtai, we will make her to be remembered."

So said Big Hard Face, with a logic as stern as his name, but Thunder Moon did not stop to listen. He lunged back through the woods toward the center of the noise of the firing, and so under the bright moon he saw what he had expected and yet could not believe.

There was a thick natural hedge of compact bushes, with a little strip of cleared ground in a semicircle behind it; and up and down that hedge rode Red Wind, weaving back and forth on her horse, and reloading and firing her rifle with such wonderful rapidity that, taking into account the different points from which she was constantly firing, it might well have seemed that the entire party of four had taken cover there.

153

The assailants had not yet worked around to the rear of the position. But when that happened, Red Wind would die. She must have known, but she did not falter in her work.

Thunder Moon, looking at her, felt his heart swell and then almost stop with wonder at the sight. He had looked upon her as a mysterious combination of woman and devil, but he never had dreamed that anything could have controlled her other than purest selfishness. And here she was offering her life for the safety of the party—offering it without braggadocio, simply.

He heard the crashing of the guns of the posse. He heard the whistling of the balls. By miracle—or by dint of her constant shifting of position—she had escaped injury. And as she rode she fired, loaded, and fired again.

For a half second Thunder Moon endured the wonder of this spectacle and then he swept down to her. She turned with a faint cry, as she felt the rush of something from behind, and as she had fired her rifle that instant, she grasped it by the barrel and swung it like a club above her head as she turned her horse around.

Then she saw who was coming and let him take the bridle of her horse and sweep away, leading her beside him.

"Who gave you authority," said Thunder Moon, "to come back here and fight like a mad woman? Listen! They still are firing into the covert! You have baffled them more than all the rest of us had managed to do. But who bade you come here? Red Wind, am I mistaken about you? Are you a greathearted woman, after all? Ah hai! What is a greater heart than that—to die for the safety of one's friends?"

He praised her as they rode. She looked neither to

the right nor to the left, but kept her face straight forward and gave no sign that she heard a word he uttered.

Thunder Moon was enormously excited. Before, there had seemed in this girl nothing but evil under well-controlled guises. But now there appeared to be something more—a self-sacrificing nobility. Courage he never had doubted that she possessed. But courage as a gentle and pure-souled power was the last quality he would have attributed to her.

What shall man say of Thunder Moon and his fickleness?

That very evening he had looked into the eyes of the white girl and told her that he loved her, but now in one instant Charlotte Keene's memory was dimmed as by the passing of a whole year. His heart began to leap and thunder as he saw the moonlight gleam on the red-metal braids of her hair, brushed out the next instant as they swept on into the shadow.

Suddenly he said to her, "Somehow I knew at once what had happened and what you had done. Well, I certainly must have thought better of you than I guessed."

This was not a polite speech, but it did not disturb the girl. She looked more statuelike than ever.

They rushed up to Big Hard Face and Standing Antelope, who were working their horses to and fro.

"It was as I guessed," said Thunder Moon, and he took the hand of the girl and laid it in the hand of his foster father. "Look, Big Hard Face, what she has done! They still are back there firing at the shadows. They are afraid to come closer. I shall be surprised if she did not kill one or two of them. Ha, my father, what will you say of warriors who are killed by women? There is more

155

danger in Red Wind than there is in three war chiefs. I always knew that. Take her. She is my sister. Twice she has saved us on this one night!"

"Keep the rear, Thunder Moon," said the chief. "Keep the rear with Standing Antelope, while I make trail with the girl in front. Shall we point quartering across that ridge?"

"Yes," answered Standing Antelope, "because I know that there is another road to the west running beyond that low hill."

So Big Hard Face turned the head of his horse and rode without haste. For though the men of Harrison Traynor had discovered that they had been firing for some time at an empty covert, still it would take them much time indeed to follow the trail by moonlight. The great opportunity of Traynor seemed to have come and gone again when he saw big Thunder Moon before him—and had his arm nudged as he drew the trigger.

Calmly, mildly, the chief spoke to the girl, "Tell me, Red Wind, if you hate us so much, why have you done such things for us as you have done this night? I cannot understand, and my head spins as I try to make out your reasons. Have you a reason, girl?"

She looked sidewise at him.

"I have a reason. It is no reason that I can tell to you."

"Is it a noble or a selfish reason?"

She hesitated, smiling at the naïveté that asked such a question. But at length she said, "It is not noble. It is not selfish. It is surely something else."

"But what else can there be?" asked Big Hard Face. "Everything in the world must be done for one reason or for the other."

"There are some things," said the girl, "that even a wise chief does not know about. Or if he has known them, he forgets afterward."

"Ha? Well," said Big Hard Face, "no matter what you may say, you have earned the right of talking freely with me and with all the tribe of the Suhtai. I shall not ask you questions you do not wish to answer. When we come safely back to the Suhtai, you will be admitted to the council and allowed to sit with the chiefs and the wise men because of what you have done tonight, Red Wind. Some old and wise chief will take you for a squaw."

"Peace!" said the girl sharply. "Listen! They are coming fast!"

Through the night the booming, chiming voices of the bloodhounds swept rapidly toward them.

26

Very deliberately, as men long used to peril in a thousand forms, the party determined how they would baffle the dogs. So much time had been lost when Thunder Moon went to say farewell to his mother that the whole countryside was thoroughly alarmed, and men were willing to risk their lives to arrest the flight of the little band.

Nothing remained, therefore, except to cut across country as fast as they could; and this they did, riding steadily, but never pushing their horses in spite of the cry of the hounds behind them. No horse in the world could have lived with dogs over such running as this, one moment through tangled woods, and the next struggling across marsh, and then fording a river and staggering up the farther slope of the stream. The hounds were sure to gain, unless the wits of the fugitives could turn them.

Presently, they had an excellent chance. They came to a broad-faced little river, so shallow that they could ride their horses into it. On its verge they looked up and down and finally decided that here they must make their attempt at a trail that would throw the dogs adrift.

Upstream, therefore, they went for well over a quarter of a mile, and by that time the voices of the hunt were breaking through the trees and finally went echoing up the river after them. Immediately afterward, they heard the sounds dying out, sure sign that the pack was in the water. Then deadly silence as every dog was swimming.

When the dogs recovered the trail, they would give tongue, of course. If the wisdom of Kingston turned them up the stream, then a crisis would come at once.

In the meantime, the fugitives came to a spot where a shelf of rock stepped with comfortable ease from the waters, and there they climbed out. From the rock, a great trunk of a tree extended to the ground beyond, and over that natural bridge they led their horses, one by one, without mishap.

That this bridge might not be suspected, after they were across, Big Hard Face directed that they should turn the trunk from its place.

That was done and the rock struck the ground with a heavy impact.

They stood listening, fearing lest the cry of the hunt would be attracted by the noise. Then, indeed, the cry of the pack did sound, but far, far down the stream.

"It is ended!" said Big Hard Face, in great relief. "Some one of the dogs has happened upon a false scent!"

158

They remounted and pushed ahead through the woods, always aiming west but taking what advantage they could of the terrain.

The cold morning was beginning when they entered a little natural pasture. All the world was silent. The fugitives were overcome with fatigue. Here they determined to make a temporary camp, rest the horses, and then move cautiously forward once more.

Big Hard Face set the example, and having loosed the girths of his horse, he stretched himself on the damp grass. They set no watch. All about them were the deep woods; there was no noise except the sound of the horses tearing at the grass, and not even a ghost could have come upon them without making a sufficient disturbance to put them on their guard.

It was not the noise of anyone passing through the woods, however, that wakened them before half an hour. It was a deep, rich burst of music as a dozen hounds gave tongue.

Their trail had been recovered! They mounted once more. There was no sign of fatigue, as yet, from Sailing Hawk, and the three horses that had been taken from the colonel were thoroughbreds. Thunder Moon made trail; the rest followed in single file.

But ever the clamor of the dogs grew. They could distinguish the separate voices as every hound gave tongue, and now they knew that they had come to the end of their tether.

They came to a natural tunnel through the woods. By the morning light they entered the path, and now they could make fair headway, letting the horses go at a trot; but even such a speed would not do, as they could tell in a few moments. Right behind them sounded the thunder of the pack, and the noise, caught as in a funnel, confused their minds. Even Big Hard Face nervously pushed his horse ahead, and Thunder Moon looked around him and saw Red Wind watching him with acute, expectant terror in her eyes.

It pleased him oddly, that sign of fear from her. It showed that she was not above human weakness, no matter how mysterious her strength.

He managed to fall behind with Standing Antelope, and the instant they were well to the rear, Thunder Moon flung himself from his horse and motioned to the boy to do the same. Clear-eyed, grim of mouth, the youngster waited for his orders.

In either hand, Thunder Moon held a revolver, and where the tunnel turned sharply to the side and made a distinct angle, he placed himself and made the lad kneel before him, a knife gripped in his hand.

"They are not like other dogs," said the boy, taking up his position. "Remember, I have seen them. They come to kill, and kill they will!"

"What pass my guns, your knife must count for," said Thunder Moon loudly, for the noise of the dogs was swelling. "Never slash at the throat. Give them the point, always the point!"

As he spoke a great, reddish-brown beast turned the corner of the path and his bay turned to a snarl as he flung himself forward. He was the tried and tested leader who never had failed in a score of battles. In midair the bullet found him; but he had sprung so far and boldly that though he landed dead, with a brief howl of agony, his weight struck full on Standing Antelope and knocked him sprawling headlong to the ground.

Two more, straining abreast, lurched bravely at Thunder Moon. He gave them a bullet from either gun. One shot smashed through the brain and the beast fell;

the second was no more than a glancing wound and, like a fury, the great beast charged.

It would surely have gone ill with Thunder Moon then, but the Suhtai boy, lying on his back, stabbed upward as the bloodhound passed over him, and the poor brute writhed in convulsions of pain, dying slowly.

But still that charge came on as though the dogs were gallant cavalry. The horn of Kingston was frantically blowing a recall, but they gave no heed. They had heard the death cries of their leaders, and they went on for their vengeance.

A double stream of lead met them. Never had Thunder Moon made better target practice. Twice a wounded dog managed to stagger on after being struck, but on each occasion the cunning knife of Standing Antelope finished the work.

The place became a shambles. Nine bodies lay there dead or dying, and the remaining dogs held back, at last thoroughly daunted. They were the weakest spirits of the pack. Now they shrank, turned, and fled yelping.

Voices of men were sounding down the green tunnel now, and particularly the high-pitched yell of Kingston, demanding vengeance for his loss; but here Big Hard Face and Red Wind came back, guns in hand, thoroughly alarmed.

"They are coming fast!" said the chief. "They will charge against us. Reload! Reload, Thunder Moon!"

He laughed, pointing to the bodies before him.

"They have lost these lives already," he said. "Do you think they will come on for more? No, no! They never will follow us here; they will strive to block us at the farther end of the path. Go with me, father! Hurry! Or they will take us like snakes in a hole!"

161

27

They came from the tunnel that passed through that jungle-smothered marshland none too soon, for on their right they could hear horsemen working through a thicket. Before them, now, stretched a long sheet of firm ground and their horses swung away at a long gallop. As they started, they heard a wild yelping well to the rear.

"It is the hounds!" said Standing Antelope, wiping his hands and knife on the mane of his horse. "They are trying to whip the dogs onto the trail, but they will never take to this line again."

He laughed cheerfully as he spoke, adding, "Tell me, Big Hard Face, were you ever on a better war trail than this? Were there ever such great odds against you? Did you ever before make such fools of so many men?"

The old chief smiled at the boy.

"We may talk afterward, perhaps. Let us think only of what our enemies are doing with their wits and with their horses. They are not following fast, my friends!"

For at that moment nearly a score of riders came out from the marsh and, seeing the distant fugitives, swung into a gallop in pursuit. But their mounts seemed to have neither spirit nor strength left to them. They had been floundering for too many hours through the steaming bogs of the marshland, pushing aimlessly here and there, rushing to meet every alarm, swarming out on many a false trail; and now the keenness was as great

162

as ever in the riders, but the horses could not answer. Whereas the fugitives had gone steadily, without undue haste, conserving their horses at every turn of the way. They reaped a harvest now for that forbearance. Without effort, without a single whip stroke, they left the whole body of the hunt laboring far behind them, and soon lost to view. Only, from time to time, they had a glimpse of a few hardy riders who were able to keep their horses at a great effort by dint of whip and spur.

In that body of skillful riders went Harrison Traynor, and at his side was the constable. Never two finer riders had dashed across country after fox or chasing pure sport. But they lacked that instinctive skill that comes to men who have lived in the saddle, and all the four fugitives had spent almost as many hours on horseback as they had on foot. They knew how to rate their mounts at a slope; when it was wisest to dismount and lead the horse; when a downpitch was too sharp to be negotiated with speed without taking too great a toll of their animals. And, in addition, when the final test came, and the run for life or death had to be made, they knew how to wring from their tired horses the last bit of speed, strength, and service.

For all these reasons, the four drew easily farther and farther away.

The country was changing, now. The flat land, the steaming marshes, the straight, well-made roads gave way to rolling country, sometimes with hills the size of mountains, and the roads were either bridle paths, or else the roughest sort of wagon ways laid down with no pretense at engineering, but simply going where streams of wandering cattle first had marked out a course.

It had an advantage and it had a great drawback, this country. In the first place, it gave them a chance to work freely ahead; in the second place it was sure to place them under observation more easily, for they had only an occasional grove of trees to shelter them.

Until noon, they kept steadily to the hollows, pressing on without remorse for their flagging steeds; but shortly after the middle of the day, they saw before them a small house and Thunder Moon declared that there they would take rest, find food for themselves, and grain for their horses. Better rest now, when there was no enemy in sight, than wait for the night. Because night was apt to bring them as much danger as it did security.

As they came up toward the house, they saw a man, a woman, and a child break from the place and rush away toward the corral where, hastily, each threw himself on a horse and plunged away down the valley.

"They are going to spread trouble ahead of us!" said Big Hard Face and he unslung his rifle. "They must be brought back!"

"They shall be," answered Thunder Moon, and beckoning to Standing Antelope, they swept in pursuit. Tired as their horses were, like all thoroughbreds they were able to raise a racing gallop. Swiftly they came up with the trio, and a shot fired over their heads by Thunder Moon made them draw rein.

They faced about in a panic of terror. The man had an old horse pistol in his hand and a set expression on his face.

"You murderin' devils," said he, "you keep your distance, or I'll count for one of you!"

But Thunder Moon rode in on him, his rifle under his arm.

"Put up that pistol," said he. "If we wanted to do murder, we needn't have stopped to talk to you. You'll have no harm from us. We simply want you to come back to the house so that we'll be able to leave the place before you go to spread the alarm. We want food, too, for ourselves and these nags. If you're there, we'll be able to pay you for what we have to take."

The man hesitated, but the woman broke in, "We might as well die there, as here, and besides, maybe he means to do what he says. It's William Sutton, Ben!"

"I know who it is, well enough," replied the man. "Sutton, we got your word for this?"

"Yes."

Standing Antelope had remained just beyond hearing distance during this colloquy, ready at any moment to shoot, but as the three turned back toward the house, the man and woman pale and sick of face and the little boy whimpering, the young Suhtai hurried to the side of his leader.

"There are three scalps and three coups for me," said he. "You don't want me to go back to my people with empty hands?"

Thunder Moon raised a sternly admonitory forefinger.

"Don't touch them," said he, "with gun, knife, or hand! These people have done us no harm, and they may do us much good!"

"No harm," echoed the boy. "Are not the whites our enemies just as the Comanches are? If you saw three Comanches, would you let them live?"

"Be still," said William Sutton gruffly. "You speak of things you do not yet understand."

Standing Antelope, however, was not appeased by this rebuke, and so long as they were in the shanty, his wistful gaze was turned upon one or another of his involuntary hosts, much like a dog eying a flitch of bacon hung just above his reach.

By the time they reached the house, they found Red Wind already in possession of the kitchen, while Big

165

Hard Face, in the adjoining barn, was finding ample rations of oats for the horses. From the moment the farmer's wife saw Red Wind, her attitude changed.

"My sakes!" she cried. "Why, this ain't no wild Indian. She knows cooking. Here, honey, gimme that bacon and I'll slice it. Willie, slap on some water to heat. Ben, you hand me that coffee can! I dunno what these folks have done, but now that they're here, they might as well have a chance to eat. They got their belts three notches deeper'n normal!"

Thunder Moon and Standing Antelope worked strongly and steadily over the horses, rubbing them down, giving them from time to time a swallow of water, and tending them with the most precise care. Then, as they permitted the horses to bury their noses in the finest oats, they stood back to watch, well contented. Indian ponies needed no such care as this. A chance to roll after a long, heartbreaking ride, a little sun-withered prairie grass to graze on, and a few hours of rest enabled them to take to the trail again with hardly diminished spirit. But these long-legged, deerlike creatures were different. Only Sailing Hawk seemed to combine the qualities of the desert pony and the racer.

No matter what happened, they could be sure, now, that they would have remade horses for the rest of their day's flight. But they were in no haste to leave the shanty. They ate and paid for a hearty meal, and then they lay down on the floor of the cabin, with Red Wind to keep guard because, as she said, she had no need of sleep.

She sat beside Big Hard Face, her eyes looking continually through the open door and down the valley, but no sign of a pursuer troubled her vision.

Perhaps the trail had been lost by those who followed! Indeed, they had come across enough stretches of gravel and rock to have discouraged even the most expert Indian trailer.

The white family gathered to watch, big-eyed, enormously curious. They had changed their opinion of these visitors a great deal. In the first place, they had suffered from no violence. In the second place, they had been handsomely paid for all that had been eaten by horse and man. And in the third place, they were beginning to see that this was a distinguished adventure that would make them talked about by all the neighborhood, and envied wherever women or men met to gossip.

The three men lay in a row. They were asleep the instant that they closed their eyes.

"How did you hear of us?" asked Red Wind, looking at the housewife.

"From the telegraph office at Stanley. Messengers were sent over the whole country around here to get folks out to watch the trails."

"What did they say?"

"That you've murdered about a dozen people up the way. There must be near onto a thousand folks out looking for you right now."

"But not in this direction?"

"No."

"At least, they haven't looked for us here," said Red Wind.

"Ah," said the woman, "why should they have to do that? Because they know that once in the valley, here, there ain't no chance that you'll get out!"

28

No chance for them to get out!

Red Wind said not a word to alarm the three sleepers. "Show me!" said she.

And straightway the farmer and his wife and son took her outside of the shanty and to the hillcrest that overshadowed the house. From that point of vantage she could sweep the horizon and now she saw what was meant. All to the west and the north, beyond the hills, rushed a river of impassable white water, and to the south lay marshes from whose boggy face a mist exhaled visible even at that distance. From the east they had come, and that way was still open; but if they returned they would find the gathered forces of their enemies ready to block the way.

Such was the prospect that she looked out upon.

And when she had seen it, she asked anxiously, "There must be some way across that river. It is not very wide!"

"Swifter than an arrow," was the reply. "You couldn't never cross it, lady. Never in this here world, I'm tellin' you; never at all! There has been some that tried. Jake Mulvaney tried last year on a bet. Poor Jake, he didn't get halfway across."

"The marsh, then!" said the girl. "Surely someone could get across that!"

"With a boat, perhaps," answered the farmer's wife. "If you was to take a boat, and drag it across the mud,

168

and then float it off again, why you might get across that way. I don't know! There's the Baynes gang. They live in there—a curse on 'em!—and they manage to get across from side to side. But who's gunna be able to get that secret out of 'em?"

Red Wind seized upon that clue, but when she made anxious inquiries, she achieved nothing. The Baynes gang of ruffians lived in the marshes, to be sure, but how they managed it was the secret by means of which they had baffled all pursuit. Many a time strong expeditions had pushed out against them, but in every instance the expeditions had failed; they were bogged down and eluded and the robbers still issued time and again to commit their depredations on the lands of their honest neighbors.

Red Wind, without another word, went back to the shanty and there she sat down in the doorway.

She turned again toward the east and looked out at the horizon to see even a trace of dust that might announce the approach of horsemen, but there was no sign of a disturbance. They were gathering there, doubtless. They were gathering and making ready to stop the entrance to the valley with a perfect security.

"An' what are you gunna do?" asked the farmer of the girl, big-eyed with fear and curiosity.

"There will be a way," said the Omissis girl quietly.

"But what way, would you tell us? You ain't got wings, I suppose?"

"Do you see the big man? The young one? Do you know who he is?"

"He's William Sutton."

"His name is Thunder Moon. The Sky People will not let him die. He has many days before him."

"Maybe he's a kind of a witch." The wife grinned.

"You will see," said the girl calmly. "He has been in the

169

camp of the Comanches. He has gone alone into the warrior camp of the Pawnees and come out carrying their medicine bags and leaving their dead behind him. You see that I am not troubled now. All is in the hands of the Sky People. Now he sleeps. When he wakens, I shall tell him!"

Again and again they tried to shake her calm conviction by pointing out the terrible imminence of the danger, but she merely smiled, faintly, in the same way that had baffled and disturbed Thunder Moon in the old days, in the tepee of White Crow.

Fatigue kept the three soundly asleep until deep in the afternoon, when Standing Antelope wakened, rose softly, and came out to the girl. To him, in her soft voice, she related what she had heard and observed. He in turn climbed to the crest of the hill and looked over the countryside before he came back to her.

He walked slowly, a sure sign that his thoughts were profoundly occupied. Then he sat down cross-legged beside the girl.

"We shall wait?" he asked at length. "What else is there to do? What could we manage in the day? We must have the darkness. In the meantime, our horses are growing strong. So is Thunder Moon. The rest is in the hands of the Sky People!"

Standing Antelope made no answer, but he withdrew a little and began to make medicine, picking up handfuls of dust and blowing gently upon it until there remained a few pebbles or shining bits of rock. According to their nature, size, and number he was receiving answers from the spirits; and the answers seemed to trouble him gravely.

"There are four of us, are there not?" said he, coming back.

"There are four," she agreed.

170

"One must be sacrificed," said the boy with great seriousness. "I see by the signs that have been given to me that only three can go free, perhaps. Tell me, Red Wind—if a life were given freely to the Sky People, would they let the other three go through to safety tonight?"

She understood his meaning instantly and caught her breath a little.

However, she answered with an air of surety, "One must be lost. But who can tell which one the Sky People have chosen for death? And what a fool one of us would be to lay down life that is not wanted?"

The boy considered this with a knotted brow. Nevertheless, he seemed relieved by this reasoning and relaxed, and began to nod his head a little.

"You are right," he answered. "They do not wish to have us presume to read their minds and understand their purposes. They are great spirits and jealous of their secrets! However, the medicine that I have made is very sure. One of us at least must die!"

Red Wind fell into a gloomy study and remained lost in it when Thunder Moon and Big Hard Face came out of the shanty.

With faces like masks they heard the story, looking sternly to east where the danger lay. Then Thunder Moon looked to the westering sun and saw that the evening was not far away.

He said to Standing Antelope, "Saddle the horses; look to the guns and see that they are clean. Tonight we shall have fighting."

And with that, he walked off by himself and was soon lost in a little copse not far from the house.

He was no sooner hidden there, than he sat down cross-legged near a tiny spring of water, and taking out the ingredients of his paints, he mixed them and began

171

to daub his face. He took off his deerskin jacket next, and his painting was continued upon his body to the waist until Thunder Moon looked more like a devil than like William Sutton, heir of Sutton House.

When he had completed his ceremonies, he stepped into a clearing in the center of the trees, and taking his dream shield upon one arm, and his rifle in the other, he extended both toward the sky, where the pink of the sunset was beginning to gather in richer and darker tones.

There he prayed as he had prayed before in the critical moments of his life.

"Sky People, all that was dim to me before I now understand. When I asked you what I should do for my foster father, you sent me with weapons in my hands to take him from the jail. You promised me safety. So I went, and it all happened as you said. There was danger, but you saved me from it. Now I have come away with Big Hard Face, but still there is a part of my heart that remains behind with my mother and the lodge of my father. I think, too, of the white girl. For this reason you are punishing me. You have drawn great dangers around me. You are catching me like a fish in the net. I understand. I do not reproach you for having saved me once and threatening me later. It is because you do not want to take me back to the Suhtai when my heart is still with the whites. But now I see the truth. I must go back to the Cheyennes and be one of them. Behold me! I have put on the sacred paint for the warpath. I denounce the God of the white man and accept you only. I give myself away from my father's lodge forever and take the tepee among the Suhtai. Let their way be my way. Let their food be my food. Let me be a weapon in their hands in the time of trouble, and let all my friends have red skin.

172

"Hear me, Sky People, and if you accept my prayer, give me a sign!"

He remained for a long moment, his shield and his gun extended in arms that began to tremble with fatigue, and great beads of perspiration formed upon his forehead and rolled swiftly down across his face.

He said again, "All that is good has come to me from your hands. All that is evil has come out of my folly. Do not ask any wisdom of me except the wisdom you have given me. Hear me, Sky People, while I make you this pledge and promise! When I come safely back to the tents of the Suhtai, where their enemies oppress them, I shall gather the warriors and go out and cover the plains with blood of the Pawnees. I shall make them howl like wolves, and then I shall take three living prisoners and sacrifice them to you to make you happy. All this I shall do for your glory, that men may recognize your power. But now give me life. Give life to the old man, and to the young warrior who rides with me, because he came into trouble through his love for me, following me from his distant country. Save the girl, too. But all that I have been among the white men I give away. Let whoever will pick it up."

He ended. His shoulders ached and his whole body began to shudder with exhaustion, and darkess swam before his eyes. But it seemed to him that the darkening sky lighted a little and turned to a deeper rose, and now, by degrees, the edge of a cloud pushed above the edges of the dark-pointed trees, a great cloud in which red fire was living, flooding the world with terrible light.

"O Sky People! O my fathers!" cried Thunder Moon. "I accept the sign, and I shall drench the world with blood for your sake!"

And he fell forward and lay upon his face in the cool of the grass.

29

Now, it was while Thunder Moon lay there, semiconscious, overwhelmed by what he felt to be the direct manifestation of the will of the spiritual world, and while the evening rapidly darkened toward night after this final burst of crimson light, that the watchers from the shanty looked anxiously at a small dust cloud coming up the valley trail.

It seemed at first, large enough to be the sign of a great body of people, but as it drew nearer and nearer it seemed more and more insignificant, and Ben, the farmer, in a reassuring voice, vowed that it could not be any large section of the posse. More likely, it was some emissary come to offer terms. For the farmer and his family had grown quite out of their first opinion, and now they looked upon the fugitives with the keenest interest. Only, at times, the keen, roving eye of Standing Antelope touched upon one of them and made them thrill with dread. But the others were filled with dignity, and their soft, quiet voices enchanted the good wife, above all.

Now that cloud of dust drew nearer, and presently the farmer, with his glass, was able to assure them that only two forms were revealed beneath the mist. Standing Antelope was in a fury of excitement and eagerness.

"I understand!" said he. "That is the sort of thing that Thunder Moon always does. And now two great warriors have come to fight against the three of us. It would be good if Thunder Moon were with us now!"

He glanced anxiously toward the trees in which the hero was still concealed.

"No," answered Red Wind, with the faint smile of assured conviction. "They haven't come to fight. If it were Thunder Moon alone that they expected to find here, no two men would dare to come against him."

The boy breathed a little easier; and yet there was a shade of disappointment in his eye—like a bull terrier glad to be freed from hopeless odds, and yet sorry to have missed a fight.

In the meantime, the riders came on with a sort of fearless directness that made Red Wind, in spite of her prophecy, stand up to look again, and now they could see that the two were magnificently mounted upon long-striding horses.

Big Hard Face had picked up his rifle and risen to his feet when Red Wind called suddenly, "One of them is a woman! Look!"

A moment later it was clear to everyone. They came up the final slope side by side—Jack Sutton and Charlotte Keene! How different was she from the country beauty, now! Her hair straggled from beneath her riding hat and blew in wisps and tangles; her wrinkled habit was gray with dust; her eyes were hollow with fatigue, and a remorseless sun had burned the tip of her nose to a sharp red.

She came boldly on beside Jack Sutton, and the pair halted at a little distance.

"Are you there, William?" called his younger brother.

"Let us go out to talk with them," said Red Wind to the boy.

And they went together and raised their right hands in Indian greeting.

175

"Thunder Moon is not with us," said the boy gloomily. "He is near, but he is not with us."

"Call him," said Jack Sutton. "Call my brother at once. I have important news for him."

"News that will take him back to your father's lodge?" asked Standing Antelope cunningly.

"No, no! God knows how he could return at once with three dead men behind him in the jail. But news as to how he can get out of this trap!"

"He is away," said Red Wind, breaking in, "asking the will of the Sky People, and we dare not disturb him!"

"Good gad!" exclaimed Jack. "What utter nonsense!"

"It's late," broke in Charlotte. "We may be followed. In any case, tell them what we've learned." She went on hastily, "We've found the leader of the brigands who lives in the marsh and we've bought his help. If you go down to the edge of the marshes a little after dark, he'll be waiting for you on this side of the bogs. He swears that he'll show you safely through to the other side, horse and man. But keep good watch on yourself. The man is a villain, and he wouldn't scruple to murder you all if he thought it worthwhile. Do you understand what I've said?"

"I understand," said Standing Antelope.

"You must go quickly," said the girl. "Because we're afraid that another man guesses what we have done."

"Tell William," broke in Jack, "that Harrison Traynor may have guessed what we're up to, and in that case he'll try desperately to block you."

"We shall tell him everything," said Standing Antelope.

"And now," said Jack, "can't you call him in? I want to shake hands with him, at least!"

"No, no!" exclaimed Charlotte Keene.

"What's the matter, Charlie?"

176

"I'd rather not. What I mean to say is we mustn't be here to worry him. You," she added, letting her horse make a step closer to Red Wind, "you came with Big Hard Face from the Suhtai, did you not?"

"I came from the Suhtai," replied the girl.

"You—you have been living with the chief?"

"I was given by my father into the lodge of Thunder Moon," answered Red Wind.

Charlotte gripped the pommel of her saddle.

"You are his wife then, his Indian wife, I mean to say!"

"I am only his slave," replied Red Wind.

Steadily for a moment, they stared at one another, and there was fire in the eyes of each.

"I've heard enough," said the white girl, her voice breaking. "Let's go back quickly, Jack!"

"But you can't believe that he has a wife, really?" said the youngster. "You understand, Charlie, that William doesn't lie about things. And he never said a word about having a—a family among the Suhtai, you know!"

"It isn't lying to be silent," she replied.

"I know you're wrong, Charlie!"

"Jack, Jack," said she in a trembling voice, "you're a child and you're blind. Look at her!"

Indeed at that moment, with the dim sunset light upon her; the massive double braids of hair glimmering in the shadow, and the brilliantly beaded dress flickering about her like a ghost of fire, it seemed that nothing in the world could be half so beautiful as Red Wind.

Charlotte gazed for one more heartbroken moment, then turned her horse and fled down the valley as if she were being hunted by armed men, while Jack followed in the rear, vainly calling to her to ride slower, or to turn back.

The boy and girl remained, for a time, looking after

177

them, and neither spoke until the pair had become once more a dwindling cloud of dust, barely distinguishable through the twilight.

Then Standing Antelope said sternly, "Red Wind, you have said the thing that is not!"

She replied with sudden meekness, "You have heard me lie, Standing Antelope. But be a friend to me. Keep what you have heard from the ears of Thunder Moon. He would be angry. He would beat me. He would cast me out from his lodge. But besides, do you want the white woman to draw him away from us again?"

Standing Antelope looked fixedly at her, but finally he said, "I have thought that Thunder Moon was right and that you were filled with evil. Well, now I begin to remember what my father said: that many women are wicked merely because they are women! Pah! For my part, I never shall take a squaw. There never is any trouble except what you creatures make!"

He turned to stride away, but she followed him with the softest of voices. "Standing Antelope, do you hate me, also?"

He wheeled sharply about and glowered down at her.

"Should I not hate you?"

"I am a wicked woman," she said, "but I am very sad. Will you have pity on me, Standing Antelope?"

She stood close to him, and looked up to his fiery young eyes until suddenly they softened and he began to blink as though a strong light had been flashed in his face.

"Will you promise me to speak nothing of this to Thunder Moon?"

"Well, I shall promise!" said he. "Red Wind," he continued, "I shall be your friend. Because I see that you are strong, and that you can make people do what

178

you want! You came out of the plains and made Thunder Moon go back with you. You do everything that you want to do. It is a strong medicine that you make! Hai! My heart is still beating because of it. As if I had seen a grizzly bear. Or something even worse that that!"

He walked away from her and Red Wind, facing toward the shanty, at that moment saw a lofty form stepping from the cover of the trees not far away. Upon his arm was a shield, and in his right hand the rifle glimmered through the dusk. It was Thunder Moon, coming back from his time of solitary prayer.

He came swiftly and proudly to them.

"I have talked with the Sky People!" he said to Big Hard Face. "And they have promised me freedom from this danger. They sent me a red sign, which means that blood must be shed. But in the end we shall have the victory. They are angry with me because I have been living among the whites. But I have given them up. I have turned my face forever back to the plains, father. And so we shall all be happy together, once more!"

Big Hard Face said nothing, but looked quickly upward; and presently he murmured, "I shall not forget!" Plainly he had made a vow.

30

It was Red Wind who told Thunder Moon of the message that had just been brought, promising a chance of release. She forgot to mention that Charlotte Keene had been there, and merely said that Jack Sutton had come to say that he had probably been able to buy his brother from danger.

"Listen!" said Thunder Moon, greatly moved. "I thought that I left only a mother behind me; now you see that I have a brother, also."

"It was the work of the Sky People," broke in Big Hard Face eagerly. "They put the spirit into your brother. Now let us start. It is deep dusk. And there are the campfires where they watch for us in the throat of the valley. Mount, Thunder Moon. Let us go!"

They took to the saddle immediately, and, saying good-bye to the farmer and his wife and son, headed straight across the valley toward the marsh.

"How great are the Sky People!" said Thunder Moon, looking toward the twinkling lights of the distant fires. "Look with what care they regard me! They hear my words. They are kind to me. I make a prayer, and first they answer me with a sign, and after that, they make this to happen naturally by sending me my brother. The miracles that they perform are all made to appear easy and simple things! What sacrifices we shall offer when we come back to the Suhtai!"

And he laughed aloud, filled with the sense of his own great power on earth and upon the spirits of the air.

They came to the edge of the marsh. They had to go carefully along its verge, for one false step might plunge a horse up to the knees in muck, but presently out of the gloom a figure appeared before them.

"Where's William Sutton?" asked the voice. "Now, the rest of you keep back and don't try no rush, because I got more men behind me, and we're ready to shoot if this turns out to be a fancy trick. Is William Sutton one of you?"

"I am William Sutton."

"Step out here a minute by yourself," said the rough voice.

Thunder Moon willingly advanced along, his fingers kept continually near the handles of a revolver.

When he was very close, he could make out a low, wide-built man, who held a double-barreled rifle of an old make under his arm with a careless ease that denoted he knew all about the uses of the weapon.

He said, now, "That's close enough. If you're what they say you are, then you know all about crooked work and dirty games, and you can cut a throat as well as the next one. Are you the Cheyenne?"

"I am."

"I had a cousin was murdered by one of them red devils. Someday I'll have it out with 'em for that, too!" There was nothing but sheer brute in this fellow, it was patent. But still Thunder Moon was patient, merely saying, "My brother paid you a sum of money to see me safely across the marsh with my friends—"

"Your friends? The talk was about you, and not the rest! What I had undertook to show the whole mob of you through to—"

"The price was paid for me and all my party," said William Sutton.

"I'll see you damned first!" answered the ruffian. "I ain't had more'n enough money to sort of get me interested in this job. But if the whole party is to come across with me, I'm gunna see another thousand in cold cash."

Thunder Moon was silent.

"What's a little bit of money to a rich man like you?" quickly asked the swamp pirate.

Thunder Moon stepped a little closer during this speech.

181

"If I paid you what you ask, you'd call for more," said he. "You'll take us across for the money you've already had."

"Why should I?" asked the pirate sharply. "I've had the money paid down to me. What for should I pay any more attention to you folks unless you'll pay again?"

He finished on a note of triumph, and from the shadowy bushes nearby there was a burst of brawling, mocking laughter.

"Well said, Stevie! Well talked up, boy!"

"You leave it to Stevie," said that ruffian. "He can talk for himself and for all of the rest of you, too!"

"Your name is Stevie," said Thunder Moon gently, stepping still closer toward him.

"Yes, it is."

"Stevie, there are two things for me to do. One is to tell you that if you see us through this trouble we'll be friends to you later on. The other is to cover you with a revolver and shoot the matter out."

"What good would you gain by shooting? Would it get you through the marsh, man?"

"It would be a comfort to finish off a robber like you, Stevie; and here you are!"

He snapped his revolver into his hand as he spoke, but Stevie merely laughed through the semidarkness.

"You ain't gunna bluff me, Sutton. You need me too bad to shoot. Now, I'm gunna treat you real fair and square. You pay me only a measly little five hundred dollars more, and I'll take you across the marsh, horse and man, all of you."

"You'll take me anyway, Stevie—no, don't try to step back! Stay where you are. You've had your money. Father! Come up! Come up, Standing Antelope!"

The party advanced behind him, and the marsh pirate, not knowing exactly what he had better do, presently found himself closely confronted by the old chief, young Standing Antelope, Red Wind, and above all by the fame and mighty hand of Thunder Moon. He had not had the courage to retreat, for fear lest Thunder Moon should send a fatal bullet after him.

But now he said loudly: "Mind what you do, Sutton. I got friends watchin' all this and only askin' a word from me to fire on you and sweep you all into hell. I guess you realize that!"

"Lead on, Stevie," said Thunder Moon gravely. "There's no danger from us. Lead on and take us across the marsh."

"May you like what you'll find on the far side of it!" said the brigand bitterly. "Come on, then, if you're gunna drive a bargain as hard as this, and may you get much good from it, all of ye, and be damned to ye!"

So, pleasantly, Steve Baynes led them toward the marsh and there followed an hour of close and bitter work. Yet, by miracle, they were actually working their way across the marsh. Often their horses were almost belly-deep in water, but there were places where there was firm sandy or rocky bottom underneath. Often, again, they were pushing through thin slush. But most of all they found themselves traveling upon firm land that was scattered in bits here and there throughout the drowned marshes, and so they crept on toward the farther shore. It could not have been more than a brief half mile that separated one side of the marsh from the other, but during the entire hour they were weaving back and forth and slowly making headway through the swamp.

"And don't think that you'll be able ever to come back and cross without me!" declared their unamiable leader. "Little Dan Sargent, he was a wise one and he said that he could do it. Well, the bog ate him up, horse and all!"

183

"If it was the bog that ate him, Stevie," broke in a voice from the nearby darkness, "how come it that you had the pickin' of the bones?"

"I found the stuff! I found the stuff!" snarled Stevie. "That's what I said to you, Chip Tucker!"

Chip laughed, with a noise more like the melancholy wailing of a wolf than the laughter of a normal man.

"I've found stuff the same way," said Chip Tucker. "It takes eyes to find such things in the swamp. Oh, it takes eyes, and it takes guns, too! Grand guns!"

"You're a fool!" answered Stevie.

They went on through the darkness, the brigands pushing in as closely as they dared until Thunder Moon and Standing Antelope warned them back again and again. Plainly these lawless ruffians envied the purses and the good horses that belonged to the people they were guiding.

They were not a hundred yards from a rising slope that promised to be good, sound land, and the end of the bog, when someone came hurrying toward them, his feet sucking noisily out of the mud.

"Stevie! Stevie!" he called. "Are you there?"

"Here, Dick!"

"I've finished off the other bargain and—"

"Shut up, you fool!" exclaimed Stevie angrily. "Have you got no wits?"

He began to confer closely with this messenger.

"There's treachery in this talking," said Red Wind decisively to Thunder Moon. "Push straight on, O Thunder Moon! These men will sell you for the value of a single hunting knife or a handful of beads. They are greedier than Comanches!"

"There is no one so quick as Red Wind," said Thunder Moon, "to see evil in anything and in everything. However, you may be right. Push on, Standing Ante-

184

lope. No, I shall go first, and find the right way. The rest of you follow me in single file, and keep close behind me!"

So said Thunder Moon, and rode to the head of the procession at once. The rest pressed close. "Here, you," said Stevie anxiously. "You can't go on that way. You'll wind up in a hundred feet of muck and bog unless—"

"Then come and show me the proper way through."

"Not until I see more color of your money."

"Keep close behind me," said Thunder Moon to his companions. "There's no trusting these devils and I think we can get through this way!"

He drove steadily ahead.

"Will you come back?" screamed Stevie in a great fury.

"No!"

"Then take this and be damned to you!"

And he fired both barrels of his rifle in rapid succession.

31

The horses floundering more than knee-deep in sticky mud and slime, William Sutton and his little single file of followers were suddenly made a focus upon which a dozen weapons began to play.

Sheltered behind the shrubs and the trees, or in hollows in the ground, the marsh rats fired rapidly; and straight ahead, from the rising slope, two or three more rifles were playing upon the shadowy little procession.

The night light, and the twisting and bobbing and heaving of the thoroughbreds as they struggled through the ooze, spoiled the aim of the ambushers until Standing Antelope heard something strike Big Hard Face with a noise like a fist pounded home. And he knew suddenly that a bullet had hit the chief.

"You are wounded!" said the boy, pressing up beside the old chief. "Tell me how I can help you, O Big Hard Face!"

The heavy arm of the warrior was raised and brushed his offer away.

Now they heard the voice of Stevie shouting behind them, "There's double money for us if ye bring down the big man! Hit William Sutton, boys. He's our meat!"

There was a loud exclamation of surprise rather than pain from Standing Antelope at that moment, to show that he also had been struck by a bullet, but he did not on that account hold back.

And now Thunder Moon felt the hoofs of his stallion bite home through the mud against firm footing, growing steadily shallower with every inch that they advanced.

Just before him he saw the loom of starlit grass on the shelving bank, and this, he knew, was the end of their journey, hardly two bounds away from Sailing Hawk.

He turned to regard his party. Standing Antelope properly brought up the rear, twisting in the saddle and firing again and again. Red Wind was next, and just behind Thunder Moon rode his foster father.

"Now, father!" said Thunder Moon. "One moment more and we are free."

"How many rifles are there before you?"

"We'll know when we reach the place," said Thunder Moon.

"Wait!" cried the old hero. "Keep where you are one minute. I have an idea. Thunder Moon!"

And striking his horse a terrific blow with his whip, he sent it bounding right past his foster son and up the slope beyond.

As he went, his voice roared above the cursing, the grunting of the horses, the sound of the guns, the calling of the bandits, one to another, "Hear me, Tarawa! I offer myself a free sacrifice for my son! Let all the rifles be emptied into me!"

Bursting past Thunder Moon before the latter realized what was happening, the big chief reached the dry, firm footing of the bank and drove his horse straight up it at a fence of brush beyond.

There was no doubt of the prescience of the old warrior then, for instantly from the close ambush half a dozen rifles flashed at such a range that hardly a single ball could have missed its target; but still, as though no single blow could down his great spirit, Big Hard Face rode gloriously ahead and straight into the little thicket, firing his rifle as he went and then swinging it like a club over his head.

There was no doubt, now, that his ambush was well prepared with extra rifles and pistols, for as the old man rode on to his doom, a second and third volley went crashing against him.

On the very verge of the thicket he fell from his horse with a battle cry cut short on his lips.

Past him, as he fell, like a furious lion and a wild young panther went Standing Antelope and Thunder Moon, charging to avenge the fall of their chief. And what a vengeance they had. The guns of these enemies had been emptied into the body of one hero. And here was the rifle and then the knife of Standing Antelope at

187

their throats. And here, worst of all, was the double revolver play of Thunder Moon. Six chosen rascals of the marsh pirates stood in the covert, and only three of them dragged themselves away, badly hurt, going like snakes or beaten dogs, close to the ground, leaving a crimson trail behind them.

The seventh man was no marsh rat. Tall and straight, yielding not an inch to his danger, this apparent leader of the ambush saw Thunder Moon and Standing Antelope drive through the gunmen before him without flinching.

His own rifle he had reserved for the last moment, and now he pitched it up and drew a bead on Thunder Moon. At that instant the latter fired and saw the tall fellow sway; the rifle exploded aimlessly; and Thunder Moon swept his victim from the ground and caught him by the throat.

"Traynor!" he exclaimed. "Harrison Traynor!"

And the voice of that gentlemen answered him, "You've killed me, Sutton. But even after I'm dead, you still can't have her. I've put up a wall between you that will last forever! I'm only half a loser, you see!"

He tried to laugh, but that instant he turned limp in the arms of his destroyer; Thunder Moon felt for the heart. It beat no longer.

There was no difficulty in making on with their journey. Now the marsh that had been so difficult for them lay between them and the pursuit. Traveling by night and resting by day, the three made swift progress. Their fourth companion lay behind them. Thunder Moon had written back to his brother and mailed the letter at the first little town they reached.

Bury Big Hard Face like an Indian, on a platform raised toward the sky with his weapons around him, and kill a good horse beneath the platform. So his spirit will be able to hunt through the hereafter when he wants to ride across the sky!

All that was demanded in that letter was done with scrupulous care, and Big Hard Face was properly interred after the manner of his ancestors.

In the meantime, leaving the white settlements behind them, the little party struck out across the plains. They were making good time. Their horses were inured to the work by this time. Standing Antelope's wound in the thigh had healed, as well as two or three scratches Thunder Moon had received during the course of the conflict. So for several weeks they beat toward the north and the west, striking out for traces that would tell them how the Cheyennes had been marching.

They found them at last among the hills; and, halting on the brow of an eminence, the three riders looked fondly down on the glimmer of the fires in all the lodges of the Suhtai.

"Look!" said Thunder Moon. "I have lost two fathers. You shall be my brother, Standing Antelope, and you shall be my sister, Red Wind—and we shall have happiness together!"

The girl rode on past him, as though she did not hear, her head inclined.

"What is wrong?" asked Thunder Moon of his companion. "Is she angry again? Has the mysterious spirit come over her once more?"

"Oh, Thunder Moon," said the boy, "the Sky People have made you very great but very blind! Do you think that you can make Red Wind happy by calling her your sister?"

"I shall call her my daughter, then," said Thunder Moon.

"You are a fool!" said the boy.

189

"Do you think that she wants to be my squaw?" asked the great warrior. "How can you speak such nonsense? From the first day when she came to the Suhtai she showed that she hated me!"

"She tried to run away because she knew that if she stayed she would want to belong to you. And she did not want to be your squaw, because you are a white man, and sooner or later she was afraid that you would leave us and go away to your people. She sent you away. It was by her managing that you went away. But afterward she was sick at heart and had to follow you!"

"Standing Antelope, you say the thing that is not true."

"I cannot give you wits if you will not have them!" said the youth.

"Wait here, Standing Antelope. I am going to speak to her!"

Thunder Moon rode rapidly ahead, and presently Red Wind came drifting back to him. At the edge of a stream she stopped her horse, and he knew that it was not from fear of the ford but because she waited for him that she had paused there. For that reason he rode more slowly. There was no moon. But even by the starlight he saw the curve of her throat, and the dull, copper glimmer of her braided hair.

PART TWO

32

Out of the hills came a red rider. He rode like the wind, his long, heavy hair streaming across his shoulders. He was a big man. All the Cheyennes were big. The pony beneath him seemed absurdly inadequate to carry such a bulk, and yet it continued to run.

It was polished with sweat that ran down to the middle of its belly, and its ears were flattened with labor and with agony, for the Cheyenne in the saddle sent it forward with the most determined cruelty, appearing to pay little attention to the direction in which it ran, but exerting all his ingenuity to torment additional speed out of it.

Yet, torment or not, it was going only at a hand gallop when the Indian topped the rise and saw before him another warrior in the hollow beneath a man who had heard that violent approach, the hoofs of the tired pony beating and scattering the rocks. So he of the hollow had halted his horse—a lofty and noble-appearing chestnut—and had swung into the crook of his left arm a long-barreled rifle. So, at wait, he regarded the new-comer.

But, from a distance seeing the rider of the chestnut, the speeding warrior began to make frantic signs, and drove straight down on him. As he came up, still he kept his animal at a gallop. The big chestnut was turned then and galloped easily at the pony's side.

"You are one of Thunder Moon's men," exclaimed the rider of the pony. "I tell you by your horse and by your rifle! Tarawa has put you here to relay the warning to our people. The Pawnees are out! Spotted Bull is leading them. I myself have lain for two hours and watched them, and counted them. They are a host. They travel slowly like men wishing to keep their horses and themselves fresh for a battle. Even now perhaps they have picked up my trail and are rushing behind me like wolves, but now you carry on the warning!"

The second warrior said not a word in reply. But he took his rifle and handed it to the speaker, who carried a war bow alone. He gave him, also, a pouch of ammunition; so that if the brave were indeed overtaken by the flying Pawnees, he might give a good account of himself until help arrived from the Cheyenne camp.

After that, he sent the chestnut flying. No Indian pony could have matched the speed of that thoroughbred. The big horse smoked on over the ground like a red mist caught on a storm wind.

Presently he broke out of the hills into a stretch of gently rolling ground. A river angled sharply out of the highlands, and then rolled smoothly away among the undulations of this fatherland of the prairies. Where the river swung in a wide bend through this pleasant country—treeless, but spotted with drifting lines of shrubs, here and there, and rich with tall grass that swished about the legs of the running chestnut—there was an Indian village placed at a suitable distance from the water's edge. One could tell that the tribe prospered

194

by the whiteness of the tepees, and by the numbers of horses that moved in herds nearby, under the care of many keen-eyed boys. A thin stream of people went from the village to the water and back—women to wash, or girls to carry in water or wood, or boys to frolic and play and make themselves strong.

The warrior on the red mare, taking note of all this, smiled a little in pride, and rode on, however, at a greater pace than ever, for the mare was keen at the sight of her home. Like a flung lance, horse and man darted into the circles of the tepees, and in the inner-most circle the rider flung himself to the ground.

There were three tepees close together, in this inner most circle, and into the nearest of these—a noble, gaudily painted lodge—the warrior turned. He first struck against the board posted near the entrance; a voice spoke within; then he lifted the flap and entered.

Inside, squatted at the back of the lodge upon a folded buffalo robe, was a chief who wore a hideous mask of a face. In close fight with the enemy he had lost one eye, his right cheek had been slashed across several times, and the flesh had gathered above the ghastly, livid furrows of the wounds. Nevertheless, to his people he was a handsome object; his wounds were proof of his dauntless valor. And he was, in fact, the war chief of this detachment of the great Cheyenne nation. He was now smoking a long pipe, whose bowl was of the true pipe rock, and he rose and greeted his visitor with a resounding "How!"

"You have brought news, Young Snake," said he. "Will you eat first and then smoke, or first will you speak?"

"The Pawnee wolves will not let me smoke or speak," said Young Snake. "Word was brought to me out of the hills. The Pawnees are on the warpath. Spotted Bull moves at their head. They are very many. Their horses

195

are good, and they count many rifles. They come straight toward our camp!"

The chief smiled, and the expression was a dreadful grimace.

"When they come to me with guns and scalp knives," said he, "they are not coming against a squaw. And our men are not children, and our boys are not girls. But these Pawnees are fools. I have heard that Spotted Bull is a wise chief. But does he think that the medicine of Thunder Moon has grown weak?"

"A hungry wolf," said Young Snake, "will try to pull down a bull moose. The Pawnees are hungry and they forget the medicine of Thunder Moon."

"Go to Thunder Moon, my friend," said the war chief. "Ask him if we shall draw out our fighting men. Or perhaps he will take down fire from the Sky People and fling it in the faces of these fools, and then send them wandering and blind!"

This pleasant thought made the eyes of Young Snake flash, as though in foretaste he already were taking the scalps of helpless men.

He left the tepee at once and crossed to an even larger one, whose skins were as white as snow, and which had recently been painted with all the skill that an Indian can show. Close beside it was another, much smaller lodge. At the entrance to the larger one he struck the board, a woman's shrill voice, quavering with age, bade him enter.

"Thunder Moon is not here, White Crow?" he asked with a good deal of respect in his voice and in his manner. Indeed, he was like one standing upon sacred ground.

"You come here with haste on your face," said White Crow. "There is trouble for the Cheyennes again, and so they remember that I have a son in my lodge!

196

Hungry dogs always have soft eyes when they smell food!"

This bitter speech did not abash the warrior. He merely asked her if she could tell him where he could find her foster son.

"How shall I tell you?" asked White Crow. "He sits by the river in a dream. Perhaps Red Wind will know."

Young Snake left the lodge and stood at the entrance of the smaller tepee, after casting one rather anxious glance through a gap among the tents and toward the open prairie in the direction from which the Pawnees might be expected. However, he dared not question the wisdom of the war leader, no matter how indifferent that hero might seem to be.

In answer to the blow of his hand on the entrance board, the flap of the tepee was pushed aside and Red Wind stood before the brave. Over one shoulder a great braid of copper-colored hair, looking as smooth and heavy as that metal in fact, dropped down even below her waist.

"Red Wind," said the warrior, "I have come to ask where I may find Thunder Moon. Do you know where he has gone?"

Her face clouded at once.

"How should I know?" she asked with some bitterness. "Does he live in my tepee? Is he my husband? I am only a stranger who lives on his kindness. Why should he open his mind to me and tell me where he moves?"

She stepped back as though about to drop the flap of the tepee, then added coldly, "Go to Standing Antelope. He is more to Thunder Moon than all the other men among the Cheyennes. Go to him and ask him. He cannot fail to know the mind of the great warrior, by night or by day."

The flap of the tepee straightway fell, and the brave

197

remained for a moment, scowling, as though he was minded to call the girl back and teach her better manners. But he altered his mind, and turning, he strode rapidly through the village until he came to a much smaller lodge, in front of which sat a handsome young brave with such feathers in his hair as denoted feats done in battle, in spite of his youth.

"Thunder Moon! Where is he?"

Standing Antelope frowned.

"I do not carry him in my hand," said he. "How shall I tell? I only know where his mind is. In the land of his white fathers!"

To the blunt answer of the youth, Young Snake, a hardened and seasoned brave, returned a baleful stare in which he surveyed the youngster from head to foot. But Standing Antelope did not shrink from the survey, repaying it with a calmly insolent glance. Correction hesitated in the mind of the older man; it was true that Standing Antelope was young, but he had ridden on long forays at the side of Thunder Moon, and from that strange and terrible man he had learned gun play with such skill that few among the Cheyennes would have been willing to stand against him.

So Young Snake contented himself with saying, "A true friend should be as one's shadow."

With that he walked haughtily away, and plied his query again of a boy at the outskirts of the town; having remounted the chestnut mare in the first place. The boy had no hesitation at all. He pointed at a clump of trees on the bank of the river, and toward this Young Snake galloped at full speed. He was growing nervous. For what if the Pawnees should suddenly appear in a rushing charge?

So he made the mare travel at high speed toward the designated clump of trees and, dismounting, he pressed through them and found Thunder Moon reclining at ease. Young Snake gazed upon that mighty form with awe. Now, as he lay at ease, his strength appeared more formidable than in action. In his hand lay a book, partly shaded by the down-showering of his hair, cut short when he had lived among the whites, but now grown long again. He brushed back this hair so that it fell more in order across his shoulders and nodded to Young Snake. Only at that hint did the message dare to speak.

"Thunder Moon," said he, "the Pawnees have been seen in force among the hills. They are coming fast, and straight toward this camp, it seems. Spotted Bull leads them."

"I am not the leader of the Cheyennes," said Thunder Moon. "This is a message for Bald Eagle."

"I have spoken to Bald Eagle. He told me to ask you if he should lead out the braves, or if you, instead, will go out and throw the fires of the Sky People in the faces of the Pawnees?"

Thunder Moon closed his book with a reluctant sigh. He stood, gathering into his hand a heavy cartridge belt that also supported at either side a long holster, out of which the handles of two revolvers appeared.

This he buckled about his waist. From the tree beside him he took the long rifle, which he carried in his left hand. In his right he took a staff and so left the wood. Young Snake pointed to the mare.

"Will you ride?" he asked.

"While you walk?" asked Thunder Moon kindly. "No, brother. I have not loaned the mare to you in order to take her back the first time there is weariness in my feet!"

They crossed the level stretch between the river and the village, Young Snake leading the mare behind him.

"Ride through the camp and gather my men," said

Thunder Moon. "We are going out to find these Pawnee wolves who dare to come so close to our village. That is to say, we shall ride out, if Bald Eagle gives me his permission."

Young Snake whirled without a word, bounded upon the back of his horse, and hastily rode off through the camp. His face was illuminated with confident joy, for the Cheyennes never took the dread of defeat with them when they rode out behind Thunder Moon.

The latter went on into the tepee of Bald Eagle and briefly stated his purpose.

"Brother," said the war chief, "whatever your mind tells you to do is good. Shall I ride with you?"

"Only those who ride my horses are going," said Thunder Moon. "But you shall ride if you will."

"I stay here, then," said the chief. "Let the young men go out and gather the scalps of the dead men whom Thunder Moon leaves on the ground!"

And he looked down as he spoke, for fear that the other would see the poisonous envy and hatred that at that moment was overflooding his soul.

33

All musters were quickly made in the Indian village, and the followers of Thunder Moon were rapidly assembled, he himself cantering a horse among the tepees and encouraging his braves to hurry, until he came to the lodge of Standing Antelope. Here he called, and after a moment the youth appeared at the entrance. A buffalo robe was gathered close about him; he appeared bowed, as if in pain or in weariness.

"The Pawnees!" called Thunder Moon. "Are you riding? Have they failed to bring you word?"

"O my father," said the young warrior, "there is hot pain in my heart. I do not think I could sit on the back of a horse! Besides, you do not need me. The finest braves follow you. Even without them, you could not fail. The Sky People ride at your side!"

"When I come back," said Thunder Moon, "I shall see you again, and then we shall talk about your sickness. Rest quietly and keep your mind cheerful. A sad mind makes a weak body, Standing Antelope!"

He rode on, and Standing Antelope stared gloomily after him. Then he retired to the quiet of his tepee and sat with the robe gathered around his head, trying to shut out the shouts of farewell and encouragement, as the braves departed on the war trail. His whole soul was on fire to join those riders. Yet he controlled himself, and for a long hour after the riders were gone, he waited. Then he got up and put on a suit of beaded deerskin.

He picked up a revolver, but remembering that this was a gift from Thunder Moon, he promptly laid it aside again. With only a knife at his belt and a staff in his hand, he walked out and went with dignity through the village until he came to the tepee of Red Wind. He spoke, and she came to the entrance and smiled cheerfully on him.

He went close to her and said in a quiet voice, "He is gone, Red Wind. Let us go, also. I have horses ready. Once we are away he never will be able to find our trail!"

She looked narrowly at him.

"Are you asking me to run away with you?" she demanded bluntly.

201

He drew himself up.

"I am," said he.

"And why should I go?" asked Red Wind.

"My tepee is filled with wealth," he said. "I have fine back rests and many painted robes, and good pipes, and also pots and everything that a woman could wish, such as beads."

"Who gave you your wealth?" she asked.

"I fought for it," said he.

"You fought under the shield of Thunder Moon," said the girl.

Standing Antelope struck the ground with his staff.

"I have counted seven coups in battle!" he declared.

She answered, "You have counted your coups with Thunder Moon riding beside you, striking down every danger that came at you!"

"You talk like a woman blind with love," replied Standing Antelope.

"Who is greater, then, than Thunder Moon?"

"Bah!" said the youth. "He never is brave, except when he knows that the Sky People are with him. Thunder Moon never has taken a scalp."

"But he has counted more than thirty coups—and in battle."

Standing Antelope bit his lip. Then he countered, "Of what use is a fine horse to the man who cannot sit on his back?"

"What do you mean by that?"

"You love Thunder Moon. But what are you to him?"

"Do you think," she answered angrily, "that I shall like you better because he likes me less?"

He said with emotion, "You do not know me, Red Wind. I am not old, but I am a man. Already I may speak in the council. The old men listen. Why will you not listen to me, Red Wind? You are nothing to Thunder Moon. He keeps you here out of his kindness. His heart is full of the memory of the white girl whom he left behind him."

It was the girl's turn to grow excited. She gripped her hands hard and her breast heaved.

"Thunder Moon takes what he wants, even out of the camp of the enemy," said she. "If he wanted the white girl he would have taken her. You should know this!"

"Among Indians he is an Indian," answered Standing Antelope. "But among white men he is a white. And among the whites, the word of a girl unstrings the arms of the strongest warriors. This I have seen, and you have seen it and know it, also. You talk to make your own heart strong, but there is no truth in your words!"

She stared at him, as though what he said had entered her heart deeply, and he went on, "Now you are sad and angry, because I have told you the truth. See what I offer to you in exchange. I am not a magician. I cannot call down the Sky People. I am not so rich as he. I have not a whole herd of such matchless horses as he inherited from Big Hard Face, who stole them from the whites—from Thunder Moon's own father! But I am a Cheyenne, and I am a man. I have ridden out on the war trail and fought hard, and gone hungry and welcomed every pain, because I hoped that in that way I could drive away the thought of you."

"Standing Antelope," said she sternly, "how do you think that I may trust you? If you could betray a friend like Thunder Moon, would you be true to a woman?"

"I give up a friend whom I love for a woman whom I love still more," said he. "Besides, I have shown you that he will never make you his squaw. He has learned among the whites their ways of marriage. His wife would have to be a real wife, and one only, and for the one woman, he already has made his choice!"

Suddenly she drew her robe about her head.

"Ah," said she, "you can break my heart, but you cannot take me away from him!"

Standing Antelope went away with a pausing step. Bald Eagle, from before his own lodge, watched him going, and motioned to him. The youth, half reluctantly, went to his chief.

"You have a sore heart?" said Bald Eagle.

"I am not happy," answered the brave.

"Patience, patience," said the war leader. "Patience will win the longest battle. And brave men know that the last blow is what decides the fighting!"

The two looked fixedly upon one another, with understanding, and then Standing Antelope resumed his way to his own lodge. It was a bitter day to him. Besides, it placed him in a quandary. He hardly could trust that Red Wind would not tell Thunder Moon of that conversation; and if this were done, how could he remain in camp without fighting against Thunder Moon? And no matter how boldly he had spoken in the presence of the girl, he well knew in his heart that he could not stand for an instant before the strength and the skill of the white man.

So he sat in his tepee and thought long thoughts; and twice he was on the verge of mounting his best horse and deserting the tribe. But always he resisted that temptation. For he was so sick with love that he hardly cared how soon death came to him!

Armed to the teeth, Thunder Moon's band of chosen braves voyaged across the prairie. In two hours they put the camp well behind them, and they had broken into the region of higher hills when the advance guard whirled and raced back. He had seen the Pawnees.

They were coming straight up the valley—nearly five-score warriors, well armed and mounted, as the first report had accurately stated.

Thunder Moon ordered his men to dismount. He concealed them in the long grass of a hilltop, leaving three men in the rear to handle the horses and keep them in readiness for a retreat; and when this was done, he rode boldly out into the valley in full view of the advancing Pawnees. It was his hope to draw them straight past his concealed force, which then could pour in a searching fire and make away to their horses and escape before the pursuit became effective.

Upon a little swell of ground in the midst of the valley he took his post and watched the irregular body of the Pawnees jogging toward him. Nearly every warrior appeared to carry a rifle; in the rear, a large herd of horses was being brought on by several Pawnee boys.

Coming still closer, the Pawnees suddenly seemed to recognize an enemy. They flogged their horses into a gallop and bore down upon the lone horsemen at a terrific speed. Still he did not move from his position, though some of the enemy already had unlimbered their rifles and were firing. But the distance was still too great for any sort of accuracy.

Thunder Moon watched that charge with grim satisfaction. He was just about to twitch his stallion around and send him flying to the rear, when he saw a chief break forward through the mass of the Pawnees and begin to make many violent gestures, shouting as he did so.

A great war chief of the Pawnees, perhaps, encouraging his men to the charge.

But then he saw that the warriors were restrained on either hand. Their pace became slower. Suddenly the whole body halted at the front, those in the rear bringing up their ponies and then stopping so as to form a fairly dense line.

The leader, in the meantime, advanced by himself and signaled from a distance that he wished to converse with the solitary rider. So that Thunder Moon, nothing loath, advanced in turn. They met in the midst of the valley, and Thunder Moon saw before him a stocky, powerful man of middle age or a little less, with a particularly gross and brutal face.

It was Spotted Bull, a famous and lucky hero among the Pawnees; particularly distinguished for raids in which he had driven off horses from the Cheyennes, the Blackfeet, and even from the Sioux themselves—a tribe that on account of its great numbers, most of the other plains warriors were glad to leave alone.

This chief came straight up to Thunder Moon, his rifle in its case, his shield slung over his shoulder, and only his long, light lance in his hand. Even this he did not carry on clear to the point of meeting, but jabbed the butt of it into the ground and rode on empty-handed. He raised a hand in greeting.

He said to Thunder Moon with such complacency, "Now that two such famous chiefs have met, Thunder Moon, let me know why we should not part as friends?"

"What friendship has there ever been between the Cheyennes and the Pawnees?" asked Thunder Moon sternly.

The other was undisturbed.

"No doubt," said he, "we are generally at war with one another, but that is no reason why there should not be peace, now and again. What are you to gain today from us? No doubt you have some of your men hidden nearby, watching with their rifles. But if you kill any of our tribe, then we must try to have vengeance, and that would mean that for many days your village would be very uncomfortable. Men are not happy when they are surrounded with stinging bees, and the Cheyennes do not sleep soundly when they hear the wolves howling in the night!"

At the aptness of this remark, Thunder Moon could not help smiling to himself a little.

"On the other hand," went on Spotted Bull, "it is very hard to win any honor from Thunder Moon. All the nations of the plains know that very well! Now, I wish to say to you that we have not ridden out to do any harm to the Cheyennes. We do not wish to strike at your young men. We have another goal," concluded Spotted Bull. "That is why I offer that we should be all friends for a few days."

Thunder Moon nodded.

"Spotted Bull, you speak very kindly. Kindness from a stranger makes the brain sleep. However, I shall try to do what you want. But if you are not riding into our country in order to make war on us, what is it that you wish to do, and where are you going?"

"A good rifle is best kept in one holster," said the cunning Pawnee, "and a secret is safest when it is lying in one mind; however, to a famous man I must give an answer. Is it not true, Thunder Moon, that not very long ago you went to live among the whites for a time?"

"That is true."

"And that you left them? That, in fact, they hunted you out?"

The frown of Thunder Moon was a sufficient answer.

"These things are talked of among all the tribes on the plains," said Spotted Bull. "The Pawnees," he added with additional flattery, "were not very glad when they learned that Thunder Moon had come back again to the

Cheyennes! But I know that after such a thing has happened, you have no great love in your heart for the whites."

"If a dog is kicked," said Thunder Moon in oblique answer, "he licks the hand of his master who beat him; but if a wolf is struck, he leaps at the throat."

"So!" said the Pawnee chief. "And Thunder Moon will teach the white men that they were fools to throw him out! This I can understand. It could not be any other way that a man would act. Then I freely tell you that I am riding against the whites."

"That will be a great war," answered Thunder Moon. "I have been in their country, brother. I know the numbers of their warriors. Since we are speaking as friends, I tell you the truth!"

"I am not riding against their towns," continued the Pawnee. "But they have sent out a party into the plains. That party has killed a Pawnee. It is right that they all should die like dogs and that we should take their scalps and their horses and their weapons!"

He added, "It is said that they have very fleet horses, but I think that they cannot run as fast as the Pawnee bullets!"

"You have told me the truth," said Thunder Moon. "I have nothing to say except to give you peace!"

"Peace to you," answered Spotted Bull, "and to all of the Cheyennes. Afterward we may meet in a different manner."

So they parted, and each rode back to his own men.

34

Out of the grass arose the twenty Cheyennes, took their twenty horses, and sat in the wind, their feathers blown sheer back upon their heads, watching the Pawnees—those ancient, traditional enemies—ride slowly past them into the heart of the valley. They looked down to the unharmed Pawnees, they looked without regarding the greater numbers. For they were invincible, they felt; they were the men of Thunder Moon, who could not know defeat. So they looked to the foe, and then they looked to their leader, and their faces grew darker.

All the Pawnees went past. They went in silence, departing through the hills, rising and dipping like a ship through green seas, streaming soon out of sight.

"Suppose they turn and ride for the village?" asked one gloomy warrior. "Suppose they are riding now with all their might, now that we cannot see them any longer."

Thunder Moon said, "If we had fought, we would have killed some of them. They would have killed some of us. And I would not kill twenty Pawnees at the cost of five Cheyennes!"

So he spoke, but one of the younger braves muttered, no louder than a whisper, "Thunder Moon, perhaps, has lost the support of the Sky People! Perhaps they no longer hear him speak!"

So he said. And their eyes widened with fear at the mere thought; there was malice, too, in their faces.

Thunder Moon, though he did not hear that malicious voice, plainly understood the meaning of those expressions, but he did not heed them. For he had known for years, if the slightest thing turned out well, it was not because of his own brain and the strength of his own hand, it was because of the Sky People.

He hardly knew what he felt about them, now—those dim beings of the upper world. There had been a day when he would have shuddered at the mere thought of doubting their existence, but now he had altered somewhat, having lived for long, long months among the white men of his own kin. He had not actually prayed to the Sky People for these many, many months. For this, even, he felt more and more guilty. Perhaps they had turned their backs upon him!

So he understood, perfectly, the shadow that ran over the faces of his men, like a cloud shadow running over a group of hills.

His thought turned back to the last thing that had disturbed him. The Pawnees rode to attack the whites. Somewhere they would strike the wanderers and wipe them out, perhaps. He was amazed and troubled by the thought. Amazed to know that it could pain him so deeply, when he remembered how those of his own color, his own blood, had driven him out with bullets!

Then he called forth Young Snake. There was hardly a better or a more seasoned warrior in his entire band.

He said, "Go back with the other men to the city of the Cheyennes. I am riding alone!"

Young Snake looked upon his master with a burning and a hungry eye.

"O Thunder Moon," he said at last, in a voice that actually quivered, "I hear you and I understand. There is no longer glory for Thunder Moon in striking the enemy with so many followers. He wants to go alone, his

210

guns speaking, and the Pawnees falling. He wants to count twenty coups in a single battle. But think of us! We follow you for the sake of glory!"

Thunder Moon could not help smiling a little as he answered. "Do you think that I would attack them single-handed, one man against eighty? Is that a wise man's thought, Young Snake?"

Young Snake answered with perfect devotion. "When the Sky People ride with you, do they count the number of the faces of the Pawnees before them?"

Thunder Moon spoke briefly. "The Sky People bid me to ride along, and not for the sake of a battle. I have told you what to do. Ride back to the village. I will not change my mind."

At this direct command, Young Snake obediently drew off. The other warriors sulkily heard his voice, and suddenly they fled across the hills on the homeward trail, like so many shadows mounted upon red streaks, so rapidly did the big chestnuts run and smoothly! But Thunder Moon rode on alone, and with the greatest caution, upon the trail of the Pawnees.

But carefully though he went, he knew that he was overtaking the Indian column. The walk of the big stallion was equal to the jog of the Indian ponies, its trot was the equivalent of a mustang's canter; whereas the long-stroking gallop had no counterpart among the hobbling, broken gaits of the prairie horses.

There was no dust cloud ahead to show him the nearness of the Pawnees; but he moved onward with the keenest caution, knowing that such a wise chief as Spotted Bull was not apt to trust to an informal treaty of peace such as had just been completed, but would surely throw out rear guards to spy against any possible surprise attack.

He came to a narrow little gorge where a stream

wound back and forth through the flat, pebbly bottom; and down this he went with a crash. The stallion struggled up the farther side, where the grass grew so tall that it brushed against the feet of Thunder Moon. And the sun glittered like the flashing of steel blades on the polished surface of the grass; like the flashing of steel blades, but not quite like the dull sheen of a rifle barrel!

Thunder Moon whirled in the saddle as the rifle jumped to the shoulder of the Pawnee. He saw a hideous face, streaked with war paint, and he flung the heavy bull-hide shield from his left arm straight at the Indian.

The rifle spoke; the shield staggered in its course and fell to the ground as the bullet ripped sidewise through it. It would have been easy, then, to finish off the man with a bullet from his revolver, but Thunder Moon was full of the white man's fighting madness. The Indian fights as coolly as a wild beast—that is to say, he always avoids risks if he can. But the white man rejoices in a sort of drunken, berserker lust of battle for battle's sake. So Thunder Moon followed his flung shield with a leap like a catamount that drove him from the back of his horse and straight upon the Pawnee.

This was a practiced and wide-shouldered warrior, bull-necked, cunning of hand, with an arm of iron. But he could not stand against the charge of Thunder Moon. He had dropped his rifle and caught out his knife just as the weight of the white man smashed into him and bore him heavily to the ground.

Then, kneeling beside him, Thunder Moon watched the stunned victim gradually open his eyes.

He made no further attempt at resistance. Blankly he gazed up at the leader of the Cheyennes, and waited for death.

Thunder Moon gathered to his hand the knife, the hatchet, the rifle of the Pawnee.

"The Pawnees keep good treaties and their word is sacred," said Thunder Moon bitterly. "Yet here is a wolf in my path, jumping at my throat!"

The warrior did not attempt an answer.

"Rise!" said Thunder Moon.

The Pawnee rose to his feet.

"Is there any reason why I should not send a bullet through your brain?"

"Dog of a Cheyenne!" answered the Pawnee with a dauntless heart. "The Sky People turned my bullet aside from your heart. Or else you would lie dead here, and tonight I should be a great man among my people. Kill me as you please. I am not sorry that I tried to end your days!"

"What is your name?"

"It is known to my people."

"I can tell you," said Thunder Moon, "by the scars across your shoulder. You are Gray Bear, are you not?"

At this the discretion of the Pawnee could not prevent a flash of pleasure from appearing in his eyes.

"A man will be known even in the lodges of his enemies," he said. "And a great warrior is named in the camps of the foemen! I am Gray Bear!"

"Where is your horse?"

"He is near."

"Show him to me."

The Pawnee whistled. A pony sprang up from the grass and came forward.

"Your horse knows you," said Thunder Moon. "Get on his back. Ride on with me!"

The Pawnee obeyed without a word, but a settled sternness of gloom appeared on his face; as though he

213

were seeing long beforehand the burning fire in the Cheyenne camp where the women would torment him to death.

They journeyed on to the brow of the rising land, and as their heads came up across the top of the grass, they could see, in the distance, the moving line of the Pawnees, with the sun winking upon the bright tips of their spears. The prisoner sighed, ever so slightly, and Thunder Moon said to him, "Keep close to my side. Ride slowly. All may be better for you than you imagine!"

The problem of Thunder Moon was now considerably complicated. He had to watch a strong and capable warrior at his side—even if that man were disarmed—quite likely to undertake any desperate and sudden attack upon him. And, in addition, he had to look out for other rear guards who might have been thrown out to watch.

However, for some time they journeyed on, having cautious sight, now and again, of the Pawnees who traveled before them over the top of some grass-grown hummock upon the prairie; and there were no further encounters with subtle watchers who lay in the grass.

And, while they rode on, the mind of Thunder Moon turned somewhat between the dangers that beset him and the glory he already had won upon this expedition. To carry into the city of the Cheyennes a prisoner, and of all prisoners, who so welcome as a grown and famous warrior? The women had a thousand wrongs and remembered deaths to avenge. They would expiate them upon the person of this brave. And the grim face of Gray Bear already acknowledged his approaching fate.

Another thought, too, interfered with the mind of Thunder Moon. He could not help remembering that the whites among whom his kin lived would never have acted thus toward a prisoner. The life of a defenseless man was sacred!

And this new standard troubled Thunder Moon, and made him scowl askance at the Pawnee. And then, almost against his will, he looked up and was aware of a small white cloud sailing across the upper heavens, filled with radiance, as though the sun were seated in its center.

"The Sky People!" he thought inwardly, and no matter how little he consciously believed in that old superstition, yet in spite of himself he was comforted and reassured.

So they came up behind another hummock and Thunder Moon suddenly reined back his horse, for he had had a view of the line of the Pawnees crouched behind a low ridge just before him, their horses held farther down the slope. And beyond, across the prairie, came a stream of wagons.

There were fully twenty of the big canvas-covered schooners, drawn by teams of oxen, a little gap between the rear of one wagon and the horns of the following cattle. With their clumsy but powerful steps they pushed on through the prairie. And around the train rode horsemen, three or four in front, and others to either side, but it seemed that they rode for pleasure and comfort rather than to keep guard, for otherwise they should have been pushed out to ten times such a distance, so as to act as spies in the treacherous Indian country.

The leading wagons had begun to mount a slight rise. The wind was dead. In the mortal stillness, Thunder Moon could hear the creaking of the great wheels upon their axles, and, dimly, the shouts of the ox drivers as they used their goads freely. For this train was long out

215

from the settlements, and the cattle were weary—soft with such lush green fodder, and weak with the long days of labor.

Those dim voices, like thoughts rather than physical facts, haunted Thunder Moon with a strange sadness, and he suddenly saw the house of his father, and the big white walls flooded with sunshine, and his mother in the stately library, her needlework in her lap.

And then a rifle shot cracked from the hollow before him; he saw the long line of the Pawnees break over the crest of the low ridge and pour with the most fearful yells across the level, brandishing their spears, shaking their rifles above their heads.

"Ha!" grunted Gray Bear. "They will swallow those white men! They will take the cattle, and the horses, and the guns, and the whisky, too! There will be much fire water among so many wagons! All is ours!"

For the moment he had forgotten that he was himself a wretched captive, and that the most unlucky white man in that train was hardly to be pitied more than himself.

The wagon train, threatened so suddenly in the plains, instantly began to act. The leading wagons turned sharply around and began to move toward the rear, while the frantic, yelling drivers goaded the oxen to a trot, then to an inconceivably heavy, lumbering gallop.

And while the head of the train turned back in this fashion, the rear likewise curled about to join the front. The purpose, of course, was to form the wagons into some sort of a rough circle, from which, as from the walls of a fort, the riflemen could keep up a steady fire and drive the enemy away.

But slowly, slowly moved the wagons; the Pawnees rode on wings to strike. Gray Bear groaned with eager-

216

ness and with joy as he saw the probable success of the charge.

There were brave and ready men in that caravan, however, and the rifles worked steadily. Three of the red riders were knocked out of their saddles, but the rest rode on, lying flat along the backs of their ponies, and yelling like so many madmen.

The head and tail of the caravan, gradually nearing, now seemed to have an equal chance of actually locking, when a bullet fired by one of the Pawnees struck a bullock that was struggling forward in the lead team from the rear. The animal dropped, dragged in the yoke, and then the wagon slued around to the side.

It was only possible to close the gap, at this point, by having the wagon next following veer outside the one that had been checked. But the driver of the second wagon, utterly confused, merely halted when the one before him was checked. It was the old habit of following the leader, which all the drivers soon learned upon the prairie.

In this case it proved fatal. The progress from the rear being stopped, the whole caravan looked a helpless thing, like a hedgehog that fails to quite curl up before the reaching paw of the lynx rips up its belly. But he who drove the lead wagon was a man of sense. Seeing that he could not join the rearmost ox team, he turned in almost at right angles, to the left, and the other wagons streamed after him, thus striving to close up a smaller circle that would protect at least a portion of the entire line.

Now, into the open gap, the Pawnees streamed, screaming like mountain lions over a kill. They rode erect, firing to either side. But they had divided attention; some turned on the nearly defenseless wagons to the rear. Some raced on to try to prevent the front half of the train from closing up. But the latter were foiled, and Thunder Moon saw them recoil as the circle was completed.

35

Well sheltered behind the wagons, the men of the circle maintained a steady fire against the Pawnees, but the latter now had a similar shelter.

They swept in a single rapid wave over the remainder of the wagons; wild cries of agony and wilder cries of triumph went up to heaven, and then the Indians threw themselves into position behind the captured wagons to open fire upon those who remained. However, after the first few moments, seeing that they were making only a small impression upon the remainder of the white fighters, they gave the greater part of their attention to the looting of the train in their hands. The wind was dead. A thin smoke cloud from the firing of many rifles began to sway out and envelop the battle. Then Thunder Moon turned to his captive.

He had come with a bland satisfaction to see the wiping out of the whites; now he found in his heart an increasing rage. Under his glare, the Pawnee chief winced, but Thunder Moon merely said to him, "You are free. Go back to Spotted Bull. Tell him that our truce is ended. He has counted many coups and taken many scalps. His hands are heavy with plunder. Now tell him to guard himself; the Cheyennes are on his trail!"

The Pawnee did not wait to be reassured. He gave merely one incredulous glance to his captor; then he sent his pony off at a jog trot. When he was a hundred yards away, as though suddenly mastered by fear, he put the whip to his horse and shot off in rapid zigzags across the grass, like a snipe flying upwind. Thunder Moon grimly watched him go. Bitterly he wished for those chosen warriors whom he had sent back under Young Snake!

He turned the tall stallion and drove at full speed back toward the Cheyenne village. In less than an hour, he sighted the smoke above the tepees; then the village itself. He sent his shout before him and the whole village roused itself in answer. As he came up, Young Snake was the first to gallop out to meet him, armed at all points; behind him streamed the rest of Thunder Moon's own private bank of adherents. With that advance guard of proved and well-equipped warriors, he headed across the prairie. He did not follow the straight line toward the scene of the recent battle and slaughter of the whites. Instead, he cut off at right angles to that line of march. For he reasoned that it would be very strange if Spotted Bull should remain to exult on the field of battle after the warning that he had received through the liberated captive. He was more apt to take the first and quickest trail toward his homeland.

If he moved to the left, it was very likely that Thunder Moon would cross that line of march; if he moved to the right, he would be free. So, with one chance in two to gamble for, Thunder Moon drove his men remorselessly.

Ten miles of prairie rolled behind them, and then a youth scouting ahead whirled back to announce that there was visible, in the distance, a column of riders coming straight toward them at a round pace. Thunder

Moon himself pushed forward and swung to his eyes the glass he always carried. Instantly he recognized the Pawnees by their cropped heads. Behind the file of warriors came the herd of horses, mixed with the cattle recently taken from the wagons of the whites. A foolish thing for Spotted Bull to have taken such slow-moving animals if he wished to move with celerity!

And there was no doubt about his haste. He had pushed out to either side two or three scouts to ride in advance, and the line came on with gaps in it, showing that some of the horses were being distanced by the rest.

Not Indians alone rode in that procession. The very first thing that Thunder Moon saw—more moving to him than the flashing of a sword—was the long waving of a woman's hair, and then he made out the bundle of an infant in her arms; and two children riding one behind another on another horse, and upon a third a man—evidently wounded or brokenhearted, for his head was sunk upon his breast.

Thunder Moon smiled, and the smile was not good to see.

His own dispositions were easily made. The horses were swept back into a sunlit hollow; the riders were thrown forward into the high grass along the ridge of a knoll which was rather a small wave of green than a hill. In a moment, the Cheyennes were out of view, peering out through the grass blades at the procession of the Pawnees.

In a murmur, Thunder Moon passed his word among his warriors—to every one who recaptured alive one of the white captives of the Pawnees, there would go in full and free possession one of the chestnut horses. It was a gift worth the risking of life!

But, in the meantime, it appeared as though this stratagem would be entirely wasted.

Far distanced by the ride of Thunder Moon's band across the prairie, a score of Cheyennes on their war ponies had clung to the trail and now these were in plain sight, coming rapidly on.

Spotted Bull must have sighted them at the same time.

Some thirty of his own warriors were dispatched to the side to confront this menace, but though they deployed across the line of the Cheyenne approach, still the outnumbered Cheyennes came on. For they well knew that somewhere in the sea of the tall grass, Thunder Moon and his chosen warriors were strategically placed.

The Pawnees, on the other hand, as though amazed by this resolute advance, wavered a little, uncertain; and Spotted Bull himself, with half a dozen of his best warriors, rode out to reenforce his advance guard, while his main body, now reduced by half, came slowly on with the captives.

All was working out for the best interests of the Cheyennes. The late-comers from the village bore straight on against Spotted Bull. Just behind that chief lay Thunder Moon and his chosen fighters in the grass; and straight toward the concealed line came on the rest of the Pawnees. One Pawnee division was already tacitly taken from the rear; the others would be swept with surprise.

To the left, from Spotted Bull's immediate adherents, a rifle cracked, and then another, but Thunder Moon, half rising to his knees, saw with joy that the Cheyennes kept on their rapid advance, merely fanning out their line so as to offer poorer targets. And now the head of the Pawnee main body was jogging close and closer. A dozen yards from Thunder Moon's concealed warriors—and then, silently—the Cheyennes rose to their

221

knees in the grass and, with a deliberate aim, they blew the head of the column to bits!

The sudden blast of more than twenty well-aimed rifles took the Pawnees so completely by surprise that it was as though the ground before them had opened and spat forth fire and destruction in their faces. They rolled back in utter confusion, and the Cheyennes leaped in among them with clubbed rifles, with knives, and with thrusting, narrow-headed lances.

Thunder Moon, his rifle cast aside, a revolver in either hand, made at the woman, and saw her Pawnee guard whirl on her with lifted hatchet; two quick shots dropped the redskin, and Thunder Moon stood at the head of the horse and looked up into a white, drawn, bewildered face, and saw trembling hands that clutched the infant closer.

"Have courage," he said rapidly to her. "You are safe. No one will harm you!"

He turned back to the battle; but it was ended already. The men with Spotted Bull, amazed and unnerved, did not even pause to discharge their rifles, but turned and fled, and as they turned, the riders of the Cheyenne ponies whipped vigorously in pursuit.

Woe to the Pawnee whose horse stumbled or proved a laggard!

And the tall chestnuts, rushed up from their hiding place in the hollow, were hastily mounted and darted away to join the pursuit, their long strides rapidly overtaking the fugitives. In another instant the sounds of battle were scattered far across the prairie and in all directions. Here was a Cheyenne group busy taking scalps; others rounded up the herd of cattle and horses; and others took the fallen plunder; and still the greater part were mercilessly hunting down the tribal enemy.

It was as great a stroke as Thunder Moon himself

ever had delivered, and yet he felt no keen pleasure as he looked on the work that was still under way. For it seemed to him then, with a stabbing suddenness of truth, that the death of one white, even woman or child, was more than enough to counterbalance all the vengeance he could execute upon the entire Pawnee nation.

Bitterly he realized this. He had been cast out from among his people; but now he knew in full what they meant to him and that an Indian name and an Indian life never could give him an Indian heart!

The white fugitives were gathered in a close cluster, surrounded by half a dozen braves, who were disputing as to which actually had rescued them—a problem Thunder Moon himself had to solve.

The two children and the woman who carried the infant were half hysterical with joy and with relief. He had them placed on the ground to rest and steady their nerves. Then he turned to the white man and found, as he had expected, that the latter had been wounded, a rifle ball having passed through his left thigh, so that it had been a constant agony for him to remain in the saddle.

Then, with all the skill he had learned from whites and Indians, Thunder Moon cut open the trousers leg and cleansed and dressed the wound. A swallow of whisky out of a flask restored the color of the face of the sufferer, and he said quietly, "Heaven knows what luck sent you here at the right moment. But if you had come a few hours before, you would have saved a horrible massacre!"

"I saw the attack," said Thunder Moon. "Tell me, did the last circle of the wagons hold? Or did the Pawnees break through and slaughter them, too?"

"No, they beat the Pawnees off. And you—"

He paused, looking earnestly at Thunder Moon.

"Will you tell me who you are?"

"I am a Cheyenne. They call me Thunder Moon."

"By heaven," said the other, "I thought so! Your hair was shorter when I last saw you, and you were not so sun-browned. But you are William Sutton!"

36

To this recognition, Thunder Moon replied in the uttermost astonishment, "And who are you? Where have you seen me?"

"I'm Charles Siegler," said the other, "and I used to see you near your father's place. I had the small farm down the road, with the row of poplars in front of it, and the pool beside the trees. Do you remember me, sir?"

Thunder Moon closed his eyes. He remembered very well the tall, slender, graceful trees, and their images ever floated on the surface of the little lake.

"I remember you, Siegler. I remember you very well," said he. "And no doubt you were one of the men who hounded me out of the country with guns and dogs? Were you one of those?"

"No, sir, I thank heaven!" said the other with violence. "I had nothing to do with that bad day's work."

"Bad day?" said Thunder Moon, darkly. "There were dead men in the jail behind me!"

"Ah, and was that it?" asked Siegler. "But, as a matter of fact, there were no dead men at all, and he who hounded on the others after you knew it very well! No, sir; since your leaving, there was never a time when a great many people did not make a stir about bringing you back! Your father and mother have gone to the expense of fitting up all these wagons and the cattle to go across the prairie and find you."

"To find me!" cried Thunder Moon. "And how many died when the Pawnees rushed the train?"

"I saw five men down, and three women, and three children," said Charles Siegler.

"Eleven dead," muttered Thunder Moon. "But why did my father send out women and children to help hunt for me?"

"Those were not all of his men," answered Siegler. "We fell in with another small train; we made one party, to travel together as far as we could into the country of the Cheyennes. After that, they were to go on alone. They were mostly in the trail of the wagon train. They went down with a crash when the Pawnees charged. Heaven help them!"

"Who went out commanding my father's men?"

"Your brother, sir."

"Jack is commanding them!" muttered Thunder Moon, with a total bewilderment.

"No man is keener to find gold than he is to find you, sir."

"Is that likely?" broke out Thunder Moon suddenly.

Then he added, "But Jack's come with the rest—to find me! It's got to be believed!" He added, "Is there any one else in the party that I know?"

"I think there are, and particularly there is—"

Siegler checked himself.

"Go on, man!"

"There's one you'd better see with your own eyes before you're told about, Mr. Sutton!"

225

Thunder Moon rubbed his chin with his hard knuckles. He looked away across the prairie, and he saw the men of his war party coming gradually back, some from such a great distance that they were mere specks; others disappearing in the hollows, in part, and growing big against the sky, again, as they climbed the slight knolls.

It had been a great victory. The scattering drew back. In that sudden assault, not a single Cheyenne had been killed or seriously injured. Not a horse had been lost. Altogether, seventeen Pawnees were dead, and seventeen scalps were hanging from the bridles of the Cheyennes, and there was not a man of the entire party who had not counted at least a single coup. It was a glorious victory. There was loot, besides, in abundance, not only from the Pawnees but from the whites who had first been plundered by the Pawnees.

Young Snake, splashed with red from head to foot— part of it running from a shallow, unregarded wound in his own broad right shoulder, came up to his leader with a face convulsed with joy.

"Take all the men, and go back to the village," said Thunder Moon. "My band is tired, and they have fought hard and ridden as only Cheyennes can ride. Go to Bald Eagle and ask him to send out some new men. The Pawnees are men. Spotted Bull is not among the dead, and he may attempt to come back and fight once more."

"Spotted Bull," answered Young Snake, "is a brave man, for a Pawnee. But he has this day seen the fire of the Sky People flung in his face. I, Young Snake, saw him ride from the battle and never look back! But I shall do everything as you wish!"

"Listen to me sharply," said Thunder Moon. "In the wagon train there are many white people who are my friends. They are to be treated as friends. They have

226

come a great distance to find me. Let the young war-riors come out and be a guard between the white men and the roaming Pawnees. Do you hear?"

"I hear and I shall tell Bald Eagle."

"Go to the tepee of White Crow, my foster mother. Give her the rifle and the clothes and all the weapons of this dead Pawnee. Load them upon his pony. Tell her that I killed him and two more with my own hand. She is an old woman, and she needs to hear pleasant news to make her heart light and young again."

"O my father," said Young Snake—though Thunder Moon was much his junior—"this I shall do! White Crow shall sing louder than all the women of the Cheyennes. Shall I go?"

"Go at once!"

The other was off instantly, gathering his men about him with shouts; and off went the warriors across the plain. There remained behind, the dead, stripped bodies of the Pawnees, the whites, and Thunder Moon.

The others gathered close around him, looking fear-fully across the plain, as though they expected terrible danger to flow in upon them from its vastness at any moment. He reassured them gravely.

"The Pawnees have lost heart. The Indians are not like the white men. When they are beaten, they go off to make new medicine."

Several horses had been left to them by the express command of Thunder Moon. The woman and the two children were mounted. The wounded Charles Siegler was slung in a rude litter between two ponies, and so they started back across the prairie, Thunder Moon riding his great red stallion, and leading the litter horses.

At last, far off, they saw the wagons, all exactly as Thunder Moon last had seen them, the small, cramped circle at the head of the line, and the rest of the wagons scattered in a broken line just as they had stood when the Pawnee charge broke into their midst.

And he said to Siegler, "Jack Sutton is in that train?"

"Him? Without him, we'd all be dead! He was driving the lead wagon—it was him that had the sense to turn in short and make the small circle—Heaven bless him! He done a day's work that would have lasted him for the rest of his life!"

He added, "And the girl, too! I seen her handling her rifle like a man!"

Thunder Moon asked no questions. An odd, stinging hope was awakening in his breast, and he looked with a scowl at the slow pace with which the litter bearers kept up the line.

Then, in profound wonder, he looked up to the broad surface of the sky, now gathering color, for the sunset time was upon them, and he saw one golden cloud high above the rest, with a bosom filled with rich fire.

The Sky People, thought Thunder Moon. They have brought my brother out to find me!

When they came still closer, they saw that all the people of the caravan, more than a score, were gathered around a mound of newly turned earth—a common grave in which the dead had been placed. Thunder Moon could see afar the man who was reading the service for the burial. And three women were in the listening group—one of them had fallen to her knees in grief.

A little nearer, and now they could see faces—and yonder he knew the tall form of his handsome brother, Jack Sutton. Hardly a brother he seemed in the old days. How different to find him here on the prairie!

A queer thrust of joy passed through the heart of Thunder Moon, and he hurried on ahead of the others, scanning the group, which had now turned away from the grave and toward him.

They began to shout. One of the women ran out with a wild cry that passed into the mind of Thunder Moon, never to leave him again.

She passed him, and reached the litter, and cried out again; but there was so much agony of joy now in her voice as there had been agony of sorrow and pain and hope before.

Yonder man who had been reading from the Bible, was now revealed as no less a person than Judge Keene, looking no less courtly on the wide floor of the prairie than he had been in his own house.

Thunder Moon brushed straight on. His brother was hurrying toward him, calling out with honest joy in his voice. Judge Keene, also, moved forward, waving his hand in wonder and delight. But these people were hardly in the eye of Thunder Moon. He looked beyond them to a woman—beautiful Charlotte Keene!

She did not advance with her father to greet Thunder Moon, rather, she shrank back into the crowd; and the more she shrank the more savagely and well he knew that she loved him as much as ever he had loved her during the long and lonely months since he left her and rode westward toward the prairies.

The instant that he felt that hot wave of confidence in her, he could turn his attention to his brother and the judge. They greeted him with the purest amazement, as well as joy. His hands were wrung. Big Jack Sutton grasped him by the arms and a thousand questions poured out.

How had he known that they were there? How had he

chanced to come that way? There was less of a miracle in this coincidence than appeared, for had not the caravan been voyaging west these many weeks, striving to find the section of the Cheyenne tribe to which Thunder Moon, alias William Sutton, was attached?

"Where's Charlotte?" said the judge. "She wouldn't let us go off without her when we started on this expedition. She wanted a taste of frontier life. Heaven knows we've had too much of it today with the Pawnee tribe!"

Charlotte was with them, at last, shaking hands, and gravely telling William Sutton that she was glad they had found him. To Thunder Moon she looked almost childishly small, compared with the tall Cheyenne women; even compared with Red Wind. And then all the other people of the train had to be met, and there was a glad hubbub of voices, except from those who had lost friends or family in the battle.

To escape from that spot Thunder Moon urged them to march straight on, because they would find water within two miles. So the cattle recaptured from the Pawnees were put to the wagons, and the train forged ahead until the darkness came. Then camp was made at the edge of a small stream; men and animals drank, and three fires were lighted, for brush was plentiful. Dinner was cooked. And all this while, Thunder Moon had little opportunity for conversation, because his presence was required here and there, directing the way, helping to picket the horses and oxen, and taking command in general.

Later, he would have a chance to talk with Charlotte Keene. But when he came back to the fires after all his work, he found that Charlotte had gone to the wagon to sleep. The other women and children, equally exhausted, disappeared under the canvas.

And all the camp grew quiet; and with low voices Judge Keene, Jack Sutton, and Thunder Moon talked together. They watched the head of the fire rise and snap off in the blackness, under the glow of the stars.

"One of you has done most of this," said Thunder Moon. "Which one is it?"

"We pulled together," answered the judge gravely. "We did everything together. We each had our motives!"

"And what was yours?" asked Thunder Moon of his brother.

Jack Sutton grew red, but his glance would not waver from the face of the other.

"I had to find you," he said, "in order to let you know I understood, at last, what a greedy fool I'd been. I had to find you and tell you that I'd wanted to rob you of your rights—that I'd envied you the estate. Great Scott, Will, I never could have called myself a man if I hadn't made some effort to find you! I'd even plotted against you—that last night."

Thunder Moon glanced at the judge.

"He knows all about it," said Jack Sutton. "I told him and I told Charlotte. I'm clear with them, at least. And perhaps someday I can be square with my own conscience!"

"It was Harrison Traynor that put the killing into your mind," said Thunder Moon.

"It was," admitted the younger man.

Now, across the firelight, reached the great hand of Thunder Moon. It was laid upon the shoulder of Jack Sutton.

"Brother!" said he.

And they looked full at one another with a world of understanding and affection.

"Now that we've fairly met," said the judge, "we

231

must put the question we've come to ask. Do you come back to your father's home with us?"

Thunder Moon frowned. He lighted his pipe, and blew a puff toward the ground, a puff into the air, and another cloud of smoke he struck with his hand.

In this Indian fashion he continued his smoking, unconsciously frowning in thought.

"I came back to my father's house," said he, "and I tried to live like a white man."

"And a good job you made of it, almost from the first," said his brother.

"The first whites whom I saw hunted me like a fox. And then I settled down in the house, and in the end, after a great deal of hard work with the reading of books, and toiling and grubbing, and wearing stiff clothes that grip the shoulder muscles—in the end of all of this, when I had learned to love my father and mother and the old white house, I was driven away, because I would not let my foster father lie in a jail!"

"It was Traynor who did that," said the judge. "Heaven rest the dead, and Traynor is among them! But I cannot help saying that I never heard of any more treacherous and malicious action than that of Traynor's against you, and the raising of the crowd to hunt you—when he knew very well indeed that there were not three dead men left behind you in the jail."

"There are other things," said Thunder Moon. "It is true that very often my heart is sick to go back among my own kind. But still, here on the plains, a man is a man. There is freedom. There is no one to say to me, Go! Come! Stand!"

"And who is there to say that to you in your own home, Will?" asked his brother.

"There are a good many things to stop me: pity for

my mother, respect for my father, and always the hard fist of convention beating into a natural man's face—to say nothing of the law that keeps its rope around every neck!"

The judge, at this, smiled and nodded.

"Of course, it's true," said he. "But, with us, you would at once be a distinguished member of society. Your father is very old. Frankly, he is not very well. We don't expect him to live through the next winter. In case of his death, you would step up as the head of the family. The head of the whole estate!"

"If I were head of the whole estate," said Thunder Moon, "could I then do as much as this?"

He whistled—a long, birdlike, mournful note—and then he raised a hand as a warning to listen. Almost at once, out of the darkness, they heard the rapid beating of the hoofs of a horse. Then, into the firelight, came a young Cheyenne. He brought the mustang to a halt close to the fire and raised a long, slender lance and shield in salutation to Thunder Moon. That posture he maintained for a moment, unstirring, except as his lithe, muscular legs gave with the heaving ribs of the pony.

Thunder Moon spoke a few words in Cheyenne, and the warrior whirled the pony and was gone in a flash.

"Can I do that, when I am head of the estate?" asked Thunder Moon.

37

That wild vision out of the night was still in the minds of the listeners; they were still half dazzled by the wild light in the eyes of the mustang, in the eyes of the Cheyenne brave.

Then the judge said slowly, "Isn't it true, William, that you're held by something else?"

"By what?"

"You have a pretty young wife among the Cheyennes, haven't you?"

"I?" exclaimed Thunder Moon.

"Let's be frank, my boy. The girl who speaks English. She herself told my girl that she was your wife."

"Red Wind!"

"She told Charlotte that I am married to her?"

"No doubt she simply meant that she had been taken as a squaw, Indian fashion."

Thunder Moon set his jaw hard.

"That explains a good many things," said he. "And your daughter believed her!"

"I want to talk frankly," said the judge. "You will imagine that I had to have a pretty strong reason for making such a journey as this. And a still stronger one for letting Charlotte come along with me. The fact is, William, that you were something more than a friend to her."

"I love her," said Thunder Moon quietly. "And I told her so!"

The judge seemed to inhale this speech like incense.

"If you care for her, that settles it," said he. "We'll arrange all the minor difficulties; and back you must come with us, my boy. Life has been a little drab and dark for poor Charlie since you left us!"

"Suppose," said Thunder Moon, "that I build a trading fort in the hills. The Cheyennes would still be around us. Would Charlotte be happy here in the open country?"

"She has a thousand friends," said the judge. "You know that, William. It would be hard to ask her to come out here. But I think she would do whatever you asked—except that you could not very well ask her to share your life with the Indian wife."

The judge had put this as gently as he could, but his old eyes glimmered with fire and contempt as he spoke.

Thunder Moon arose.

"I go back to the village," said he, "and there I shall see Red Wind, and bring her back with me to tell your daughter the truth. I have had no wife among the Cheyennes. Old White Crow, my foster mother, is the squaw in my tepee. I have placed a lodge for Red Wind near us. She was left alone in the world. I was a friend to her, and she has hurt me when my back was turned! But you will hear the truth from her own lips!"

The judge fairly groaned with pleasure.

"My dear boy!" said he. "My dear lad! Bring her as fast as you can. Start with the morning. We'll head on in this direction."

"There will be Indians in front of you and around you," said Thunder Moon. "They are my friends, the Cheyennes, and they will keep you from trouble. Go to sleep now. You are all tired. In the morning I start for the village."

They took his word for it and went to their blankets, but Thunder Moon sat by the fire, the blanket huddled closely around his shoulders.

He knew that he had come to a parting of the ways, where he must choose one of the roads that branched before him. Drawing him toward the house of his father was his affection for his family, and the love he felt for Charlotte Keene, and there was the pull, also, of his own blood and kind.

But on the other hand, among the Cheyennes he was a force. He was like a king of the body and the spirit. And though he half knew that his mysterious authority was based upon a sham, yet in a way he could not be sure. The Sky People were to him half a superstition and half a fact.

Here upon the prairie his was a name that rang through all the red nations—Thunder Moon! But far to the east, where his father's house stood, he was simply William Sutton, vaguely known as a man raised among the Indians—a nonentity—a thing without being, so far as the minds of other men were concerned.

He sighed as he thought of it.

And looking up from his thoughts, he saw that it was the first glimmering of the gray dawn.

Now he rose, and mounting the red stallion, he started back across the prairie. The Cheyennes swung in like gray ghosts to meet him, but he waved them back to their watch and bade them bring on the white men in the morning.

Then he went on swiftly.

The sun was half up over the horizon when the stallion waded through the creek and went up the slope beyond toward the village, which already was up, for the Indian begins his day with the sun. Young women were coming down to the river for water. Boys stood

236

about, shivering with the early cold. Warriors began to appear, wrapped in their buffalo robes.

But when he was sighted on his familiar horse, what a shout went up in welcome! So they brought him, in a tangle of cheers and exulting shouts, to his lodge.

He went in and found White Crow busily laying out the trophies he had sent her. She turned to her foster son with a toothless grin of joy that almost made nose and chin touch.

"Last night a woman sang in the scalp dance," she said. "I told of the coups you had counted, O my son! I told how you had laid your braves in the tall grass. I told how the Pawnees were like puffs of smoke. You struck them, and they disappeared forever! Spotted Bull is a great chief. He is a lucky warrior, also. But my son is Thunder Moon. Hai! My soul is hungry to see the spirit of Big Hard Face. He must have leaned low from the happy hunting grounds last night to hear. All the people shouted your name together! Thunder Moon!"

He listened, delighted.

If there was something childish about this, there also was something magnificent. Then he pushed the pleasant thought away.

"Where is Red Wind?" he asked.

The jealous old squaw exclaimed, "Asleep, perhaps— that lazy creature! Or whispering with Standing Antelope. She makes his eyes as bright as the eyes of a hungry wolf. Is that a good thing? Be wise, Thunder Moon! Send her away. Or else give her to Standing Antelope. Let him have her!"

"He is my friend," said Thunder Moon, cheerfully. "If he wants her, then he shall have her. But first I must talk to her."

"Give her away—and talk to her afterward!" insisted White Crow. "She will not want to leave you. Now she

237

has a lodge to herself. She only has to work for herself. Why should a useless woman wish to keep a lodge and do all the work for a warrior?"

Thunder Moon stepped outside the lodge and saw Red Wind coming up from the river, carrying water, and a great braid of her copper hair shone like golden fire as it slipped down over her shoulder. She came to Thunder Moon with a smile and paused before him; but he waved her into her tepee and followed her in. She, putting down the skin of water, turned to him and offered him the place of honor on a folded robe, with a comfortable back rest behind it. He refused with a curt gesture.

"Red Wind," he told her with the dignity of anger, "you have made me not happy."

She clasped her hands loosely before her and looked at him with submission.

"I am not wise," she said meekly. "Tarawa has not given me a mind like the sun or the moon. But all of my days here seem to have gone by me like the wind over the prairie grass. Surely I have done nothing to make the great chief angry, but I have had a dark thought, perhaps, and he has made medicine, and he has read my mind!"

Thunder Moon scowled upon her.

"Are you talking to some other person?" he asked. "Are you talking to some foolish other person, Red Wind? Between you and me there is an understanding. You know that you have no real belief in the Sky People!"

"But do you deny them?" she asked him quickly. "Would you stand under the open sky and tell them that you deny them?"

He sighed and shook his head.

"There is no more strength in my mind than there is

238

in a chain of grass," he admitted. "But that is not true of you. There is no foolishness in you, Red Wind. There is nothing in you except thought. You laugh at the Sky People and at all the Indian ways, and at all the Indian medicine. Tell me if that is true?"

"How should I say that?" asked the girl quietly. "Who am I not to believe what my master believes?"

"I am not your master."

"What are you, then?"

"I have only tried to be your friend."

"The lodge that I live in is yours," said she.

"I have given it to you," he answered. "Why do you act as though you were a slave?"

"What else am I?" she demanded. "I am not your daughter or your sister. If I were, you would sell me for a few horses to one of the men in the village. Perhaps you could find one who wants me. I am not your squaw. What am I, then, Thunder Moon?"

"Whenever you choose to play the child and be helpless," he grumbled, "there is no way that I can talk with you. I think that you know it!"

"Tell me how I must speak to you?" she asked. "The will of Thunder Moon is my will!"

He stamped upon the floor of the tepee.

"Do you want a husband?" he asked. "Twenty times I have begged you to tell me which one of the young men among the Cheyennes pleases you! Young Snake I have seen looking at you!"

"What pleases you is pleasing to me," she replied.

"Answer me!" he commanded. "Tell me what you think!"

"Do I dare?" she asked plaintively. "Young Snake is a great friend of yours. He is your bravest warrior, next to Standing Antelope. If I should speak a bad word against him, you would beat me and leave me weeping!"

Thunder Moon went closer to her; he towered above her darkly.

"I never raised a finger against any woman or against any child," said he. "And this you know. Why do you speak to me in this fashion?"

Her eyes closed.

"O Thunder Moon," she murmured, "whatever I say is wrong. Whatever I do, I cannot please you!"

"Speak truth, and be yourself," he begged. "Why do you act in this way? Is it because you are partly white and partly Indian?"

Her eyes remained closed. He saw the long dark lashes against her skin. He could not tell why she had closed those eyes, or what thought was in her mind, or weariness, or disgust. She was a problem beyond his solving.

"How can I tell what is the evil in me?" she asked. "But Thunder Moon sees me, and understands much better!"

He drew back from her, shaking his head.

"Is it true that you hate me?" he asked her suddenly.

At this she opened her eyes. They were dull and empty.

"Hate?" said she.

"You saw the white woman whom I loved. You told her that you were my wife among the Cheyennes! That was a lie, Red Wind. Why did you lie to her?"

For almost the first time in his knowledge of her, he saw that she was taken aback. Her color altered. She rested a hand against the nearest lodgepole.

"There were many rich men and wise men who loved her," said Red Wind at last. "Why should she have you, too?"

There was no acting now. Manifest fear was in her face.

So he said slowly, "In spite of that, she has found me again!"

"She!" cried Red Wind, starting almost violently.

"She is one of the women in the wagon train the Pawnees raided."

"And they could not find her body with a bullet!" cried the girl with a sudden outbreak of savagery and despair.

Something like fear stirred in the heart of Thunder Moon. He looked at her in amazement.

"She is alive and well," he answered sternly. "You would gladly have seen her dead in the attack. Is that true?"

She did not answer but watched him with a sort of sullen defiance, as one who realized that she had said too much to retract.

"After this," went on Thunder Moon, "there is only one thing you can do to help me. You must come with me to the white camp. You must go before her, and tell her that on that other day you lied to her, and that you never have been my squaw!"

Red Wind turned pale indeed.

"When must I go?" she asked.

"At once!"

"Thunder Moon," said the girl in a trembling voice, "do what you wish to me today. But let me stay here till tomorrow in quiet. The wagon train will come close. It will be easier, then, for me to speak to her. I need a little time to think of what I must say. It is not easy even for a woman to admit that she has lied!"

The man sighed with pity.

"That is true," said he. "Because of your pride, Red Wind, there are times when I admire you as I admire strong men. We shall wait until tomorrow before you speak to her. In the meantime, it is not right that you should remain any longer as a part of my family. I see that bad talk has started. Everyone must be made to know that you are not my squaw. And it will be better for you to pick out a husband from among the Cheyennes!"

She listened with great dark eyes that suddenly narrowed in thought.

"Then I must choose a husband?" she said.

"It is better. You see that. When you do not have me to take care of you, you must go into the tepee of some warrior of the tribe."

"Then let it be Standing Antelope, if he will have me!"

"Shall I send for him?"

"No. I shall ask a boy to go with a message to Standing Antelope. When he comes, then I shall talk with him and ask him if he would have me for a wife."

"There is little doubt of that!"

"And I shall ask him how many horses he will pay you for me. How many would you demand, Thunder Moon?"

He flushed at this.

"You think," said he, "that I have kept you in order to make myself richer by giving you to some chief for a wife? No, no! This lodge and everything in it is freely yours. Besides that, Standing Antelope will be as rich as any man in the tribe when he takes you for a squaw!"

She bowed her head.

"My master is like one of the Sky People," she said. "Where he gives his kindness, he gives greatness and wealth, also."

"You will be happy, then, Red Wind?"

"Happy?" she exclaimed.

She threw up her head and broke into such wild laughter that Thunder Moon backed out of the tepee with trouble in his heart, and went slowly into his own lodge, where he found White Crow waiting for him, a smile of cruel satisfaction on her withered lips.

38

Left now to herself, Red Wind pushed away the grief and the rage that invaded her mind. Since that old day when her father had brought her among these Cheyennes and palmed her off, as it were, upon Thunder Moon, she had worked cleverly, insistently, in her own way, to win the love of that hero of the ugly face and the wide shoulders. A dozen times she had told herself that she was victorious, but never with more certainty than when she had gone into the white man's land, to the very house of Thunder Moon, and there had managed to draw him away from the woman he loved. The triumph had seemed complete. She would have wagered her soul that before another moon passed she would be installed in the lodge of her hero. And still, while many a moon came and went, she seemed as far from him as ever!

Now was the end. She knew it beyond doubt and beyond hope. He had learned of the artifice and the lie with which she had kept the white girl from him and there would be no forgiveness.

Then, from the door of her lodge, she called a scampering boy and asked him to carry her message to Standing Antelope. Then the girl retired once more into the lodge and sat down with her thoughts. The extent of her failure was clearer and clearer, and a boundless malice rose in her. All that love she had felt for Thunder Moon turned swiftly to poisonous grief, and then anger, and then settled hatred. She had offered him her soul in the palm of her hand, and he had turned his back upon her!

A voice at her lodge entrance; she called; Standing Antelope was before her.

He was as different from Thunder Moon as were their names. The one was like a lordly bison bull, able to overawe the hearts of the strongest warriors. The other was like a soaring flame, as swift, as light, as dangerous.

A painted buffalo robe was now gathered about the youth, but in spite of the swathings she could see that, like flame again, his whole body was trembling. And his black, eager eyes gleamed at her.

Here was fire, and it would burn at her bidding!

She stood up to greet him, gravely, and gently, as she well knew how to speak to men, and she said in the metaphorical speech into which an Indian could always drop in time of need, "A woman should be like a child and never speak to warriors until she is first noticed. A shield that is cast down cannot leap up into the hands that own it, and a lance cannot strike if it has fallen to the ground and lies there unregarded. But I have been bold, and I have sent for you, Standing Antelope. White Crow will scold me for this; she will beat me afterward!"

The warrior's hand made a convulsive movement; the robe parted, and she saw that he instinctively had grasped the handle of a knife.

"The tongue of an old woman," said he, "is like the tail of a puppy; it cannot stop wagging. But there are ways to prevent the falling of blows. Red Wind!"

"What could I do?" asked the girl, making her eyes

244

large with helpless grief and fear. "When Thunder Moon speaks, all the Cheyenne warriors tremble. When he lifts his hand, they all bow their heads. How should I dare to speak against White Crow, or stop her hand, if she raises an unstrung war bow to strike me."

"To strike you!" said Standing Antelope, half choked with emotion.

She had slipped on the bank of the river and bruised her arm against a rock only the day before. Now, with a swift movement, she exposed her arm to the elbow, and showed the discolored bruise.

"That was to keep the blow from my head!" said she.

The young brave folded his arms across his breast, as though by the strength of his own hands he were striving to compress and control his excitement.

"There is a chief in this tribe," said he. "Bald Eagle is a chief!"

"Shall I complain to him? He would laugh in my face and send me away, for fear lest Thunder Moon should give him back luck on the warpath."

Standing Antelope drew softly a step nearer. "You speak as people speak who do not know the whole truth. It is true that many of the warriors fear Thunder Moon. Many of them ride behind him. So do coyotes follow the grizzly bear, for the sake of the leavings after the kill has been made and the killer has feasted. So the warriors are glad to ride behind Thunder Moon, because after he has struck, the least of the young boys are able to count coups and to take scalps! But it does not mean that they follow him because they love him!"

She looked down to the ground, to hide the burning exultation she knew was springing up into her eyes. Then she sighed and said slowly, "If you give a horse grass from your hand, he is grateful, and if you throw meat to a dog, he kisses your hand. Therefore, of

245

course, the Cheyennes are grateful to Thunder Moon, and love him for the good he has done for them!"

"They are not horses," said the youth, "and some of them are not dogs! Some of them know that Thunder Moon despises them. He treats them as men treat a dog—to carry a burden, to run on an errand. He treats them at best like children. The council is called and all the old men speak, and the chiefs, and all the experienced warriors who have taken scalps and counted many coups. After they have ended, Thunder Moon speaks like a voice from a cloud. He tells them that they have talked very wisely and very well, but he himself has wisdom from the Sky People, and therefore they must do only what he advises them!"

"But is it not true that the Sky People protect him and guide him?"

"Have you forgotten," said Standing Antelope, "how he had to run for his life from the white people? We have seen him hunted with horses and dogs and guns, like a wolf. We have seen him running! And therefore I say that all his talk about the Sky People is a great lie!"

Having said this, Standing Antelope's glance rolled anxiously upward, as though he half expected that, in reward for such a blasphemy, the thunders of the actual sky might at that moment descend upon his head.

The girl saw; and a faint smile of understanding and contempt flashed upon her lips, glimmered in her cold eyes, and was gone again. This boy was a tool, and no more than a tool; but with him she could strike a glorious blow of revenge, she felt.

She summoned an expression of terror and wonder and ran to the youth.

"Standing Antelope!" she whispered. "Beware! Pray quickly to Tarawa before you are stricken! Pray for protection!"

His lips were pale with fear, but presently he mastered himself again and said as stoutly as he could, "You see that nothing happens! I am safe. I am safe because I am not afraid of Thunder Moon!"

She affected an air of intensest admiration. "O Standing Antelope," said she, "is it true, then? Are you alone among the Cheyennes able to stand Thunder Moon? Are you alone able to save me from him?"

"Are you in danger from him?" asked the brave. "Does *he* also strike you?"

"The heaviest blows are not given with the hand!" said she.

He waited, keen as a knife for more.

"See how he keeps me here!" said she. "I am neither his slave nor his sister nor his squaw. I am nothing! I am like a dog on a chain. It can only be seen! So am I! Thunder Moon keeps me here. He keeps me here so that he can point me out to strangers and to the whole tribe. It is because I satisfy his pride. He shows them what I am. She is not worthy to be my squaw, is what he means to say to them.

"What life have I? If he will not have me, why will he not let others have me? What am I to him that he should want to keep me here? But if a warrior or a young brave so much as looks at me, Thunder Moon frowns terribly, and the warriors turn their heads away and pretend that they were not looking at me at all!"

She allowed her voice to rise softly to a little breaking point of vexation and grief.

Then Standing Antelope, his voice as shaken now as his body had been before, exclaimed, "This is wonderful, Red Wind! We all have thought—all the warriors and the young braves—that you cared for nothing except Thunder Moon. That you lived because he willed you to live, and breathed because he willed you to breathe! Have we all been wrong. Have you hated Thunder Moon?"

"Ah, Standing Antelope," said she, "you have drawn the truth out of my heart! I could conceal nothing from you! And now you will go to Thunder Moon! He will kill me for speaking as I have spoken!"

The warrior answered with a strange quietness, "What you have told me is as much a secret as though you had spoken it only to your own heart! Will you believe that?"

"If you have said it! There are no lies on your tongue, Standing Antelope. All the other Cheyennes might scorn a woman so much that they would not tell her the truth. But you are too proud to lie even to a woman!"

He said, "You want freedom, Red Wind?"

"Ah, yes! I die for the lack of it!"

"I have not," said the youth, "a herd of great horses like Thunder Moon. I have not many rifles. I am not followed by many braves. But if you will come with me, as I tried to say to you not many days ago—"

"Would you take me?"

"I? Tarawa, see my heart!"

"Thunder Moon would follow us."

"Perhaps he will not pursue. He might simply let us ride away. I do not think that he would beg a woman to return to him after she once wanted to go away!"

"Then why has he kept me here, like a wretched slave?"

He was silent, brooding, upon this point. And, remembering his old affection for Thunder Moon, his heart failed him a little, and he looked at the girl with a keen thrust of suspicion.

She met that glance with a steady boldness of eye. And he sighed. He could not face her and remain true to himself and the better heart that was in him.

"If we fled away together," said the girl, "he would remain behind us not long. He would soon pursue. And who can outride the red horses?"

He struck his hands together.

"It is true," he admitted in despair. "It is very true that no one can ride away from the men on his great horses!"

Then he added, "You are wise! Even Thunder Moon has asked for your advice and followed your counsel. Be wise now, Red Wind, and tell me what I can do. Look at me only as two hands that are willing to work for you!"

It was exactly the point to which she had wished to bring him, but now she affected sorrow and despair in her turn again.

"There is only one way," said she.

"Then let me know!"

She shook her head.

"You beg for your freedom; you will not open the door to it!" he exclaimed.

"It would be my freedom, and your death!" said she.

Sobered a little, he stared at her. And then, with the slender staff he carried in his hand, he struck upon the hard-packed earthen floor of the lodge.

"Who can tell when death will come?" said he. "I have done something in my life. I have counted coups. I have taken scalps. Now, why should I be afraid to die? I am not afraid! Tell me in what way we can go free then?"

"I am his captive," she said slowly, "as long as he lives! But a dead man has no hands to hold even a weak woman!"

At this sudden suggestion, no matter how she had tried to lead up to it, the warrior shrank a little and looked at her as though she had opened a pit that looked down to the bottom of the world.

He said at last, rather huskily, "To murder Thunder Moon!"

She did not answer. Passion, vengeance, envy, jealousy, dead love, were all in her face. But no matter what feeds the fire, it casts a light. So her beauty flared before the eyes of Standing Antelope and dazzled him.

"Do you know," said he, "what comes to the man who murders in his own tribe?"

"He is outcast forever!"

"It is true," said Standing Antelope. "I should be a man without a people."

"Let that be true," said she. "Ah, Standing Antelope, if you were with me, I think that I could make you happy, even as a man without a people!"

He did not touch her; merely a dazed look came in his eyes.

"It is done," said Standing Antelope simply. "When shall I kill him?"

"This night, this night!" said the girl with a wild eagerness. "Kill him this night, and then we shall ride under the cover of the darkness!"

Amazed, he stared at her.

"Will you love as you hate?" he asked her.

"You will see!" said the girl. "There is no flesh in me; there is nothing but fire, Standing Antelope. Kill this man, and then we may be happy together. If he lives, I shall burn up like a leaf in the autumn sun!"

He hesitated, his eyes wandering swiftly from side to side.

"And the best of all that is in the lodge I shall take!" she assured him.

But she had mistaken his meaning. He answered hotly, "This was the gift of Thunder Moon. There is nothing here that is really yours. Take nothing."

"At least, we shall ride off on two of the red horses."

"Not for a single stride!"

"But he has given two of them to you."

"They are his gift," said the youth sullenly and sadly. "I want nothing that is his! I shall not take the rifles he has given to me. Look! Nearly everything that I have is his gift. But I shall throw everything away except the little that is my own. And I wish that Tarawa would give to me the power to strip off from my mind the things Thunder Moon has taught me. That I cannot do. But if he has made my hand skillful, he has only given it the skill that will take his own life!"

At this, as though the saying of the word brought up the vision of the deed brightly before him, he straightened himself with a swelling breast before her, and with great, desperate eyes. Then he turned and went out of the lodge without speaking another word.

She, following to the flap of the tepee, looked after him and saw him going off with a rapid but uncertain step; and she gripped her right hand hard. Standing Antelope was a keen knife, to be sure, but the metal was apt to snap under the strain, she felt!

39

In the heart of the afternoon, the wagon train came up.

It did not cross the river, but remained upon the farther side of it, at the express suggestion of Thunder Moon. He, too, often had seen that white men and red cannot agree very long together, and the first gladness of meeting rapidly turns to trouble. So he decided that it would be best to keep the current of the river between the two camps.

Almost immediately, however, there was a flood of the red men among the wagons, their eyes and then their hands prying everywhere. So Thunder Moon stood in the center of the camp and raised his great voice. Great as thunder it boomed and when he had finished his brief admonition in the Cheyenne tongue, the Indians slunk off toward the river.

Only their chiefs remained.

Bald Eagle had come bearing a present of beaded moccasins and three Indian ponies, the fattest and therefore the best of his herd.

Judge Keene received him, with Thunder Moon acting as interpreter, accepted the presents, made others in return, chiefly of good knives, of which the tribe at this moment was in great need. For, working on the hides of tough buffalo bulls and cows for tepees wears out knives faster than anything in the world.

The exchanges being made, the chiefs departed. Judge Keene then set about looking for William Sutton in person, but that unreclaimed white man was seated in a corner of the wagon circle lost in conversation with Charlotte Keene. And the judge, after one long look, turned otherwhere.

Thunder Moon had said to the girl, "The Cheyennes do not tell lies except to public enemies. I am going to call the biggest of the chiefs. You shall hear him say whether or not I have a wife among his people!"

But she answered frankly, "Do you think that I've come all these hundreds and hundreds of miles to argue with you, or to take testimony? I don't care! There's only one important thing—which is that you and I are sitting on the double trees of this particular wagon in this particular place. I know that; and I don't care about the rest!"

"If you've come here," said he suddenly, "would you stay here, Charlotte?"

She looked down to the ground. He could feel that she had been struck a blow, but she glanced up to him again almost immediately and said, "I can stay here."

"It would be a wilder and a harder life than you've been accustomed to," he assured her.

"Not so hard as my life since you left me, William."

He was silent for a moment, listening to an echo of her voice, as it were, pronouncing his Christian name—so long unfamiliar in his ears.

"I could build a house for us. Do you see where the hills begin to go up there?"

"It looks like blue, rolling smoke?"

"Yes."

"I see them more clearly, now."

He smiled at her.

"You will learn to use your eyes in this country! If you look still harder, you'll see the mountains beyond the hills."

"They're almost lost against the sky," said she.

"And the flecks of white—those are the snowcaps of the mountains. There the hills and the mountains divide?"

"Yes, I see the gap, I think."

"A great river comes down from the highlands there. I've chosen the valley. We could build there."

"Yes," she said.

"Does the thought of it make you sad?"

"Nothing really makes me sad today," she answered obliquely.

And this humility in her disturbed him more than any

253

prayers that he should go back with her to her home among the whites.

"You think of your friends," said he after a time.

"Yes, I think of them."

"If you think of them a little today, you will think of them a great deal, later on."

"Perhaps. But that will not keep me away, William. And I'm not a weak thing, to sit and mourn and complain. You must trust me in saying that!"

"I *do* trust you! And out of this we're going to find happiness, Charlotte."

She turned her head and smiled at him, and by that single glance he knew truly the depth of her love, which had brought her here to him.

He went to the judge and told him the conclusion briefly.

"Charlotte agrees that she'll try to live out here with me."

The judge sighed. "Charlotte would agree to anything," said he.

Then he added, "Now, my lad, I won't begin with giving you advice. Your lives are your own. Only permit me to say, no one gets something for nothing in this world of ours. We pay as we go; and a bad investment leaves you bankrupt in the end."

"I don't quite understand that."

"I mean that the sorrow you cause is the sorrow that you will eventually have to feel."

Thunder Moon, turning this thought in his head, went back toward the village. There was to be a feast at which all the chief men would appear, and the judge and Jack Sutton would be there.

Indeed, he found Jack already in the village, having broken through the express orders that no one was to leave the wagon circle.

Jack was surrounded by a large and curious throng. Men and women pressed about him. Children dived recklessly among the legs of their elders, and so strove to creep through the forest and come to the sight of the white man. And as Thunder Moon came up, he heard over and over again the simple phrase, "It is the brother of Thunder Moon! It is the blood brother! It is the brother of our medicine man!"

And he smiled a little, with a lifted heart. Standing Antelope at that moment went by, hastily, with his light, noiseless step, and Thunder Moon reached out to him and caught him by the shoulder.

"Have you seen my brother, Jack?"

"No."

"What? Not seen him yet? See how they crowd around him. But we'll break through, I think."

Thunder Moon strode on, dragging Standing Antelope with him, and exclaimed at last, "Here is my brother among the Cheyennes, Jack. You've not forgotten Standing Antelope?"

And Standing Antelope, who understood the words perfectly, closed his teeth hard, to keep back a groan.

It was Bald Eagle who noted the wild and unhappy look of Standing Antelope and took occasion to draw him a little apart from the crowd.

"Brother," said the war chief, "your friend has become greater than ever on this day. Therefore, you are greater also; and yet I see a shadow on your forehead. How can this be?"

The boy answered nothing for a moment, but considered the older man. At length he said grimly, "Your arms have been filled with presents. Another such a day and you will have to live in two lodges; one for yourself and one for your wealth. But still you do not seem happy, Bald Eagle."

That battered chieftain frowned at this readiness of tongue in so young a warrior, and he said sternly, "A youth listens; an older man speaks!"

"To what do *you* listen, then?" asked Standing Antelope. "To your own heart, do you not?"

"All men listen to the voice of the spirit," said the chieftain.

"Let me tell you, then," said the boy, "that your heart has been beating so loudly that even I have heard it."

Bald Eagle could not make a reply, but it was plain that he was startled.

"I have heard your heart say," went on Standing Antelope, "that the young men follow Thunder Moon on the warpath. How do they regard Bald Eagle? He is only a name, and no more, to them!"

The chief was thrown into such a frenzy of anger by this speech that, for a moment, he seemed about to leap at the throat of the youngster, but he controlled himself long enough to say in a voice like distant thunder: "Has he sent you to me to give me these taunts?"

Then Standing Antelope answered quickly: "Look at me, Bald Eagle! It is not as a stranger or a spy that I have understood what is within you!"

Bald Eagle's wrath was quite dissipated by astonishment as he listened to this speech, and he answered, "Are you telling me that Thunder Moon no longer is your friend?"

"How can he be my friend?" answered the boy. "He keeps in a lodge beside him a woman, like a dog on a chain. He would not give her to me for the price of a hundred good horses!"

"Red Wind, Red Wind!" exclaimed the chief softly. I know that friendship is more powerful than rawhide ropes, well twisted. But a woman is stronger still. With a touch of her hands she snaps stronger ropes of kindness

256

than these! The Sioux give us war outside the camp; our women give us battles inside our lodges. And that is what has happened to you, Standing Antelope?"

The boy, somewhat heated by the implied reproach or contempt in the words of the other, said hastily, "When a man is sick of a great fever, does he laugh at the medicine man who can cure him?"

Bald Eagle's eyes narrowed to slits.

"One says to the medicine man, how will the cure be made? With prayer and medicine—or how?"

Standing Antelope looked swiftly about him, and then stepped closer.

"With the knife!" he whispered.

The nostrils of Bald Eagle expanded.

"Come with me," he said. "It is plain that we have much to say to one another!"

Never in the history of the tribe had there been a greater feast. For an Indian feast is not made with food but with conversation, and here present among them were the kin of that man of mystery, Thunder Moon. They looked on the thoughtful face of the colonel, and upon the handsome, pale features of Jack Sutton; and then they said among themselves, "Truly Thunder Moon has something more than an Indian name and a Cheyenne tongue. He has also no little part of the blood of a Cheyenne, by sympathy. See his face! It is almost as dark as ours! His features are those of an Indian. His hair and his eyes are as dark as ours. His way is our way, and he is one of us!"

While Jack Sutton was saying to his brother, "You are a great man to these people, Will."

"Do you wonder," said Thunder Moon, "that I can't leave them forever?"

257

"You could come out to see them every year or so!" suggested Jack Sutton.

"Perhaps I could. But the tribe would be wandering. They might be scattered to the four winds before I came back again. For, as a matter of fact, I think that I have had some share in holding them together."

"They admire you; they know that you're useful," said Jack Sutton, "but how many friends have you really among them?"

"There is Standing Antelope," answered Thunder Moon. "He's young, but he's a man. I've seen him tested in fire."

"Where is he tonight?"

"Sick; in his lodge. I've been to see him. He has a fever. Hands dry and forehead hot. Tomorrow I begin a course of medicine for him."

"He has a dark look, that youngster," said Jack Sutton. "Who is that about to speak?"

"They are passing the coup stick," said Thunder Moon, smiling faintly.

Briefly, and in murmurs, he translated the sum of the tales that were narrated, and the two white men beside him listened, fascinated, to bloody and wild deeds done in the midst of fierce battles, or in the camp of the enemy in the dead silence of the night.

The night grew old. The feast ended, and Thunder Moon accompanied his brother and the judge out of the tent.

A crowd followed, but left them at the edge of the village.

"As odd and interesting an evening as I ever passed," said the judge. "But why are you downhearted, Thunder Moon?"

"Because," said the other, "I cannot understand this. They should have sent out twenty young men—with

258

torches, perhaps—to show us the way to the wagons. I don't understand it. What's in the mind of Bald Eagle?"

"He's forgotten, of course."

"Indians never forget their manners until they are about to run amuck," replied Thunder Moon, and still gloomily thoughtful, he went with the others down the slope toward the bank of the river.

"I go first," said he. "Watch the rocks that I step on. At this height of the water, there's no need for you to so much as wet the soles of your boots. Watch me across, and then follow."

So he went lightly, jumping from rock to rock, across the river. And as he reached the farther shore and turned toward his two companions, who were about to follow, silent, shadowy forms arose from the brush behind him, with the gleam of steel in their hands.

40

The quick eye of the old judge saw the danger first. His shout of horror was not a word—simply a vague, piercing cry—and it turned Thunder Moon about to find bright-edged steel gleaming in his very eyes, and in his ears the voice of Standing Antelope exclaiming, "No bullets! No bullets! Bullets never can kill him! Only the edge of the knife! Only the edge of the knife!"

But if bullets could not kill Thunder Moon, knives surely were at his throat. He leaped far back from the rush, his revolver coming into his hand as he sprang, and he made out, with horror and bewilderment, that one of those close assailants was no less a person than that trusted lieutenant, Young Snake. Two more came behind the first pair, with Standing Antelope rushing into the lead, swift as a panther.

A gun boomed heavily from across the river. It was Jack Sutton's rifle, for he had carried the gun with him, and now, with a shot that was partly skill and partly luck, he sent a bullet through the head of Thunder Moon's right-hand man. The fellow toppled without a sound, his shoulder striking literally across Thunder Moon's knees. A shot from the Colt doubled up the second of the leaders, and there was Standing Antelope, coming in with the scream of a wild cat. There was time for a bullet, but in the last instant, Thunder Moon could not draw the trigger. Instead, he swayed aside from the flash of the steel, and struck at the lithe body with his fist. Hard upon the ribs the blow struck home, and Standing Antelope, stunned, bruised, breathless, dropped writhing cruelly upon the river bank.

The fourth man had swerved like a football player as he saw the mischief into which his companions had fallen, and now was merely a crackle of faint sound as he shot off through the brush.

Thunder Moon did not follow.

Heartsick and bewildered, he leaned over the fallen. Young Snake was gasping out his last breath. And over him Thunder Moon leaned as his brother and the judge came floundering through the water to get to his side, quite missing the way across the dry rocks.

And as he leaned over Young Snake, Thunder Moon saw hatred in the face of the wounded brave.

"Young Snake," he said, "I have mounted you on one of my best horses. I have led you on to much honor. Why, therefore, have you tried to murder me like a wolf of a Pawnee?"

"Because I am not your dog, to come and go when you whistle. And because—I hated your pale face!"

So spoke Young Snake, and snapped at the air over his shoulder, with a last convulsion of savagery and fury, and died.

Thunder Moon leaned above Standing Antelope, who was raising himself to his hands and knees. And now he stood upright and folded his hands across his breast. He was naked to the waist. He was painted as for war. Two eagle features were thrust into the long black masses of his hair, which glimmered in the starlight. He waited in silence for the falling of the blow as the judge and Jack Sutton came breathlessly ashore.

"Standing Antelope!" cried Jack in horror.

Thunder Moon waved the two aside and drew the boy apart.

"I am sick with sorrow and trouble," said Thunder Moon bitterly. "You, too, like Young Snake, always have hated me?"

The boy tried to answer, and at length he forced from his lips a gasping, "The Sky People still watch over you! Strike me now to the heart. I shall not speak again!"

"Lad," answered the older man gently, "we have traveled too many trails together. You are as free as though you still were my best of friends among the Cheyennes. Tarawa forgive you, and purify your mind. Will you not tell me what made you come at me—in the night—with three fighters to help you? Murder, Standing Antelope! Thank the spirits who have saved you from it!"

Then Standing Antelope, trembling like a leaf, answered, "I have not hated you always, as the rest have done. It was because you would not take Red Wind for yourself, nor give her to anyone else!"

Thunder Moon exclaimed in bewilderment, "This

261

very day I told her that she should take you for a husband. This very day, Standing Antelope! Are you mad?"

"You?" cried the boy. "You told her that?"

"Yes, yes. This morning. When I came in to speak to her, because she had said among the whites a thing about me that was not true!" Thunder Moon spoke vehemently.

"Ha!" breathed Standing Antelope, and reeled heavily.

The arm of Thunder Moon supported him

"My young brother," said he, "she has lied to you, also. Is it truth?"

"Why?" groaned Standing Antelope. "What evil can be in her?"

"I shall find her for you, if you want her, and give her to you, for that is my right," said Thunder Moon.

"Shall I make a lie into my squaw who keeps my lodges and raises my children?" asked the boy fiercely. "But now I see more things, and more clearly! It is the white squaw, O Thunder Moon, that has driven Red Wind mad with jealousy! On account of her she has tried to bring about your murder; and she has simply used my knife! She said that she would wait for me up the river at the three trees. But now I know that she will not be there! She has betrayed you. She has betrayed me. Why was I ever born?"

And he turned from Thunder Moon and ran off through the brush, heading swiftly up the river.

Thunder Moon turned back to his two white companions. Down from the village, on the farther side of the river, came dancing lights, as men and boys ran to learn what had caused the wild shouts and the explosion of guns. And the light of the torches fell like tresses of gleaming red hair, spread over the surface of the water.

262

"See," said Thunder Moon slowly. "The river flows between me and my life as a Cheyenne. The river is between, and I never can cross it again. There is blood upon the water. This night my friends have gone from me. I was a Cheyenne. My name was Thunder Moon. All the prairies knew me. But Thunder Moon is dead. Do you hear? The knife of Standing Antelope found the heart of that chief. He is dead. He will return no more."

He started resolutely ahead, drawing the two with him.

"I was two people in one," said he with a sudden calmness, "but now one half of me is dead, and I am going home to my own people. I am William Sutton at last!"

But farther up the river the Cheyenne boy, Standing Antelope, leaped breathless out from the covert and ran beneath the three trees, where Red Wind should have been waiting for him.

She was not there. There was no sight of her. There was no sound. Only the wind rushed through the leaves of the trees with a hissing sound.

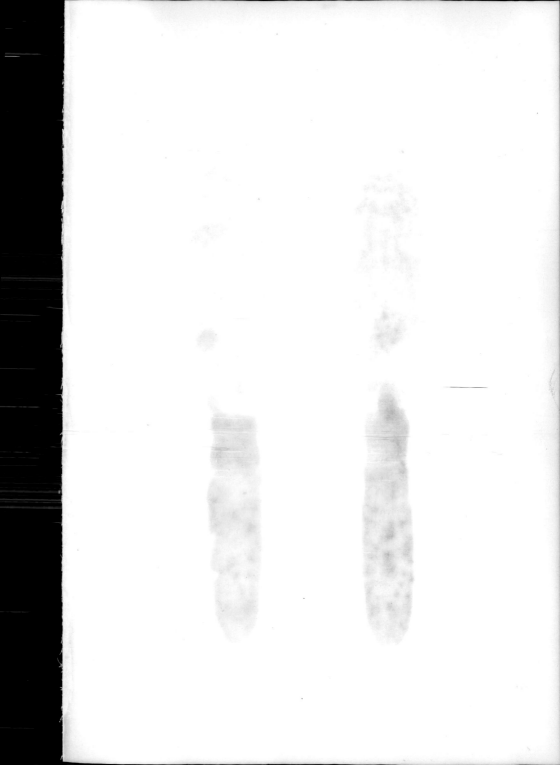

W   Brand, Max
            Thunder Moon strikes.

                                    $12.95